Café Du Jour
Risking It All

ROBIN'S

PRESS

B K Robinson

Other books by B K Robinson:

Defending Earth, an art installation in four dimensions

The True Story of Tuffy the Squirrel

The Three Sisters

Café Du Jour: Risking It All

First Edition
ISBN13: 978-0-9995097-0-8
ISBN10: 0999509705

B K Robinson

Author's Note:

Café DuJour is a work of fiction. The names, characters, places, and incidents portrayed in the story are the product of the author's imagination or have been used fictitiously. Any resemblance to actual persons, living or dead, or other settings is entirely coincidental.

➡

"… great love and great achievements involve great risks."   -   Dalai Lama

B K Robinson

ONE

Patty Townsend huffed out a big breath and shook her head, trying to clear it in the hopes sleep might finally come. She'd been lying in this unfamiliar bed in this strange hotel room in the absolute darkness for some time but still couldn't put her mind to rest so she could sleep. The darkness swirled around them in layers, surrounding her body and confusing her mind.

"Still awake?" Jon whispered from his place in bed beside her.

"No, I'm sound asleep. That's why I didn't hear you whispering," she answered, exasperation making her voice sharp, although she too kept her voice low. She didn't need light in the room to see her husband of almost twenty-five years in her mind's eye. Most of the time, even when she could see him, she still saw him the way he was when they first met, first married, and had their son, Jon Jr, or "JJ" as they call him.

Now forty seven years old, he wasn't all that much different. He was still one inch over six feet tall and had kept pretty close to the 195 pounds he'd weighed on their wedding day. So what if now there is a little less muscle and a little more thickness around his middle? His dark brown wavy hair had new silver highlights emerging at his temples but his eyes were still the same deep coffee brown, flashing equally with humor or anger, under his thick eyebrows.

Patty's mind abruptly shifted to her own changes. Her hair was still thick and sable brown, no silver threads in her hair. Yet. The stylist cut it to allow her natural waves to cascade in layers down to her shoulders. Her hazel eyes still shone with golden highlights. At forty six, she was still only two inches past five feet tall but her college weight of 105 had ballooned to 125 pounds.

"Sorry," she said, sighing. "I didn't mean to snap at you. I'm too scared to sleep."

Jon turned toward her and found her hand in the darkness. "Me, too," he said. "This is pretty frightening."

"What have we done?" Patty asked, her voice tight, rising with tension. "What in God's name have we done?"

"We haven't done anything yet," Jon replied. "We can still back out, if that's what you want."

"Is that what you want?" she asked. "Do you want to back out?"

"No-o, I don't think so," he said, his usually sure voice hesitant. "What about you? Are you ready for this? It'll mean some pretty big changes for us both."

Patty could feel the bed shift as Jon pulled himself up into a sitting position, fluffing his pillow and propping it behind him. He rearranged the sheets around him and sighed out loud.

"Wanna talk about it?" he asked. "I mean we're not sleeping anyway."

"Okay, might as well I guess. Let's go back to the beginning," Patty suggested as she too pulled up her pillow behind her and sat up. "Maybe if we trace the steps that got us here, I'll feel better about all this, a little more confident."

"That's my girl, always organized, keeping track of the pros and cons." Jon said, again taking Patty's hand, finding it easily in the darkness. "Okay," he began. "This all started when we got a letter from that probate lawyer about Aunt Maude's estate."

"Technically, it began months ago when she died," Patty said.

"Yeah, I remember getting notice she'd died, sent to me 'cause her only family was my father and he'd died years ago."

Patty could feel Jon nodding along in the darkness, even if she couldn't see it. She thought back to when both his parents had been killed by a drunk driver, deciding not to bring it up, not to sour this conversation further with that unhappy reminder. "You're stalling," she said. "Get to it."

"Right," Jon said. "Anyway, I didn't think much about it. I didn't even know she had an estate, didn't question if there were other heirs, didn't give a second thought to any of it." Jon paused to shift in the bed. "Then the letter told us about her leaving me her property here. Here, in the middle of nowhere, in north San Diego County, almost 50 miles north of San Diego, more than that south of Sana Monica, and way inland "

"And we decided to use our annual fall trip for our anniversary to come see it first hand before putting it on the market," Patty said. "It seemed like such a good idea at the time. It was all so simple. We'd take a look at it so we'd know how best to position it for sale." She shook her head again. "But that's not exactly what happened, is it?"

"No," Jon admitted. "We visited and fell in love, well, I fell in love with this little community, this simple lifestyle, so different from the life we've been living in Santa Monica. I won't speak for you."

"No, you're right. I fell for it, too. I felt almost as though we'd traveled back to a simpler time and place," Patty said. "But everything shifted when you saw that 'for sale' sign in the window of the local weekly newspaper. That made all the difference." She turned to face him in the darkness. "Has that always been your dream? To own and run your own newspaper?"

"Naw," Jon answered immediately. "My dream since J-School was just to work on a good paper, a respected paper, to follow wherever the story led me, to see my Jon Townsend byline in print. To write." He huffed out a loud breath. Patty felt the cheap mattress shift with the vehement shake of his head. "But the newspaper business has changed so much - not for the good - since I started, I don't know, more than twenty years ago. Now the newsroom is a prairie dog town with a hungry hawk circling overhead."

"Prairie dog town?" Patty asked. "What're you talking about?"

"You know, there've been so many rounds of cuts, everyone on the news floor stays hunkered down in their cubicles, afraid to stick their heads out, afraid their job will be the next one on the chopping block."

"But then, how come your position has been safe?" Patty asked.

"That man-in-the-street series I've been doing for the last couple of years is really popular and it's protected me so far, but who knows how long that'll last."

"I knew you were more stressed at work," Patty said, "but I didn't know the full story. Some reporter you are," she teased, half-heartedly.

"Well, what about you?" Jon asked. "I don't hear much positive from you about your job either."

"Yeah, that's true," Patty replied and thought for a moment before answering. "When I started teaching, twenty plus years ago, I was all starry eyed about molding young minds, changing the future through my classroom. What a dope."

"Come on, Patty," Jon said. "I've seen you with some of your students. I know you've changed their worlds, if not the world. If you're not ready to leave it, we don't have to do anything. We can just keep going the way we have been."

"No," Patty said. "I'm pretty well fed up with all the red tape, paperwork, and all the standardized nonsense. I became a teacher to work with the students, not to be a tool for the administration."

"There's my firebrand. I knew you were still in there, in spite of the crap wearing you down."

Patty could hear the smile of love in his voice. "Thank you, sweetheart," she said. "So how exactly would this work? If we do it?"

"The property is ours, free and clear," Jon said. "There's nothing that needs to be done for it. We would need to close the deal on purchasing the paper here. We'd both need to quit our jobs, put our house up for sale. I don't know what all else."

"We should check and see what retirement benefits we've accrued." Patty added. "I'm not so worried about the finances. The sale of our house will pay off what little mortgage is left on it and we can put the proceeds into our retirement accounts."

"After the purchase of the paper at a bargain

11

basement price," Jon reminded her. "That won't put much of a dent in our savings. With Aunt Maude's place paid off, our expenses won't be much."

"Yeah, all that's true," Patty agreed. "But you'll have the paper to run. What will I do?"

"Anything you want?" Jon said. "Nothing, if that's what you want."

"I don't see that happening, me doing nothing." Patty took in a deep breath and let it out slowly. "So that's it then? We're just abandoning our lives, leaving everything we know, everything we've built up to start all over again?"

"Leaving what?" Jon asked. "We're leaving our jobs, which we both agree are not what we bargained for all those years ago. We're selling our house, which will give you the opportunity to decorate our new home exactly the way you want, playing with colors, finding ways to mix what you like with what I like. You know you love that."

Patty smiled into the darkness. It was true, she did love fixing up a place. "Yeah, and this time the budget won't be as tight as it was we bought our first place. That'll be good," she said, warming to the idea in spite of herself.

"JJ's not at home any more. It's not like we'd be asking him to drop everything, change anything, to come with us." Jon's voice got stronger with each point. He was definitely getting excited by this opportunity.

"Okay," Patty said with a yawn. "Let's see if we can sleep on it. We can discuss all this some more tomorrow."

○ ○ ○

When Patty awoke the next morning, Jon was already up and she could hear him singing in the shower. She smiled, he was off-key but happy. She got up and opened the heavy curtains over the room's one window. The hotel room seemed more hopeful with the morning sunlight streaming through the window, the ghastly yellow flowers on the wallpaper brightened. The whole world looked better in beaming sunlight.

Even their big new plan looked better without the web of darkness that had strangled her last night. Patty cringed as Jon hit a particularly wrong note, ready to swear that the Gerber daisies on the wall paper had flinched.

Once they were both showered and dressed, they left the hotel in search of something to eat. Finding nothing open this early, a couple of nice restaurants open only for dinner, they returned to the hotel for the continental breakfast that was included in the room rate.

Patty sniffed deeply as she perused the breakfast buffet. Eggs, bacon, sausage, waffles, and syrup, all the regulars were there. All that was missing was imagination. Over breakfast, they discussed what they'd seen of the town while looking for a breakfast place. "Did you see the intersection with the big grassy circle in the middle? Of course you did, how could you miss it?" Patty asked. "There were three big churches on that one square. Only the fourth corner had something different."

"Yeah, some sort of park, a continuation of the grassy circle in the middle. If you walk north of the town center, that big square, you start to see some really nice homes," Jon said.

"Aunt Maude's property is two blocks, two long blocks south of there, in the opposite direction," Patty said. "It looks like it used to be outside of town center but the town kept growing until it got there."

"It filled in with some necessary, but maybe less desirable, businesses," Jon said, nodding excitedly between bites. "I bet when they put the newspaper building there they thought the printing noise would be outside of town."

"Yeah, and they probably didn't want the Fire Station or the Police Department in their residential neighborhood either. They thought they'd be away from the respectable center of town and the wealthier areas for people who expected peace and quiet," Patty said.

"So our new place will be on the wrong side of town," Jon teased. "Right where the likes of us big city escapees belong."

Patty chuckled appreciatively. "I saw at least one antiques and collectibles shop, a laundromat, and a hardware store. So there ought to be some foot and vehicle traffic."

"Foot traffic could be important once you decide what kind of business you want to open downstairs," Jon offered. "What else did you notice?"

"Mostly, it was what I didn't see," Patty said. "I couldn't see the air or smell it. Living so close to LA, I'm not sure I even knew what truly fresh air smelled like. And I loved seeing more green than concrete." Patty smiled at Jon and stretched across the table for his hand. "I think we're really going to like it here."

They got up and headed toward the desk to

settle their hotel bill. "Did you see all the birds in the park?" Jon asked. "All the brightly colored feathers, the sweet birdsongs?"

"And squirrels, did you see the squirrels?" As they reached the exit doors, Patty asked, "Do you think we have time to drive by Maude's place one more time before we hit the road home?"

They drove toward what would become their new home, appreciating the brick structure, set perpendicularly to the street, with windows on three sides of the first floor.

"I want the second floor for our living space," Patty began. "We can completely gut it and make it our own."

"What about the first floor?" Jon asked. "Yoga studio? Pottery workshop? Yarn and quilting center?"

Patty shook her head in dismissal. "I don't know yet but I have an idea for that old attic space. Let's head back to Santa Monica, it looks like we have a lot to do."

As they approached the freeway heading home, they spotted a small pocket of gas stations and fast food places. "I'm glad we didn't wait to grab breakfast on the way. I'd rather have that sorry excuse of a continental breakfast than fast food," Jon said.

o o o

As soon as they got on the freeway headed home, Jon turned up his favorites on the CD player and began chattering excitedly about their new future.

But Patty wasn't ready yet. *This anniversary trip was certainly nothing like our honeymoon in the French countryside,* she thought with a scowl, still disturbed by her late night thoughts. *What have I agreed to? Who will I be if I'm no longer a teacher? What will I do with my life? What do I want to do?*

She closed her eyes and consciously tuned out Jon and his aggressively upbeat music. *Am I jumping into a void here, following wherever my husband goes? I never thought I'd be* that *wife, the one who gives up her dreams for those of her man.*

She gazed out the window at the scenery passing by and sighed. *Just like my life is passing by,* she thought.

TWO

Three Months Later

Patty stepped back to evaluate her progress, making their new place into a real home. Their old house in Santa Monica had sold quickly, and for almost as much as they'd hoped. The purchase of the Valley Gazette had closed smoothly with only a few minor changes recommended by their lawyer.

They'd completed most of the major work on their new home before moving in. The second floor now had shiny new hardwood floors throughout and a brand new kitchen with all the top of the line appliances, work and storage spaces that Patty, who loved to cook, could ask for.

They'd taken the original bathroom and transformed it into a guest bathroom. They'd made the entire east end into their master suite to catch the morning sun and added an en suite master bathroom. Patty loved waking up in the morning to the sunshine, awakened by birdsong instead of traffic noise. She couldn't yet identify the birds by their songs but she already preferred them to the city noises they'd left behind.

Theirs was the last house at the south end of town. Patty got up early each morning, partly out of habit developed from needing to get to school before the first bell and partly to share a cup of coffee with Jon before he left for the paper, but now she could return to bed afterward to read and watch the birds gathering outside the bedroom window. She happily opened the blinds and the windows and rejoiced in the view. Over the treetops she could make out mountains in the distance. She looked forward to watching the leaves change color next fall and hoped to see a little distant snow next winter.

All the rest of the second floor was open space. They'd added wrap around windows in the open space area facing south, west, and north, to catch the sunlight. Patty and Jon were both happy with the effect, a bright, sunny, place with soft, comfortable seating to welcome them, and their guests, into their new home.

Patty recognized she was just delaying the inevitable, keeping herself busy getting their new home all fixed up. She'd yet to decide what she wanted to do with the rest of her life. *I'll think about that tomorrow,* she thought. *Yeah, 'cause that worked out so well for Scarlett O'Hara.*

Most of their personal and kitchen things had been unpacked. Today, Patty was putting up some of their pictures and artwork, finishing touches to make the place feel like their home.

Jon had come in while she was unpacking a big picture for the dining area and settled himself in near the windows at the west end of their new living space. Patty hoisted the picture up on the wall and asked, "Is that centered? Too high or too low?"

When Jon didn't respond, Patty called, "Hey, you over there, I need some help here." When he still didn't answer, she twisted her neck to look over her shoulder at him. Seeing him sitting with his elbows on his knees, head hanging in his hands, she rested the picture on the floor, leaning against the wall, and walked over to him.

"Hey, what's up?" she asked. "How come you're home in the middle of the day?"

"Honey," Jon started, he paused and shook his head. "What if I've made a mistake? What if I've dragged us away from our careers and our home and it was all a big mistake?"

"Mistake? What mistake?" Patty asked.

"I don't know anything about running a business," he said. "Sure I can report a story, I can investigate and write rings around a story. But what do I know about running a newspaper? I'm afraid I may be in over my head."

"You've been like a puppy with a new toy, learning all about running this newspaper," Patty said. "Why all of a sudden do you think it might be a mistake? What happened?"

Jon blew out a breath through his nose, his shoulders slumped further. "When we were doing the walk through for the closing, Shepard pointed to the rolls of newsprint and barrels of ink, indicating they were included in the sale as supplies. What he didn't say was that several of those ink barrels were empty and one of the rolls of newsprint paper was water damaged and unusable." Jon got up and began to pace. "And I'm such a business novice, I didn't check. Replacing that newsprint and refilling those barrels is going to eat into my budget before I even get started."

"That rat," Patty exploded. "He knew what he

19

was doing. He had to know. He took advantage of you."

"Yeah, and I made it easy for him." Jon shook his head and came over to sit again. "I've got a call in to our lawyer. I'm going to ask him exactly what the contract says. Can I hold Robert Shepard to giving me full ink barrels and usable paper? At least I can use the last of my newsprint and ink supplies to expose his perfidy in this next edition."

"No. I mean yes, go ahead with the call to the lawyer. Let's see what he says," Patty said, stretching one hand to touch Jon's hands, to relax the fists he was holding tight. "But no, let him believe you knew what you were getting when you accepted the deal. He'll think he underpriced the paper, let him worry he should have asked for more. Make him sweat it."

Jon looked up at his wife of twenty-five years with new appreciation. He nodded at her plan, chuckling at the idea Robert Shepard would never know how much his little trick had cost him. Seeing his wife anew, he focused on the one major change to her appearance.

Since they'd left their old lives and moved here, Patty had cut off her long wavy locks in favor of a new short style. Really short, no more than an inch, covering her head like a thick brush. Jon hadn't liked the idea at first but now he loved the feel of it against his palms. Patty had been right. This had been the perfect time to change her style, saying it was as good a time to re-invent herself as she would ever get. No one from the high school where she'd taught, none of her old friends would see it and none of the people here were accustomed to the old look.

Jon's ring tone interrupted them. Checking the

caller ID, he said, "That's the lawyer. Let me tell him what's up."

"You just learned a valuable lesson about running your own newspaper, for the price of one roll of newsprint and a couple of barrels of ink. Pretty cheap lesson at that price," she told him.

"Whatever else he did," Jon replied, accepting the call, "he left me a good man operating the press. That Henry Walker is worth his weight in, well if not gold, at least in printers' ink. I'm learning a lot from him and I plan to keep him around."

○ ○ ○

While Patty spent large stretches of her time inside their new space, turning it into a home, Jon spent his time getting to know the community. As a newsman, he needed to know where to find the local news, who in town, which townspeople, always seemed to be in the know.

Of course, he pursued all the usual sources. He spent some time with the police chief, getting to know him and finding some good leads for future stories. He immediately liked the police chief, Alec Harrison, who introduced him to a couple of his deputies and, most importantly, to Wanda White. "Wanda is a civilian employee, our dispatcher. She's the center of our operation, knows everyone, and knows everything." As they walked away, Alec had leaned close to Jon and whispered, "Keep on her good side. You don't want to see her bad side."

"I heard that," Wanda called. "You listen to him,

Mr. Newspaper Man. He's giving you some good advice, there. Uh hmm."

"At 68 years of age," Alec said once they were out of hearing range, "she only works part time. She could retire, probably should retire. But I don't know how we'd get along without her."

Jon liked the guy even more. At 6'1", Alec was Jon's height but a good fifteen to twenty pounds heavier, every bit of it solid muscle. He wore his nappy black hair very short, high and tight, military style. Appropriate, given his time in the military police when he'd served in the marines. His ebony skin covered an elongated face making him appear very stern. But his sharp, intelligent eyes sparkled with humor.

One of the first stories Jon did was a piece about a rescue mission carried out successfully by the local volunteer fire station. Jon turned this story into a profile piece on the fire chief, the only full time paid position, and the all-volunteer crew.

Interviewing the aging fire chief was hampered by his seemingly endless stories of the history of the fire station, interrupted often by his constant coughing and wheezing. Jon's journalistic style, honed by his years of man-in-the-street reporting, was fueled by his genuine interest in the old man and all the history contained in his memory.

"Looky here," Chief Stewart had said, as he led Jon to a glass case displaying old photographs and other memorabilia. "Some of these date back to when photography was new and fire wagons were pulled by horses."

"These are terrific," Jon had replied. "Would you mind if I reprint some of them in the paper?"

"Sure, that'd be nice," the old man had said, as he searched through his key ring for the tiny key to open the glass case. "Course it's all different now. All auty-mated, all run by fancy new machines. I don't know how half this stuff works. But I know which of my volunteer guys got it all figured out." He nodded, succumbing to another deep coughing fit. "We could probably hire more full time fire fighters or maybe some of them paramedics for what we paid for alla this fancy stuff."

Jon thanked him for his time and took several of the pictures to scan for reprint. He excused himself to make his exit as several of the volunteer fire fighters left for their day jobs.

O O O

The lawyer called back a few days later, after he'd had time to review the sales contract, telling Jon there wasn't anything there they could use to force the seller to make this right. By then Jon was ready to let it go as a necessary learning experience. He had the money, that wasn't the issue. He could make it up with the aggressive campaign for ad revenue he was planning. And with Patty's suggestion, he wouldn't have to let Shepard think he'd gotten away with anything.

As part of getting to know their new community, Jon and Patty had attended each of the three churches on the square at least once. They'd gone to a different one each Sunday until they'd found the one they wanted to go back to on a semi-regular basis. As a reporter in a small community, Jon needed to keep contact lines open everywhere he could and churches were a great place to make social connections.

At the church Patty liked best, Jon had recognized Wanda, the civilian police dispatcher. She was as Jon had described her, no more than Patty's 5'2" tall, about 135 pounds with a heavy lower body. Her dark brown hair was worn short and naturel, and her big brown eyes shone with intelligence. Her skin tone could only be described as deep coppery brown with mahogany highlights when the light hit it just the right way. But it was her voice that was her most distinctive feature. Jon hadn't been able to put it into words and neither could Patty. It was flat and a little nasally and raspy. However you might describe it, it was loud and immediately recognizable.

Wanda held herself separate from most of the congregation but was clearly friendly with Doris Shepard, the one lady there Patty most liked. Even at 78 years of age, Doris was the community services committee for the congregation. A skoosh shorter than Patty, maybe 5'1" tall, her 165 pounds made her look short and sturdy, body by bulldog. She wore her brittle blond hair, looking much like cotton candy, in a grandmotherly perm.

The committee had other members, but Doris was the glue that held it together and got the work done. The project closest to her heart was the food bank. Patty's soul responded to Doris' get-it-done attitude when it came to helping those less fortunate.

"Some of these people just need a little help until their next break," she'd told Patty when they first met. "Others are going to need help for a while. Either way, that's what we're here for, to help."

Patty had felt an immediate sense of family with Doris and Wanda and looked forward to getting to know some of the other members of the church.

○ ○ ○

One evening Jon was sitting at the table finishing up a story for the paper while Patty put the finishing touches on their dinner. While they worked separately together, they talked about nothing and everything, the town, new people they'd met, the progress on finishing their new home, and a recent call from their son, JJ.

Picking up a bright green flyer Patty had left out on the counter, Jon said, "So, ceramics, huh?" Jon's story was now complete and his laptop closed. "You've decided to open a ceramics studio downstairs? That's terrific."

"What?" Patty called, pausing in dinner prep to look over to Jon. She saw he was reviewing the flyer for a ceramics class she'd picked up down the street at the laundromat. "No. No, honey. That's a class I'm going to take at the community college." She absently reached for a stray lock of hair that was no longer there and shook her head. "I still don't know what I want to do with the downstairs space. Don't push. Please don't push."

Jon put the flyer down on the table and came over to sit at the island bar and talk with Patty while she dished up their dinner. "What smells so good over here?" He settled himself onto a barstool at the counter, sniffing deeply. When Patty didn't respond to his attempt at distraction, he returned to the topic. "I'm not pushing. I just want to see you happy. I seem to remember an interest in pottery from a while back."

"Yeah," Patty said, nodding. "Ceramics was one of the things I always wanted to pursue but I never had the time when I was teaching and raising JJ." She shrugged and sighed. "Now's as good a time as any to find out if I have any talent."

"No, that's great," Jon said, his voice warm and caressing. "I don't care what you decide to do with the downstairs. I don't care how long it takes you to decide. It's all good."

"I know, sweetie. I'm getting a little tired of my own indecision." Patty knew Jon's intentions were supportive. That was part of the problem, she couldn't even get mad and yell at him for pushing. *It isn't his fault the move is working out so well for him, that he's so happy. It isn't fair for me to resent him for his happiness as I flounder with my own lack of direction.* Together, they carried their plates to the table and sat down to eat. "But I do have a plan for the attic space."

"Oh really," Jon said. "And that would be?"

"I want to build it out as guest rooms, you know for JJ and his family when they visit."

"You know, as a journalist, I hate it when I miss a big scoop. Did JJ get married?"

"Not yet. But a mother can plan," Patty said, all the while thinking, *easier to plan my son's future than to face my own.*

THREE

Patty settled into her workspace in the ceramics studio, only half listening to the instructor welcome the students. "This course is intended for those studying ceramics for the first time and will be a comprehensive introduction to the craft of clay working," Claudia, the instructor, said. "Our primary focus will be on studio work leading to a portfolio of finished pieces by the end of the semester."

Patty gazed around at the other students in the ceramics studio, seeing mostly women with only a few male students. The women appeared to range in age from late teens to senior citizens. She found several who looked to be about her own age.

"The main goal of the course is for you to be able to create as well as appreciate expressive, beautiful three dimensional clay forms. I'll also demonstrate some techniques and give you some more technical assignments. And on occasion, I'll show slides or films to illustrate what you're learning."

Patty continued looking around. Most of the other students were dressed casually for the class in t-shirts and jeans, with aprons, smocks, or hoodies. *I guess I need to go shopping before the next class,* she thought.

"You'll gain an understanding of other cultures

and periods of human expression in clay and finally you'll begin to be proficient at forming clay objects yourself." Claudia, tall and blonde with strong arms and hands from years of clay work, returned to her desk and picked up her roll book. "As I call your name, let me know what previous experience you've had working with clay."

Patty half listened as each of the others explained what, if any, previous experience with clay they'd had, thinking about her own answer. When the name Patty Townsend was called, she replied, "I tried some ceramic work many years ago when I was in college, was first in college," she quickly self-corrected. "But then life just got too busy. Now I'm ready to try again." Claudia nodded, made a quick note in her book, and moved on.

Many of the younger students wore t-shirts with a message. Patty sneaked a peek to read some of the statements, amused by how succinctly they each introduced themselves with their casual apparel. One shirt proclaimed, *Lettuce Turnip the Beet,* supporting vegetable gardening or music? Another depicted a magic wand under the words, *You had the power all along, my dear,* movie lover or feminist? One of the older students wore a shirt in neon pink declaring boldly, *I do not intend to tiptoe through life only to arrive safely at death!* I'm going to like her, Patty mused, smiling. *Maybe I won't need to go shopping after all.*

Finally, one of the other, younger, students asked the question Patty had been worrying over, "What supplies do we need to bring?"

"Your $50 lab fees cover all the expenses," Claudia replied. "All clay, glazes and firing will be purchased for you by the course. The school provides all the tools we'll need." Claudia pulled back the sleeve of her faded blue, clay spotted, smock to glance at her watch. "Let's take a fifteen minute break and then we'll begin our first lesson."

Patty got up and left with most of the other students. An older lady, walking nearest to her asked, "You new around here? I don't remember seeing you before."

"Yes," Patty replied. "I mean, I guess I'm pretty new here. We moved a couple of months ago."

"Why here? Most younger people move away from here, not to here," the older lady said, waving over some of the others to join them. She sure seemed to know everyone and everything and wasn't at all shy about asking personal questions in a direct manner. This was new for Patty who was used to big city don't-ask-questions, stay-away-from-strangers, ways.

"My husband, I mean we, bought the local weekly newspaper, the Valley Gazette, from Robert Shepard. My husband's running it now."

"That's right I heard something about a change in ownership there. You moved into old Maude Townsend's place, right?"

"Yeah," Patty agreed with a warm smile. "I'm trying to get us settled in there."

"You'll be able to fill it up with all your new ceramic pieces soon, right?" Another lady asked.

"I don't know about that," Patty said, shaking her head. "We'll see how well I do."

"Time to go back in and find out."

That evening over a dinner of homemade pastitsio and a Greek salad, Jon asked Patty about her first day of class.

"It's sure different on the other side of the teacher's desk," she replied. "That's for sure. And I like it." Patty chuckled softly. *I may not know what I want to do next, but I'm ready to leave teaching behind*, she realized. "After class, several of us went to the campus coffee shop for tea. Well, I had tea. The others had coffee. Whatever. The campus is really a pleasant space, with lots of newly planted water smart succulent ground cover in shades of green, big bushes of rosemary and oleander, and a few tall eucalyptus trees." A sly smile slowly spread across her face. "What do you know about Alec Harrison's wife's leaving town about a year ago?"

Jon paused, fork in midair, his thick eye brows beetling. "The police chief? Not much. He doesn't talk about it. I wasn't sure whether she'd left or died, or what. And since it isn't relevant to any news story I'm covering, I haven't pushed it. Why? What do you know?" He waggled those eyebrows playfully.

"Well, it was all the talk of the coffee shop ladies," Patty said. "It seems she left overnight, no warning, with some other guy."

"Huh?"

"Yeah, apparently at first there was some question maybe he'd done away with her. But then she made contact with the son and everyone let it go."

"I guess we can't know what someone else might be capable of," Jon said. "But I don't see him murdering anyone."

"Apparently this Chris Woods, one of his detectives in the police department, thought he was capable of it. He continued to bring up questions about it every chance he got."

"Friction within the police department?" Jon asked. "That's good information. I may have to put you on the paper's payroll."

"There's more. According to one of these ladies, Chris wanted city hall to name him the new chief of police. He had the backing of the mayor and your old friend, Robert Shepard. Between Woods and Shepard, the rumors and innuendos kept popping up until the final decision was made."

"Wow, I'd think with the backing of the mayor and the local paper, it'd be a done deal." Jon had put his fork down now and was completely focused on the conversation. "Maybe there's more going on at city hall than meets the eye."

"Yeah, the ladies' talk kinda dried up about then," Patty said. "The only thing more I could get was some background. Alec was born and grew up here, a big star in high school athletics, track and field, no team sports."

Jon nodded, filing this tidbit of information away in his reporter's brain until it might prove useful.

Patty stood up to collect their plates but Jon held on to his, playfully smacking her hand away and resuming his meal after the distraction of Patty's gossip. She took her plate in and returned with two pieces of her homemade Dutch apple pie. She put Jon's across the table and started on hers. Jon eyed the pie for a moment and went back to work on his

31

favorite Greek baked pasta dish.

Patty returned to her story about Alec Harrison. "The story goes that after marrying Darla, his high school sweetheart, he left town to join the marines and didn't come back much for the next twenty years. So a lot of the town considers him somewhat of an outsider. His wife raised their son pretty much by herself. Some people took her side."

"In the marines, that's where he got his police training. He was an MP on bases all over the world, working his way up to command and a place in their MP training program." Jon pushed his plate aside and reached for his pie. "No ice cream?"

"I think there may be some in the freezer," Patty said. "Help yourself."

As Jon served himself a scoop of vanilla, Patty continued, "Did I mention his wife was white? A blue eyed blonde? Some of the community took exception to their marriage and the racial stuff may have been why they were so quick to take her side."

"Her side?" Jon asked, returning to the table. "What side? It's not like he abandoned her. Lots of guys with careers in the military are gone for long periods of time."

"I didn't really get a full story, I'm piecing it together, but it sounds like sides became an issue when she left town with another guy," Patty said, nodding. "She'd raised their child alone all the time he was gone but when he retired, came home, got on at the police department, she didn't want to stay together any more. 'Took off with the first guy who came along,' that's what one of the ladies said."

"First guy who came along? In a small place like

this?" Jon said. "How does that even happen?"

"Word is she worked part time at one of those places near the freeway," Patty said. "I guess maybe she met someone passing through town."

"Whoa," Jon said. "He must have passed through more than once." He shook his head. "So much going on below the surface."

"The worst of it seems to be," Patty said, "that now that he's back and she's gone, the son's really struggling with it all. How old is the son? Do you know? Have you met him?"

"Just once, really briefly," Jon replied. "Come to think of it, he was pretty quiet, maybe a little sulky. I just thought it was typical teenage attitude crap." Jon's eyes lost focus as he thought back, his fingers absently keeping time with the Motown music Patty had put on to play during dinner. "Still, I think Alec's MP training and experience makes him the better choice for chief."

After dinner, Jon took over the clean-up duties and Patty searched out an old box she hadn't planned on unpacking any time soon. But now she'd had a change of heart. As a teacher, she'd dressed fairly casually but still within certain limits of decorum. Some of the younger teachers wore message t-shirts to class but she'd always stuck to polo shirts and henley collared shirts in solid colors. When she'd first started teaching she'd made a conscious decision to teach her class without allowing her personal beliefs to show.

Over the years, JJ had given her many cute message shirts that she loved although she hadn't worn them often. Now was their time to shine. She located the box of neatly folded shirts and began digging through them for favorites, finding some of

Jon's mixed in with hers. She sniffed, raising her left eyebrow at the dusty smell wafting off the old shirts. "I'll launder the lot," she said to herself. "Then I'll see which ones I want to show off."

Bundling the old t-shirts up to take downstairs to the laundry room, Patty smiled broadly. "I feel young again. Going back to school, seeing these old shirts. Look out world, here I come."

FOUR

Patty bustled into the church basement, struggling under the weight of a couple dozen of her homemade muffins. Today, in just minutes, would be the first bake sale she'd worked in years.

Doris had asked her to bring something that could be sold to benefit the food bank, and Patty had thrilled at the chance. She was still struggling with ideas of what to do with the rest of her life and this presented a perfect distraction.

Just this morning, she'd frozen in place passing a mirror. She was finally getting used to seeing herself with her new short hair. But this morning, she was arrested by the sight of her face looking back at her, not just older, but stressed and lined with wrinkles. How can that be? Here I am facing what should be the happiest of choices, what to make of the rest of my life. But instead, I feel more stress than when I was working full time, raising a rambunctious young son, and dealing with monthly budget challenges.

Maybe that's the problem, she thought. *Maybe by making it about the rest of my life, I'm making it too big a deal. Maybe I should be asking myself what I want to do next.*

Doris greeted her warmly, relieving her of the containers of muffins, opening them, and inhaling their delicious aromas appreciatively, before setting them out for display. "How much do you want to ask for these?" she asked Patty.

"I don't know," Patty replied, looking around to check the pricing on some of the other items already on the tables. "What do you think they'll bring?"

"They're huge and they look, and smell, better than any of the homemade stuff we usually get," Doris said. "Where'd you get them?"

"Get them? Why, I made them myself, last night and this morning. They're some apple walnut, carrot raisin, and lemon poppy seed. Three of my favorites."

"Homemade? Fantastic!" Doris said. "I want to price them at $5 but I don't want to insult the other ladies who brought muffins. Let's go with $2 each."

Patty joined Doris and the two other ladies working the sale, time passing quickly. They chatted with each other and business was brisk, for a while at least. Around noon, Wanda came in to help them close up and close out.

"How'd it go?" Wanda greeted them. "Did you sell any of those hippie pillows of yours, Doris?" Doris' own contribution to the sale wasn't anything baked at all. She'd brought some throw pillows she'd made out of old doilies and t-shirts, some lovely, some funny. Patty particularly liked the ones that were animal faces, one a cat and another a bunny with suede whiskers and ears made of gray velvet, stuffed separately and extending out from the body of the pillow.

"A couple. But Patty's muffins were the big hit of the day," Doris said, beaming. "They sold out first, with several people coming back to buy extra to take home." Turning to Patty, she added, "You know you could sell these for $5 each for real."

Patty smiled, thanking her, saying, "Funny you should say that. Just this morning I had a real heart to heart with myself in the mirror. I've never been an idle person. I don't know what to do with myself when I don't have multiple projects going. And I find I don't like too much downtime. I need to figure out what to do with my time and my energy." Patty stopped, suddenly feeling this might be too revealing a conversation to share with these two nice ladies who were virtually strangers. "Thank you for inviting me to work with you on this bake sale." She shook her head. "Still, I somehow don't see selling muffins door-to-door as my next chapter."

"There, there, dear," Doris said, patting Patty's arm. "We'll find something suitable to keep you and your hands busy."

"Anything left we can turn into our lunch?" Wanda asked.

Doris pulled out a little box of things she had hidden under the table for just that purpose. "Come on Patty, stay and have lunch with us while we count up the bank. You earned at least that."

"Sure," Patty said. Once the accounting was finished, they sat down to eat and chat.

"You get that callback from your brother yet?" Doris asked Wanda.

"Yeah more complaining about taking care of my mother. I don't know what they expect me to do from here," Wanda said. She turned to Patty. "My whole family still lives up near Chicago and my mother isn't aging well."

Wanda shook herself and turned to Doris. "But I don't want to talk about that. You wouldn't believe what

37

those devils are up to now," Wanda confided to Doris, her dark eyes once again twinkling gaily in her mahogany face.

Doris fidgeted nervously, patting her cotton candy hair and straightening her apron. She shot a quick glance at Patty.

"It's your husband who's the newspaper man, right? Not you?" Wanda asked.

"Right," Patty confirmed. "But don't worry, it's time for me to get going anyway. I can't tell him anything I don't hear." She stood up, gathering her jacket and purse. "This was great, Doris. Be sure to count me in for the next one. Good seeing you again, Wanda." Patty sighed deeply in satisfaction and headed out of the church basement for home.

○ ○ ○

Over a dinner of braised lamb shoulder chops that evening, Patty told Jon about the success of her muffins at the bake sale. Or she tried to. Jon was quiet, distracted, not really paying attention. "So, how was your day?" she asked him.

"Oh, the usual, a little this, a little that," he replied. "Nothing outstanding."

"Then perhaps you can explain to me what has you so preoccupied," she prompted.

Jon put down his fork, looking her straight in the eye. "I'm afraid I'm becoming one of the hawks circling overhead, looking more at the bottom line than what's in the news. This is not what I wanted."

"I don't get it," Patty replied. "Why are you worrying? I thought the paper only had to pay for itself.

We're okay here if it takes a while for it, for you, to get on your feet financially."

"Yeah," Jon sighed. "But it turns out that's easier to say than to mean. I've, we've, never been well to do."

"Don't I know it," Patty agreed. "I've been the one handling our finances all these years."

"Right, but it's an attitude thing. I don't know how to relax and enjoy it without worrying about the balance sheet."

"Okay, honey. What are the expenses? What all does the income need to cover?"

"Mostly the supplies and labor. Paper and ink, printing and distribution." Jon's eyes focused as he listed the costs. "The paper and ink aren't much but they're necessary and Henry handles both the printing and the distribution."

"So until you begin taking a salary, which we don't need, at least for now, his is the only labor expense?"

"Yeah and I can't cut that expense. I couldn't get the paper out without him." Jon nodded, running his big hands down his tired face, doing nothing to erase the stress apparent there. "Lately, I've been thinking about ways to increase the ad revenues and decrease print expenses."

"You really are turning into a publisher, as well as editor and chief reporter." Patty leaned forward to look him directly in the eye. "I don't know if I've said it, but I really am proud of you, proud of the way you're stepping up and growing into this challenge. Just keep going, I have faith in you."

"Thank you, I count on it." He picked up his fork and returned to eating. "Speaking of reporting, I'm beginning to get a look at the seedy underbelly of this little community."

"Oh really?" Patty teased, "Then you probably already know what Wanda was talking about this morning."

"What?"

"I don't know really, I left before she got into any details," Patty said. "All I heard was something about 'what those devils are up to now'. I wondered what it could be but maybe you know."

"No," Jon said, shaking his head sadly. "And being new in town, I need to develop some sources I can trust. So far, it's just my spidey senses picking up a feeling around city hall and money. You know, the way people stop talking suddenly, or look over toward the building. It feels like something's going on that everyone suspects but no one wants to talk about."

"So sad, in such a pretty little community," Patty said. "But I guess people will be people everywhere you go." She brightened, smiling wide. "Oh, I almost forgot. Doris said I could make a living selling my muffins. Waddaya think? A muffin and cupcake shop downstairs?"

"If that's what you want, I'm in," Jon said. "I'll buy the first dozen."

"No, I don't think so," Patty replied, slowly shaking her head back and forth in refusal. "It sounds like a lotta work. How many cupcakes would I have to sell to support the paper?"

"That's great," Jon laughed. "Holding a bake sale to support journalism. Okay, I feel better."

○ ○ ○

Patty continued her class at the community college, learning about ceramics and enjoying the process. But so far she didn't show the level of talent required to become an artist. Nothing lost, she was having fun and meeting nice people. One of the younger students in her ceramics class, Nathalie who led yoga classes, introduced her to the growing community of Buddhists living not too far away.

Patty was intrigued. She visited a couple of times, attending services and even joining in a discussion group. She was disappointed, not really surprised, but disappointed none-the-less to find some of the older students distancing themselves from her when she talked about her experiences with the Buddhists.

"Where's the harm?" she asked Jon one night when they were reading in bed. "Buddhism is completely peaceful, it doesn't ask you to give up your beliefs from any other religion."

"You'd think they'd welcome them into the community as customers, if nothing else," Jon said.

"I know," Patty agreed. "Anyway, I think meditation could make me a more pleasant person to be around."

"Are you thinking of taking up yoga again?"

"I don't know," Patty said slowly, dragging out each word. "Nathalie doesn't have any classes running right now. Her last location kicked her out for another renter who wanted the space full time. She said she'd let me know when she'd found another place."

41

Jon made calls and scheduled time to visit Alan, "call me Woz," Wozniak, the head of the Computer Sciences Department at Valley Community College. The guy had presumed he wanted to write a story on the program for the Valley Gazette. Jon let him. That would be easy to do. He'd develop a puff piece on the program, then get to his true purpose.

Jon entered the professor's office and introduced himself. Wozniak introduced himself in turn, saying, 'no relationship' with a merry twinkle in his eye. It took Jon a moment to realize he was referring to Steve Wozniak, the famous cofounder of the Apple computer empire. He liked Woz, his sense of humor, immediately.

Later, interview done, Jon smiled at the rumpled professor, "I'd really like to talk to you about an idea I have for the paper, if you have the time."

Woz looked at his watch, "Sure, my next class isn't for a half hour. How can I help you?"

"I'd really like to explore some ways to cut costs for the paper," Jon began. "I'm thinking about doing less print and more online. But I don't know where to begin."

The professor leaned in, more interested now. "Good idea, it's the way of the future and it could really go a long way to cut your costs."

Jon and he threw ideas back and forth for a while, until it was almost time for Woz's next class. As they walked to the door, the professor had one more idea. "Would you be interested in a student project to test some of these ideas? How about if I brought in some students from Business Sciences to look at it from that point of view?"

Jon's expression went slack as his eyes grew round. "That would be great!" he said. "You want to set up a meeting with him and let me know when and where?"

"Her, with her," he replied. "Sure, she's going to be as excited about this as I am."

Jon told Patty about the ideas for improving the paper's bottom line that evening over dinner. "Woz has this really terrific idea about a student project with some of his students and some from Business Sciences to improve the paper," he told her, talking with his hands waving in excitement. He shook his head in wonder. "I guess I'm still coming to grips with the idea of the paper not needing to make a profit. It just feels strange to be so free."

Patty could sense Jon was struggling with some of the issues still plaguing her. She heaved a great sigh and reached across the table for his hand. Their eyes met and they shared a moment of empathy for each other. She broke it with a smile. "Did I tell you Doris invited me to enter a pie in the Valentine Festival next weekend? They do both pie tasting and pie eating contests. I don't know which of my pies would do better, the Dutch apple or the lemon meringue. Which do you prefer?"

"Neither," Jon said, watching his wife's face fall with a twinkle in his eye. "It's your pecan pie or nothing!"

O O O

Days later, at the festival, Patty did indeed enter her pecan pie, which took third place. "Not bad for your first entry," Jon said.

"Shoulda been better," Wanda said, her left eyebrow sharply arched, dark eyes flashing in her smooth mahogany face. "Her pie was hands down better than Miz Johnson's berry pie. Sumthin' wrong with those judges, you ask me."

Jon cast his eyes to the ground. He'd been thinking the same thing about one of the judges in particular, Robert Shepard. Maybe Shepard held a grudge against him for taking over the paper and refusing to let it fail. He excused himself to get a few photographs for the paper.

"They want the old faithful to win," Doris said. "Don't want to encourage newcomers."

"I'd almost forgotten that one of the judges, Robert Shepard, is your son," Patty told Doris. *Easy to forget,* Patty thought, *since prickly Robert is so little like his warm, generous mother.*

Doris sighed and looked away for a moment. Turning back, she said, "He's still angry. An angry young man that's becoming an angry old man."

"Stop making excuses for him. What's he got to be angry about?" Wanda asked, absently smoothing her t-shirt which read, *I'm not saying he's lost his marbles but there's definitely a hole in the bag,* over a colorful display of loose marbles. "He's had a pretty sweet life, you ask me."

Doris explained to Patty, "His grandfather started the paper, it was his life's mission. His son, Bob, Robert Sr, my Robert, he loved that paper more than anything in this life. He gave it more attention than he gave little Bobby. Then he had a stroke." Doris sagged against her friend Wanda.

Wanda pulled her into a hug and continued the story. "Robert Jr dropped out of college to help his daddy run the paper during his recuperation but then his daddy never got better. And Robert never cared about the paper, to him it was just a chore."

"Robert Sr," Doris said, "went to his office at the paper every day for the rest of his life but he was never able to take over again. By the time he died, it was too late for Bobby, I mean Robert Jr, to go back to college. He never got to lead his own life, never got to find out how wonderful he might have been." She blew her nose and shook her head sadly. "He never got over it and he's taken it out on the paper all these years. He was so happy to sell it, leave it behind, I thought maybe he'd finally be happy."

Wanda patted her friend's back. "There, there, now. It could still happen." She shrugged her shoulders and sent a sad smile to Patty over her friend's head.

Patty suspected Wanda didn't see any changes in Robert's happiness level but, understanding Robert Shepard a little better, she couldn't help but wonder at what might have been.

FIVE

Patty swayed and hummed along with the Motown music she'd found on Pandora. The pizza crust had risen to fill the twelve by eighteen inch pan and was ready to receive her homemade sauce. She ran the big block of fresh mozzarella cheese through the food processor and scattered it in a thick, even layer. Chanting "Toppings, toppings, toppings," she quickly dealt out pepperoni, strips of roasted red pepper, fresh oregano, and sliced black olives.

She heard the door downstairs open just as she slid the finished pizza into the oven. *Perfect,* she thought, *Jon's home from his run with just enough time to clean up before dinner. Wait a minute, that's too many footsteps on the stairs. Who does he have with him?*

"Come on up," Jon called. "It's pizza night, I promise there'll be plenty." Patty heard deep male voices respond but she couldn't identify them or understand what they were saying. She looked down at her t-shirt - *I'm not short, I'm built low to the ground for speed and accuracy* - stained with pizza sauce, wondering who she would be entertaining, dressed so casually.

The door opened and Jon led Alec Harrison and a young man into their home. Patty recognized the police chief but she hadn't had much of a chance to get to know him before now.

"Patty, look who I bumped into on my run," Jon said. "Alec and his son, Trevor. They passed me like I was standing still and then they were going around again just as I made it home. I asked them to stay for dinner, okay?"

"Of course it's okay," Patty said. "There's more than enough pizza and I love company."

"I'm going to go freshen up, you guys can use the front bathroom if you like. Do you need fresh shirts?" Jon asked, looking them over. "No, of course you don't, you're not sweaty at all. Are you sure you were running?" Jon headed to the back while Alec and Trevor took turns in the front bathroom.

Patty re-set the table for four and the guys all returned to the table, sniffing appreciatively at the air. Patty cut the pizza into large sections and brought it to the table. Jon and Alec had cold beer, Trevor, denied a beer with just a look from his father, had milk, and Patty poured herself a tall glass of iced tea.

Patty stole the opportunity to watch while everyone helped themselves to pizza. Jon and Alec discussed their run times, heart rates, recovery times, and running shoes while Trevor listened but didn't join in. Patty noticed that Jon had replaced his sweaty shirt with one of his message shirts, the one that asked the question, *Listen and Silent have the same letters. Coincidence?*

Turning to look at Alec, Patty noticed his khaki colored t-shirt not only still looked fresh, the creases from pressing and folding were still clearly visible. *How does he do that? I can't see them through the table, but I bet his running shorts have matching creases.* At least Trevor's shirt, declaring, *I stopped understanding math when the alphabet decided to get involved,* looked a little rumpled. Patty wasn't sure she would've recognized Trevor as Alec's son if she hadn't already known. He was almost the same height as his dad, probably about 5'11", but rounded, maybe still carrying a little baby fat. His skin looked like liquid caramel and his eyes were a warm, clear, pale smoky quartz color.

"Wow," Trevor said, smiling at Patty, revealing deep dimples. "Miz Townsen', this's the best pizza I ever had. Where'd you get it?"

Patty smiled at him. He reminded her of so many of the students she'd known as a teacher, making her like him immediately. "I didn't get it, I made it."

"So, frozen then," he replied. "What brand?"

"No, I actually made it," she said patiently. "I use a version of my great grandmother's bread recipe for the dough and my own recipe for the sauce."

"Yeah, that was fun," Jon interrupted. "We had pizza every week for a while as she fiddled with the recipe, getting it just the way she wanted. It wasn't a hardship really," Jon said, waving both hands to dismiss the complaint. "They were all good."

"And our son was a teenager then," Patty smiled in fond memory. "He could eat all the pizza I'd make."

Everyone reached for seconds and the talk turned to the town, shifting from the pizza places in town to some of the community's other highlights, and finally landing on the local history.

"All those big places on 'mansion row'," Alec said with a tilt of his head toward the town circle. "Those were the homes of our founding families, from back when this valley was mostly farming or ranches. One's the home of the descendants of our first banker and another one's owned by the family who gave us our first mayor."

"And then there's all those new big places for rich people north of town," Trevor added.

"Yeah those," Alec nodded. "As some of the founding families began to spend their wealth, they sold off big parcels of land to developers who built McMansions for people willing to pay big bucks for 'em and commute to their jobs."

"Commute? From here?" Patty asked. "Isn't that a pretty long commute?"

"That it is," Alec agreed. "Even when traffic's light, it's over an hour each way to San Diego. They're gone so much each day that they're really more like part time residents. There are even a couple of guys who commute to LA. They stay there three or four nights, only come home weekends."

"I can't imagine loving a job badly enough for all that," Patty said.

"Your husband tells me you taught high school before you moved here," Alec said to Patty. "Do you think you'll teach here?"

"No," Patty replied quickly, perhaps a little too quickly. Hearing it, she explained herself. "I really enjoyed the classroom, working with young minds, open to learning. But I think I'm ready for something new." Before anyone could ask the obvious follow up question, Patty turned to Trevor. "What year are you, Trevor? Junior, senior?"

"Just a junior, ma'am," Trevor answered, squirming in his seat, eyes cast down, clearly uncomfortable talking about school. "But I made varsity in track and field."

"Just like his old man," Alec said. Seeing his son cringe at the comparison, Alec changed the subject, "Looks like we just about ate you outta house and home. You know, if you're looking for something to do, you could do worse than opening a pizza place in the space you have downstairs. We'd be your first customers."

Patty smiled at the compliment and dished the final piece of pizza onto Trevor's plate, earning a grateful smile. "No," she said. "That sounds like too much work to me."

As Trevor finished his last bite and downed the rest of his milk, Alec pushed back from the table and patted his flat belly, saying, "We're going to have to run twice as far tomorrow to burn off all this good food. Thank you."

They said their good-byes and Jon walked Alec and Trevor downstairs to the door while Patty cleaned up.

"Need help?" he asked upon his return.

"Naw," Patty said. "It's part of what I like best about pizza night. The clean up's so easy, one pan, plates, cups, and silverware. All done," she said putting the final plate in the dishwasher before turning around. "Waddaya say tonight, sitting area or straight to the bedroom?"

"I have some computer work to finish up but I can do that either place," Jon said.

"Straight to bed it is, then," Patty replied.

After they'd brushed their teeth and changed into their sleep wear, they met in bed, Jon with his laptop and Patty with a new novel to read. Over the years they'd perfected their discussion technique. Patty brought her teacher's probing questions, queries to determine whether the learner truly understood the lesson or was merely repeating by rote what he thought the teacher wanted to hear. Jon brought his journalist investigative questions designed to discover how the pieces of the story fit together. One topic tonight was in dire need of their combined examination.

"I almost forgot to tell you," Patty said. "I had a particularly revealing conversation with Doris and Wanda today."

"Hm, you don't say," Jon said without looking away from his laptop.

"Yes, it was about Robert and some of the history of your new paper." Patty smiled as she watched Jon close out, turn off, and put aside his computer.

"I thought that might get your attention," she said, her voice purring in satisfaction.

"Okay, it's not nice to tease. What'd you learn?"

Patty told him about Robert's grandfather starting the paper, about his father's stroke and about Robert's loss in taking over the paper for his ailing father.

"So he saw the paper as a ball and chain representing everything that held him back all his life, all his unrealized dreams," Jon summarized.

"Yeah, he grew to resent it and couldn't wait to get it off his hands."

"He probably lumps me with his father in that I love the paper."

"Yeah, he thought unloading the paper was a

smart move now that papers are a dying business," Patty said. "It must be really difficult for him to see you succeed with it. That would mean the paper's failure was his fault and not an economic trend."

"Yeah, I guess it would," Jon mused. "I get that." He turned to Patty, smiling, and asked, "What would I do without you?"

"Let's make sure you never have to find out."

○ ○ ○

Jon was working on the floor of the big printing press room, all high ceilings and industrial lighting. It still smelled of lubricant but at least it was quiet when the press wasn't running. He suspected Robert was telling all of his old friends that since newspapers were a dying business, putting ads there was a waste of money. Jon had decided he could fill the lost ad space with public service announcements while he sought replacements. He and Henry were re-working the layout for this week's edition when a man with a vaguely familiar face walked in.

The man walked up and stuck out his hand to shake saying, "Hi, Jon. How are you today?"

The second Jon heard his voice it came back to him, this guy was the minister of one of the big churches in town. Unfortunately, though he could remember seeing him behind the pulpit, his name didn't come to him. "Hi, Reverend," he said. "I'm doing pretty good. And yourself?"

"Good, good enough," the reverend replied. "Look I can see you're busy here, so I'll get right to it. I saw the nice ad you ran last week for the Methodist pancake breakfast and I'd like to do something like that for our car wash. How much does something like that cost?"

"Cost?" Jon asked, brows furrowing, mentally searching desperately for an answer. He'd run the ad for the pancake breakfast for free as a public service announcement. PSA's were usually run for free, space donated by the paper. He didn't have a price sheet for that kind of thing. If he charged this guy it wouldn't be fair to him, but he couldn't go back to the first church and charge them retroactively.

"The first ad is free," Henry spoke up. "With an agreement to purchase more after that."

Perfect! Jon thought, *Thank God for Henry. Again.* "Yes, step into my office with me so we can work out the layout for your ad." He shot a look of gratitude over his shoulder toward Henry as he led the man into his small, cozy office space. An interior space, it had no windows but Patty had added a comfy sofa for Jon to use when thinking or napping.

"I brought a copy of the flyer with me," the reverend said, pulling out a bright yellow sheet of paper. "It has all the details you'll need. Will that help?"

When they were all finished, the reverend filled out the required paperwork and signed it. Jon immediately recognized his name, Reverend Langley. Of course! When he was gone, Jon sat down to work up a plan to differentiate between true PSA's and ad's for local events and to solicit more of these ads for the coming weeks.

○ ○ ○

In the meantime, while Jon was happily busy with the expansion of his ad program, Patty was returning home with bags of groceries. She carried them upstairs, slammed the door, and all but threw them onto the counter. One bag fell over, apples and oranges rolling across the counter, falling to the floor and bouncing away.

Patty stood still a moment, listening intently. *Good, Jon's not home, no one here to witness my childish behavior.* She pulled out a chair and sank into it, her head dropping to her hands. Patty shook her head. "This isn't me. I'm not like this," she whispered to the empty house. She looked around at the lovely home she'd made here. "What is my problem?"

It's that empty space downstairs, the answer came to her. Every time I enter or leave my home I have to walk through it and be reminded that I still don't have a plan. "It taunts me," Patty muttered.

Her cell phone rang, interrupting her own private pity party. Patty assumed it was Jon and immediately felt guilty for giving in to her feelings. She pulled out a tissue and reached for her phone.

But it wasn't Jon calling, it was Nathalie from her ceramics class, the young lady who taught yoga. *Great timing,* Patty thought, *maybe she has a new place to hold her classes and I can sign up for one. I sure need it right now.*

When Jon got home that afternoon, Patty told him about the call from Nathalie. She was still looking for a place for her yoga classes and wanted to know if Patty would be willing to rent her the small side room off the downstairs area. "Whadaya think?" she asked him.

"I don't know," he replied. "I guess I'd be okay with it as long as you can renegotiate once you've decided what you want to do downstairs."

"We'll cross that bridge when we come to it," Patty said, all the while thinking, *but first, I'll have to build that bridge.*

SIX

Patty rolled up her yoga mat and took it upstairs, where she retrieved the basket of muffins she'd left there for just this purpose. This was the second yoga session Nathalie had led in her new space downstairs. The students all brought their own bottled water to re-hydrate after class. After the previous class, Patty had decided to offer some fresh homemade muffins.

She checked her t-shirt, proclaiming, *Those who love teaching, teach others to love learning*, for freshness, shrugged, and headed back downstairs with her muffins.

The muffins disappeared quickly and, in ones and twos, the students said their goodbyes and left. Nathalie packed up the remainder of her equipment and stored it in the corner cabinet. "Am I too late to get one of those muffins?" she asked.

"Don't worry, I put one aside for you," Patty replied, pulling out the one last muffin and handing it to Nathalie. "The class today was great, just what I needed. How's the space working out for you?"

"Great," Nathalie said. "There were more people here this morning than last week and I expect more next week. Soon I'll be able to add more classes for people who can't come on this day of the week or at this time for whatever reason. And that'll mean I can pay you more for the use of the space." She smoothed her t-shirt which said simply, *Namastay happy*, and looked through the open doorway to the larger space. "What're you planning to do with that big space?"

"I haven't decided yet," Patty said, all of the emotional well-being from an hour's yoga workout leaching away. "Just lately my decision making skills resemble those of a squirrel crossing a street. I swear I never used to have trouble making a decision."

Nathalie quickly changed the subject, asking, "Where'd you get these muffins? They're great."

"Oh, I make those," Patty said. "I have a couple of variations on the recipe. I'll probably have a different version for next week. Is it okay to bring them for after class?"

"Sure. I don't want them eating before class, but after is fine. What do you charge for them?"

"Charge? Nothing, they're free," Patty said, shaking her head. "I guess I just enjoy feeding people."

Nathalie beamed. "And, speaking for people, we're happy to be fed by you. You know, you could use that space to sell your muffins. People would pay for these and there's nobody else in town offering anything like them."

"Oh, I don't think so. It sounds like so much work, never knowing which ones will sell, how many to make of each kind, what to do with any that don't sell. No," she said, shaking her head again, more firmly this time. "That's not what I'm looking for." *Great,* she thought, *I'm getting really clear about what I don't want. Maybe I'm zeroing in on what I do want.*

○ ○ ○

Patty continued her ceramics classes, learning more about turning raw clay into useful, if not always beautiful, pieces. She was surprised to run into Jon on campus one afternoon as she was heading home. "What are you doing here?" she asked.

"It's an open campus," he replied. "I'm allowed and I'm not checking up on you." Jon teased.

"I'm sorry. I was just surprised to see you here. I didn't mean to accuse you of anything."

Jon glanced at his watch. "I have a meeting with Woz to review our student project. I can't wait to tell him how pleased I am with the progress. There's one young guy, Carl, I'd like to hire if I can find the money."

"That's great, honey. Go get to your meeting. We'll talk over dinner."

○ ○ ○

Jon seemed a little more subdued over dinner, not quite as excited as he had been before his meeting. "Did something go wrong with Woz? With the project?" Patty asked.

"No, it's all on track. It's just that now I realize this might get us out of the red, but it'll be awhile before I'll be able to hire anyone on to help." Jon heaved a great sigh and fiddled idly in his chopped salad with his fork. "Woz had talked to Carl, the lead guy I mentioned, and he would be interested in being hired but I don't see where I'd come up with the money for that. We think the online version will eventually bring in revenue, but it'll be a while yet."

Patty watched Jon as he explained the financial

aspects of online journalism. She didn't care about the details but she was suddenly aware of changes in his appearance. His evening runs were having a positive effect on his waistline even as hers was expanding from her relative inactivity.

Jon still mostly wore khaki colored chinos every day but since moving here, he'd started wearing polo shirts with a sports jacket instead of dress shirts with ties. When he changed into his running clothes each afternoon, he put on one of his message shirts. Tonight he was wearing one with a grammar joke, *The Past, Present, and Future walked into a bar. It was tense.* The message was funny but the humor did not extend to Jon's face, where aging showed clearly.

More silver in his hair at his temples than I ever noticed before, she thought. *And I could accept the new wrinkles around his eyes, they're mostly smile lines. But when did he develop that deep vertical crease between his eyebrows? And where did those long sad lines coursing down past his mouth come from?*

Patty was suddenly reminded, out of the blue, of an earlier time in their marriage. They'd been young professionals, absorbed by their careers and the demands of parenting a young son, drifting apart for lack of time together. Patty had been tempted by a fellow teacher. He was average looking, nothing special, but he gazed at Patty attentively and hung on her every word. She'd been drawn to his company, reveling in the attention.

Nothing had happened. The flirtation didn't go anywhere. Patty had woken up to the danger before she'd fallen prey to that cliché`. But she still carried guilt that she'd even been tempted. She never knew for sure if Jon had suspected anything, but somehow his instincts kicked in. He became more thoughtful around her and they'd reconnected. It was the turning point that had made what could have been a terrible situation into a new beginning for their marriage. *Why ever did I think of that right now? Am I so absorbed in my problems that I haven't been paying enough attention to Jon's?*

Patty consciously set aside her thoughts about planning for her own business downstairs to focus on Jon's issues with the paper.

"I'm feeling more empathy for those old vultures," Jon was saying. "Even with our positive finances, I can't help but feel the pressure to make ends meet."

"I think you need to give the new ideas a chance to play out, see how well they work," Patty said. "Maybe you could see if that guy would be interested in a, oh what did you call it at the paper in LA? A 1099 contract position for a private contractor? until more money is coming in."

Jon perked up. "Yeah, that might work," he said. "With a 1099 set up, he wouldn't be exclusive to the paper. It may even work out better for him in the long run if he could arrange several contracts at different places. In today's economy, it might be a good idea not to put all his eggs in any one basket." Jon's whole demeanor changed. He sat up straighter, his smile erased the long lines around his mouth and decreased that nasty vertical crease between his eyebrows. "Yeah, I can work with that." He nodded and dug into his favorite salad with renewed enthusiasm.

○ ○ ○

Beyond what she was learning in her ceramics classes, Patty really enjoyed getting to see her new community through the eyes of the other students. And she was feeling more youthful in her message shirts, today's - *Earth without art is just 'eh'* - printed over a picture of the planet on a black background. They all talked while they worked with the clay and Patty sought out excuses to go out and about to visit people and places she never would have had the time for when she was teaching full time.

One of the younger girls shared some of her experiences volunteering with the nearby refugee community. "San Diego County has taken in more refugees than any other region of California for the past seven years," she said, nodding proudly. "LA County, about three times larger by population, runs a distant second."

"I had no idea," Patty said. "You don't hear much about that."

"Yeah well, the refugees just want to be accepted. They're seeking a sense of community, of belonging, and there are so many other refugees here, it all works for them."

"What kinds of things do you do?" Patty asked. "What's your volunteer work entail?"

"I tutor groups in English, speaking, listening, reading, and writing. But the IRC, the International Rescue Committee, runs other groups to help them find housing, jobs, healthcare, and other services, I don't know what all. I'm just blown away by how determined they are to make a better life here for their children than what they've known in their homelands." She looked at Patty with renewed interest. "Hey, didn't you used to teach? There are citizenship classes and GED classes, too. I bet they could really use you."

"Oh, I don't know how much time I could... " Patty paused, mid-sentence. *How can I say I don't have time to give? I'm not doing anything.* "I guess it wouldn't hurt to meet some IRC people. But no commitment, I'm just going to meet them."

Patty's excitement was obvious as she told Jon about her visit to the IRC offices, she paced around the room, talking with her hands. She walked over and turned off the music on the sound system, to focus Jon's attention. "They do so much. Jon, you have to go interview these people for the paper. There's a story there. At least one story, probably a series. Wait 'til you talk to them, see for yourself what all they're doing."

"Okay, okay, okay," Jon said, holding out his hands, palms up in surrender. "I'll go. I'll talk to them. I'll get them some coverage." He smiled at her. "I haven't seen you this fired up since we moved here. Will you be joining their efforts?"

"I don't know," Patty said. "It's tempting, to be involved in something so positive. These people need so much. But I'm pretty sure I don't want to go back to teaching and I don't think I should make any new commitments until I'm sure about what I'm doing downstairs."

"Do you know?" Jon asked, frozen in place. "Is it time to talk about that?"

"Not yet," Patty replied, smiling nervously and

wringing the dishtowel in her hands as she headed back to the kitchen. "But I think I'm getting closer. I'm pretty clear on all the things I don't want to do."

"That's a start."

Jon's series for the Valley Gazette covered the nearby refugee settlement, the services offered by IRC and some general background stories on refugees by groups, including several stories of select individuals. The final piece of the series addressed the fears and prejudices some of the refugees had faced coming from their new community.

"I'm surprised by some of their prejudices, disappointed really," Patty said after reading it. "I might have expected it of the older generation, but it's disheartening coming from young people on campus."

"Yeah," Jon said. "I'm beginning to uncover the crumbling foundation of the community beneath its idyllic facade."

"Crumbling foundation, wow, those are pretty strong words. Is it really that bad?" Patty asked.

"Probably no worse than anywhere else," Jon said. "People are people wherever you go."

○ ○ ○

Patty watched Jon getting ready to head off to his office at the Gazette. Thursday was the day each week he and Henry 'put the paper to bed', finalized it for distribution Friday morning. He was distracted by all the details of that. She didn't want to start any important discussions until he got home this afternoon, his plate clear until next Thursday.

63

Jon crossed to Patty to give her a quick peck on his way out the door, the look on her face giving him pause. "What is it?" he asked. "You look distinctly disturbed."

Only Jon would say 'distinctly disturbed' in casual conversation, he's such a wordsmith. "Not now, honey," Patty replied. "You go put your paper to bed. We'll talk when you get home."

"Are you sure? I can be a little late if it's anything urgent."

Patty chuckled and shook her head as she turned him toward the door. "Nothing urgent. It'll wait 'til you get home."

She had today to organize her thoughts, to line up her plans. She wanted to roll out her idea for the space downstairs. Her plans weren't yet clear. She had her own problems with it all and she needed Jon's full attention to help her figure it out.

SEVEN

When Jon got home later that afternoon, he found Patty had set up a folding table and chairs in the big open space downstairs, with dinner plates all laid out. As he looked around for a place to put his computer case and jacket, he heard Patty coming down the stairs.

"Oh good, you're home," Patty said, pushing a bottle of wine and a pair of their best wineglasses toward him. "Here, take these and I'll go back up and get dinner out of the oven."

Jon took them to the table where he found white candles in their best silver candlesticks. "Hmm, wine, candles, a basket of hot rolls. This is starting to look pretty special. I wonder what's up," he muttered as he lit the candles, too tired to do more than wonder.

Patty returned, using pot holders to carry a heavy covered pot. She placed it in the center of the table saying, "I decided to make a one pot meal tonight so I wouldn't have to make so many trips up and down the stairs to serve."

Inspired by the formal setting, Jon made the effort to pull out a chair for Patty. She curtsied and sat, chuckling. "I don't know what's proper when one's wearing jeans and a t-shirt." Looking down quickly to a favorite shirt she'd brought back from France which suggested, *If your glass is half empty, pour it into a smaller glass and quit your bitching'* she added, "Some of that wine, please." Patty passed the paella to Jon and helped herself to a dinner roll.

After Jon's first bite he sighed deeply, melting into his chair, and said, "I don't care what this is all about. One bite of your paella and I'm a happy man."

"Hold that thought," Patty said. "I'm ready to talk about plans for this downstairs space and I'm more than a little nervous about what I want to do."

"It's about time," Jon said, speaking quickly, more focused on feeding his face than listening to her. Seeing the hurt on Patty's face, he quickly added, "I mean, I'm sure it'll be great. I know you've taken your time and put a lot of thought into it."

"Yeah, but it still seems a little half-baked to me. I've never seen anything quite like it so I can't find anything to model it from."

"Hit me with it," Jon invited, stretching across the table for another of Patty's homemade dinner rolls.

"Let me start at the beginning," Patty said, choosing to ignore Jon's inattention. "Remember the time we spent in the French countryside after college graduation and before starting careers?"

"You mean our honeymoon, yes, I remember," Jon replied, stopping eating long enough to gaze questioningly at Patty over the wineglass he was refilling.

"In some ways, that was the best time of my life. Don't get me wrong, I wouldn't trade anything for JJ or our years together. But every time I tried to figure out what I wanted to do with this space, I found myself longing to go back to there, to then."

"What was it you wanted to go back to? What about that place and time was drawing you?" Jon, ever the reporter, asked. He put down his wine, pushed aside his plate, and was finally completely focused on this conversation.

"Wow, perfect question. You ought to be a reporter or something. You really zeroed right in on the heart of it," Patty said. "I wish I'd asked myself that question sooner." She blew out a big breath. "It took me a long time to make the connection and come around to the right point of view."

"I don't know about right point of view, but maybe the most helpful point of view," Jon said.

"People kept telling me I could sell my muffins, my pies, my pizza, but I knew that none of that was what I wanted to do. What I'd liked so much in France was the experience. Sure the food was good, but what I was remembering was the feeling of sitting around tables with other people, no one in a hurry, just enjoying the time."

"Yeah, those were some pretty special times together." Jon caressed Patty's hand, displaying the boyish grin she'd fallen in love with all those years ago. "Of course I thought it was special because we were there together."

"Oh, don't go looking for compliments, old man. You know I love you." Patty looked around the space. "So that's what I want to create here, a place where people can come to relax over some good food and enjoy the food, the time, and the company."

"You want to open a di-," Jon began.

Patty quickly held up a hand to stop him. "Don't say diner. A diner is the last thing I want to do. Too much work. With a diner, you have a menu with dozens of items and you have to be ready to cook to order, anything anyone wants. No, I am not interested in that at all." Patty shook her head firmly then slumped in her chair. "But that's where the doubts begin."

"Okay, no d-i-n-e-r," Jon said, spelling it out to avoid saying the hated word. "But why any kind of restaurant? You know restaurants fail more quickly than any other kind of business. Why would you want to set yourself up for failure?"

Patty frowned at Jon's response. She had her own worries about her idea and here he was shooting it down before she'd even gotten to the risky part. She looked away, lip trembling, afraid tears were next. She hated women who cried during an argument. "I don't know. Maybe it isn't such a good idea."

"No, I'm sorry. I'm always a little mentally spent on Thursdays. I'm sorry, really I am. Tell me your idea. I promise to listen with an open mind."

"Maybe we should postpone this discussion," Patty offered. "We could talk about it tomorrow."

"No," Jon said, wiping his hands on his napkin and pushing away from the table. "I really want you to do what you want here. So tell me, what do you have in mind?"

Patty stood up and walked over to the existing front door. "I figure we can leave the yoga space as it is and this front door works as an entrance. I want to replace these windows with ones like we have upstairs, with embedded blinds." Patty swirled around the empty space, pointing first to the row of windows along the north facing wall and then to the bare west wall. "And add more just like them wrapping around this area. I'm picturing three booths along the wide front wall, a big corner one here, and two more booths down the west wall."

"Okay six booths, I guess that fits. What else?"

Patty turned to the long wall parallel to the north and south walls dividing the space into two large spaces. "I'd like to keep that and build in waist high cupboards with a counter top. I can put coffee pots and ice water jugs there and a daily dessert display at one end. I saw the most darling little sign I want to put up over the dessert display." She returned to the table to grab Jon's hand. "Come on. We need to go in the smaller space for the rest."

They entered the dark, quiet room Patty envisioned as her cafe's future kitchen. Her voice echoing off the hard surfaces, she described her plans for the area, waving her arms and pointing to illustrate the workspace she had in mind.

"That all sounds reasonable enough," Jon said. "But I still have one big question, one you've been avoiding, if not a d-word, what kind of a place do you have in mind? That you think will somehow be less work?"

Patty took in a deep breath and sagged against the stairway leading upstairs to their home. "Okay, I guess I've avoided it as long as I can. What I want is a café, only open for breakfast and lunch. This town has some nice dinner places and people can head toward the freeway if they want fast food but remember our first visit here? There were no nice places for breakfast. I think, at least I hope, the key to making it be less work is to limit the number of choices on the menu."

"Makes sense, I guess," Jon said, but his

beetled eyebrows belied his stated agreement.

"I'm thinking about an 'of the day' kinda place," Patty offered, bracing herself for Jon's response.

"Waddaya mean?" Jon asked, leaning back, physically distancing himself from her and her strange suggestion. "You want a restaurant that only serves one thing a day? That's, I don't know ..." He sputtered to a stop, eyebrows bunched, mouth hanging open, hands open in surrender position.

"And that's exactly why it's taken me so long to get to this point," Patty said, making a conscious decision to ignore Jon's body language and forge ahead now that she'd gotten this far. "My current plan, subject to change, is a muffin and a frittata of the day for breakfast and a soup and a pizza of the day for lunch, plus a dessert of the day." She stopped talking, allowing Jon time to process her idea.

"I don't know," Jon said. "What about people who want something different? I've never heard of anything like this crazy idea."

Patty flinched at Jon's use of the c-word. She sighed. "Look, I admit it. I don't know anything about operating a café. But, I figure I won't have an expensive monthly rent to pay and if I can keep it simple enough, I'll be the only labor needed. With all that in mind, it seems to me that the secret to managing costs is to manage the surplus. With seven muffins, scones, cinnamon rolls, and sticky buns every day, without knowing how many of each will sell, I'd end up with way too many leftover. And they wouldn't be fresh to sell the next day. If I just make one, people can take it or leave it, or come back when what they want is offered."

"Okay, that sorta makes sense and Lord knows

I don't know anything about running a diner."

"You said the d-word," Patty accused, glaring at him until he raised his hands in surrender. "But yeah well, neither do I," she admitted. "I figure this limits my expenses. Everything fresh, just a few items for each day."

"You've had some time to plan this," Jon said, yawning. "I need some time to think about it, look at it from a couple of different angles, see if we can avoid any problems before they hit us."

"That's good," Patty said, tension leaking out of her posture and her voice, relieved that Jon seemed willing to consider her idea enough to at least think about the best way to do it. "I've been focusing on the menu choices and the kitchen build out, I can use any business tips you can bring."

"If you're looking for business acumen, why not ask the professor from Business Sciences at Valley Community College to review your plans?"

"Oh, that's good. I can do that," Patty said nodding as she began loading up things to take back upstairs.

"You know we didn't use all of the money we set aside for the remodel upstairs," Jon said. "You can use some of that money for the café remodel."

"Yes, I mean no. I don't want to use any of that money. That's our retirement savings. I'll apply for a business loan. That'll keep me honest about the costs and the interest will be a tax deduction. I need to make sure I document every cent I spend on the remodel. They'll be more business expenses to offset the taxes for my new business."

"That's right," Jon said. "Our first step needs to

be to meet with an attorney to incorporate your new company."

"Oh, that's right," Patty said, happy to welcome Jon's ideas. "I should have thought of that."

○ ○ ○

Patty rinsed the dishes and loaded them into the dishwasher while Jon went in to change for bed. She sniffed deeply at the homemade flan she'd prepared for their dessert, forgotten, melting into a messy puddle and oozing off the edge of the plate. She stared straight ahead, slumping, looking at nothing as tears coursed down her cheeks. *Maybe Jon is right, maybe this is a crazy idea.*

Patty wiped her tears with her dishwater wet hand and shook her head. *But I expected more support from him. Didn't I support him when he wanted to move here and buy the paper, even when that didn't go so smoothly?*

She blew out a breath. "I knew he'd be tired on a Thursday evening. I was all excited and he just wasn't feeling it. I should've waited for better time. 'Shoulda, woulda, coulda.' What's done is done," she muttered to her reflection in the dark window above the kitchen sink.

She found him a few minutes later sitting up in bed with his brand new reading glasses perched on his nose, clearly sound asleep, his chin resting on his chest. She decided she didn't want to crawl into bed with him tonight. She'd do a little more work on her planning and sleep on the couch.

EIGHT

When Patty woke the next morning, she stretched the kinks out of her neck from sleeping on the couch and followed the sounds of activity downstairs, where she found Jon with his measuring tapes and his laptop open and running. She watched quietly as he took another measurement and entered it into whatever software he had running. "What's that?" she asked, finger combing back her sleep messed hair.

Jon jumped a little and turned to her in surprise. "Good morning, Sleepyhead," he greeted her with a big smile. He was still in the sweats and old t-shirt he slept in but seemed fully awake and full of energy. "I worked on your new café all night in my dreams. I think we'll have space leftover for some small round tables along here between the booths and the counter."

"What's that?" Patty asked again, pointing to the laptop with suspicion.

"I pulled up a CAD program to help me visualize the space the way you described it," Jon said. Then, seeing the confusion on his wife's face, he explained, "CAD, Computer Aided Design. See, this is how it works. I put in the dimensions and we can see how the plans you have in mind will work before we put any money into building it out."

Patty was taken aback by this reversal of energy

levels, by his overnight turnaround. He seemed back to his usual caring, supportive self. *He called it a café.* She rubbed her eyes and came away with smears of last night's eye makeup. *Did I completely misread his reaction last night? Did a good night's sleep really make this much difference?* As much as she longed for the change, she didn't entirely trust it. "Yeah maybe, but I don't want to put them in to begin with. I can add them later if there's enough business to fill them."

They had several more productive discussions about the proposed café on Friday, Patty slowly accepting that her old familiar Jon really was back. Patty called Jon's contact in Business Sciences at Valley Community College to make an appointment to meet with her about reviewing Patty's ideas.

Patty and Jon continued to work together on the planning on Saturday and again on Sunday. By Monday, Patty was ready to call the attorney they'd used to buy the paper about incorporating. He said he only did commercial real estate law but he referred her to another attorney, Denise Crane, who took the information over the phone, promising to file the incorporation paperwork within the week.

Patty then contacted the contractor they'd used for the remodel upstairs. They'd liked him and were satisfied with his work. It was important that he had a subcontractor who was familiar with the special windows she wanted. Plus, she'd been more than satisfied with the guy who'd done the major build out of her kitchen upstairs. The new kitchen would be the most important part of this project. It had to be right.

Since most of the remodel would be interior, they didn't need much involvement from the city building inspector. But they still had to file their plans and get the necessary permits from the building department and schedule time for him to come out to review what of the remodel was exterior. He referred her to the county health department, whose inspection would be required.

Between the contractor and his subcontractors, the café slowly took shape into Patty's original vision, with a few of Jon's suggestions thrown in. Once she'd given the guy her ideas and he'd produced his own CAD generated plans, Jon had happily returned to the newspaper business and left Patty to the creation of her dream.

○ ○ ○

Opening day, finally, Patty sighed, remembering all the work and all the delays getting to this day. She pulled the apple walnut muffins from the oven and slid the Cajun frittata in. She rushed back into the café dining room to check that the shades were all even.

Nothing had changed since the last time she'd checked, five minutes ago. She sniffed deeply, the coffee and decaf were brewing beside the stacks of mugs. She checked her watch. Time to put out the ice water carafes. She darted back into the walk-in fridge to get them.

She took a deep breath, smoothed the front of her apron and turned over the 'OPEN' sign. She hadn't slept well last night, worrying about this moment. What had she forgotten? What might go wrong? And now she was too keyed up to stand still. Everything seemed to be simultaneously moving too fast and too agonizingly slowly.

Exactly no one rushed in. Business that first day was whatever the opposite of brisk might be. A little before noon, Patty took the platter of fresh baked date nut cookies, dessert of the day, and placed it under her beloved new sign in its fancy calligraphy script, *Stressed is Desserts spelled backwards.*

She surveyed her empty café. Other than the near complete lack of guests, it was exactly as she'd envisioned it. Patty was swamped by her emotions, the tensions of first planning each and every detail and then making sure all of it actually happened, and the stress of worrying about whether or not her idea would be accepted.

The north and west walls were filled by her beautiful new windows, with blinds encased between two of the three panes to prevent dust from collecting and falling into diners' food, over comfortable booths, six in total. The south wall, which separated the dining and cooking areas, held the counter top for drinks and the dessert of the day under her newly hung sign and over closed cabinets where she stored other necessary items. At the east end of this wall she'd had saloon style swinging doors installed to obscure the kitchen. The last wall, the east wall, separated the café from the yoga space. It had a small table for two, which she learned was called a two-top table, the stairs leading up to their living space, and the clearly marked door to the public restrooms, shared with the yoga studio.

She settled herself into one of the booths. The windows sparkled. The ceramic tile floors gleamed. The cushions for the booths were soft and inviting. The paint on the walls was a shade of off white with just a hint of pink undertones. It was all very inviting. But, it was still pretty empty, few paying customers.

It hadn't been completely empty all day. Jon had brought Henry for breakfast. Patty's friends, Doris and Wanda, came in for lunch. The student assigned from Business Sciences had dropped by. And that had been about it.

Patty had planned to take the leftovers to the food bank but, on her way there, she noticed the fire truck returning to the station from a call. On a whim she decided to give them some of the muffins and most of a veggie pizza. The food bank could have the rest. Little did she know this would be a smart marketing move.

Every day for the rest of that first week, Benjamin Rodriquez, or one or two of the other volunteer firemen, came in, either to sit and eat or to order takeout, sometimes for the station and other times for their families.

Tuesday after her yoga class, Nathalie stopped in for a blueberry scone, along with several of her students. That was a big increase to the breakfast sales but did nothing for lunch.

Wednesday, Alec and Trevor stopped by to pick up whatever pepperoni and sausage pizza was leftover to take home for their dinner. They ended up buying the leftover lemon poppy seed muffins for breakfast the next morning.

Thursday, a group of 'ladies who lunch' came in and Patty thought she recognized one of them from the yoga class. One older lady asked, "My daughter-in-law recommended your wild mushroom soup, but I don't see it today. Can I order it off menu?"

"No," Patty replied. "Your daughter-in-law must have been in on a Tuesday. I don't have any of the mushroom soup today, it's only available on Tuesdays. I make everything fresh each day. Try the cream of broccoli soup, I'm pretty sure you'll like it."

"But I had my heart set on the mushroom, she just raved about it," she said, making a pouty face that Patty felt certain she used with great effect when she wanted something from her husband.

"I'm sorry," Patty replied, forcing patience into her voice with a smile. "It'd take a full hour to get it ready for you and I wouldn't be able to serve any other diners in the meantime. If you don't want the broccoli soup, there's a bacon and brie frittata or I have barbecue chicken pizza today."

The lady returned her attention to the menu, her face a perfect picture of disappointment. Her younger companion looked up to Patty and mouthed "I'm sorry." A perfect microcosm of my café, Patty thought. For every difficult person there was at least one who was understanding.

Friday, Wanda came over to pick up a platter of pecan sticky buns for a meeting the chief of police was holding with some people from city hall.

Slowly, bit by bit, business picked up to a level that kept Patty busy without overwhelming her. By the end of the first month she was feeling better about it. Not good yet, but better.

Sure, there had been some people who wanted to order items not available that day. Patty invited them to come back for the appropriate day to get what they wanted. Most people settled for something available. A few walked out. *Oh well.*

Patty was surprised the day Claudia, the instructor for her ceramics class came in for lunch. "Welcome to my café," she said, seating her at her best booth, the one in the middle on the north wall of windows. "What can I get you today?"

Claudia looked over the selection and returned Patty's gaze. "I was hoping to get one of your stuffed potatoes, you know like you brought to our class potluck."

"Oh, I'm sorry," Patty replied, her shoulders dropping. "Those aren't on the menu. But now that you mention it, they should be. I could work those in easily. Have a bowl of soup - on the house for you today - and I promise to have stuffed potatoes the next time you come in. The menu, the whole café really, is still a work in progress."

"Perfect, I'd like that and if the soup is half as good as your potatoes, I'm sure I'll be back."

O O O

Later that afternoon, after the diners had left and Patty had turned the 'OPEN' sign over to 'CLOSED', she settled herself at the two-top table she'd set up on the east wall. She resisted seating customers there because of the lack of windows, but it was her favorite spot to sit and work. From here she could keep her eye on all of the booths and quickly catch any signal a customer might need something. Now, with all the customers gone for the day, she added the stuffed potatoes, a different one for each day of the week, to the menu.

She let her gaze drift around the empty space. The remodel had worked well, although getting the Health Inspector to show up for his scheduled reviews had challenged her time line. Forget about it. It was done now and that troublesome inspector was now one of her steady customers. As expected, the special windows and the walk-in refrigerator had been the biggest expenses and brought the worst of the problems. Now that they were done, Patty was glad she'd insisted.

From the moment Patty had decided on what she wanted her café to become, she'd known the perfect name for it. It'd come to her in a dream and she'd thought of it as Café Du Jour, in French to honor her fond memories of the cafés there, from the very beginning, absolutely wouldn't consider any other names, and now with the sign on the door, it was a reality.

She'd ordered several polo shirts for herself in a peachy shade of pink with a "Café Du Jour" logo over the left breast pocket and a couple of half aprons with generous pockets in a darker shade. Worn with khaki trousers or a skirt, it wasn't really a uniform, but it reminded Patty her café was real.

Patty looked around appreciatively. Her café was beginning to come together for her. It wasn't crowded, wasn't a booming business model. But more and more, customers lingered over their coffee and chatted, long after their empty plates had been removed. Her favorite customers enjoyed her cooking alright but spent more time simply sitting and talking with each other.

It wasn't there yet, but her little café was well on the way to emulating what she'd liked most about the cafés she remembered so fondly from their time in southern France. It was becoming more about the experience than the meal.

The biggest problem she faced now, open for a little over a month, was time. With at least half of the tables full, at least some the time, Patty was beginning to have difficulty getting the food prepared, the orders taken and delivered, keeping the coffee mugs and water glasses filled, and collecting payments. She didn't have time to sit in her own little café and enjoy the experience. *Maybe I didn't think this through,* she thought. *Maybe I didn't anticipate success.*

Her whole plan had been arranged around the ideas of controlling the expenses by limiting the menu options and of keeping it simple enough she could manage it by herself. Patty had always been an optimist, even in tough times. She had a history of bulling her way through rather than re-considering her idea. Now, here she sat, adding to the menu and looking for ways to work more efficiently.

○ ○ ○

When he was in the café, Jon used the same two-top table as his unofficial office. He set up his laptop and worked on stories while surreptitiously observing the community, listening for news or at least for news sources. Patty was happy to see that he'd walked back his earlier reservations about her café, now capitalizing on it for his own purposes.

He glad handed sources here and personally poured coffee refills for prospective advertisers. Patty knew she needed help and she took satisfaction in seeing him happily interacting with the customers. She could always pick out his familiar baritone voice over the clatter and chatter of her café.

"This is working out better than I expected," he said to her one Thursday afternoon shortly after Patty closed the café and he returned from putting his paper to bed for the week.

"There's been some resistance to my of-the-day style menu," Patty replied. "And income some days is almost enough to cover the cost of the groceries, but there's still not enough to pay me anything."

"Remember Patty, we talked about this. We never expected the café, either of our businesses really, to support themselves this first year. That's not realistic." Jon absently scratched at his stubble as he tried to recall some fact. "I almost remember the research for a story I did a long time ago. It was something about the percentage of businesses that fail in the first five years."

"That sounds like a happy story," Patty said, her tone and the quirk of her mouth conveying her real feelings.

"Really what I remember most clearly is that the stats were based the DBA, Doing Business As, filings. They have to be renewed every five years so they figure any business that doesn't renew, didn't make it." Jon shook his head and shrugged his shoulders in wonder at the minds of bureaucracy. "Anyway, my point is, we can't expect either of our new businesses to support themselves, much less us, anytime soon."

"Yeah," Patty agreed, relaxing into her seat and nodding. "We enjoy a really unique financial situation, able to support ourselves while we work to see if they'll make it."

"I'm pretty sure my paper would have folded already if I had to take a salary to make a house payment. This café is just beginning to gather a following. Remember this whole of-the-day idea is pretty new to everyone."

"Yeah, I don't know yet if it's going to work. It's a good thing I have the rental from the yoga studio to cover the payments for the remodel loan."

Jon took her hand. "Give it some time."

"Time. That's the problem," Patty lamented. "It isn't that there's so many things to do, it's that they all have to be done at the same time and there's only one of me."

"Really Patty, what did you expect? No one, not even you, can be two places at once."

That's not helpful, Patty thought. *Truthful maybe, but still not helpful.*

NINE

Patty worked the daily stuffed potatoes into her plan and they were very popular right from the start. She'd made a point to schedule them taking advantage of any leftover soup from the previous day as often as she could. That cut down on waste right away.

Since opening, she'd posted the daily choices on a big whiteboard near the front door. From the beginning, she'd had to spend too much of her time explaining what was available on other days.

This week she was starting something new. She'd put her full weekly menu, seven daily options each for Breakfast Bread, Frittata, Quiche, Soup, Stuffed Potato, Pizza, and Dessert, onto one page and had it printed onto twelve by seventeen inch place mats. The specialty print shop had printed them on peachy pink paper to complement her color scheme and had given them graceful scalloped edges.

"I wish I could have them laminated so they could be wiped off and re-used," she told Jon when they went to pick them up.

"I understand you want to be environmentally responsible, but is it a good idea to do that before you know there won't be any more edits? You'd end up throwing them all out if you decide to make any other changes."

"When," Patty said, tugging at the ends of her

short hair. "Not if. I know there'll be more changes." She sighed, watching the scenery flow past the window as Jon drove home. "I'll let it go until the first anniversary. Then I can look back and see how frequent the adjustments have been."

O O O

In the meantime, Jon continued to cover local news while investigating the rumors about financial misdeeds at city hall.

One source had emerged who seemed reliable but who refused to be quoted or listed as a source in any way. Jon hated that, but he could understand it. This is a small town. Anyone who hoped to continue to live here needed to be careful.

"What is that old saying, 'If you shoot a king, you must kill him'?" Jon asked Patty one evening over dinner, frowning and stretching his long arms over his head. "As long as the sitting city council is in office it wouldn't be advisable to speak out. My problem is that until someone is willing to speak out, I can't expose the issue, much less who's involved."

"What exactly is going on at city hall?"

"I'm not entirely sure yet," Jon replied, the furrow between his eyebrows deepening. "According to my source, too many of the city council's recent decisions have awarded contracts directing city funds to their top campaign contributors. This includes any spending for the fire and police departments, schools, parks, and public services like road repairs or trash pickup."

"I get it," Patty said. "If that's really what's

happening, wouldn't it mean that overall, the city is paying too much for what they get?"

"Exactly," Jon said, nodding absently, his eyes focused somewhere in the middle distance, between Patty's face and the setting sun framed in the west windows. He shook it off. "So far I haven't uncovered any direct evidence of bribes. I need to spend more time on this until I either find a more willing source or stumble across written evidence. This isn't going to be a quick reveal."

"Yeah, and you're loving it aren't you?" Patty grinned at her husband, knowing him so well.

Jon looked down at his empty plate and smiled sheepishly at being caught in his guilt. "I'm really a terrible person, aren't I? It isn't like I wished this problem into existence or anything but this is exactly the kind of story a good investigative reporter can sink his teeth into."

"And like the bulldog you are, you won't let it go until you get to the bottom of it."

"It looks like I'll be following the money from campaign donations to votes on spending city funds for the foreseeable future."

"Just remember," Patty said, getting up to clear the table and bring in dessert. "You may feel like a terrible person now, but in the end, you're doing a good deed for our new community."

"My source doesn't want to be named but she, I mean he or she, is directing me to a couple of good specific issues I can research for myself," Jon said.

"Won't the city clerk be able to tell what you're looking into?" Patty asked.

Jon grinned, looking much like their son JJ as a

teen with his hand in the proverbial cookie jar. "No, ain't technology grand? All the city council meetings are available for review on the internet. I can watch entire meetings to see not only the final vote counts, but all the discussions. That's what's really revealing."

O O O

Patty waved goodbye to Doris at the door as she left with some packaged leftovers for the food bank. Now all she had to do was her nightly chores so she could get a head start on the next day's food prep. Once that was finished, she could do a final clean up and take the leftover soup and stuffed potatoes she'd set aside up for their dinner.

When she finally got upstairs, three hours later tired and rumpled with a pizza sauce stain on her shirt, she found Jon working on his laptop at the dining table, covered with papers. Startled by her arrival, he glanced over to the west facing windows, checking the time of day against the setting sun. "Already?" he asked. "How did it get so late? You need help with that?"

Patty put the foodstuffs down on the counter top and heaved a great sigh. "Already?" she asked. "Funny, it didn't seem quick to me. I'm exhausted. You know, sometimes I think my favorite thing about this café idea is that I don't have to prepare any dinner unless I just want to. Tonight, we're having leftover corn chowder and Stroganoff stuffed potatoes. I hope that's okay."

"Better than okay," Jon said. "I've been smelling it up here and it's got my mouth watering."

Patty went back to the master bedroom to freshen up and re-emerged wearing shorts and an old shirt reading, *I'm not short, I'm fun sized*. She put the soup and potatoes into the microwave and began pulling out bowls, plates, and silverware. She took them over to the table and stared silently at Jon and his mess of paperwork until he took the hint and began clearing space. "What is all this, anyway?" she asked him.

"This is exciting, is what it is," Jon said getting up to turn off the news station he'd been ignoring and collect all the pages into organized stacks. "My source suggested a couple of specific city council meetings to review. The major topic for two of them was the new trash collection system. I printed out their final vote count approving these increased costs then went to the campaign page for each of the council members who voted in favor."

"Okay, that makes sense," Patty said, nodding her head as she set the table.

"Wanna guess what I found?" Jon asked, sounding like a cat with a canary still struggling in its mouth might sound. "Each of the council members who received the maximum in donations from the company benefitting directly from the new plan, voted for the new plan and neither of the two who voted against it, did."

"Alright, that looks like you've found some solid circumstantial evidence, but what's it all about? What difference does it make?" Patty put filled soup bowls and plates with stuffed potatoes in front of each of them.

"Let me start with a little history," Jon said. "Before we moved here, the trash was collected in one pass. The trash truck would drive down each alley or street, collecting all the trash from both sides in one trip. Now multiple trash trucks make a total of six trips down each alley and street to pick up trash from brown cans, recyclables from blue cans and yard clippings from green cans, collecting first one side then the other."

"From one trip to six!" Patty cried. "How is that environmentally responsible? Or financially? Wait a minute, how did they handle recycling before? Maybe there's a good reason for the change."

"It used to be delivered to a big county facility where it was mechanically sorted into trash and recyclable. And get this," Jon said, his excitement level rising. "A portion of our monthly payment to the city for water and trash pick-up still goes to pay our share for that county facility. Even under our new system." He huffed a big sigh. "I still need to investigate whether this new plan is actually an improvement or not."

"Yeah, 'cause if it is, it doesn't matter who donated what to whose campaign."

"Exactly," Jon said. "It only matters if a council member is looking out for their own good over that of the citizens."

"Wow, pretty big story in a small community," Patty said. "I guess that's one big difference between writing for a major paper in a big city and writing about your neighbors in a small place like this."

"Yeah, it is. And according to my source, this is just one example. I need to keep digging."

"Have you discussed any of this with Alec?" Patty asked.

"No, I'm not ready to take any of this to him yet."

"Why not?" Patty persisted. "He is the chief of police and corruption is a crime, isn't it?"

"Maybe, but the way I see it is, either he's involved, at which point I don't want to tip my hand or he isn't and I don't want to put him in the middle. The city council is his boss after all. Besides, I'm not through investigating. There may not be anything criminal here at all."

○ ○ ○

Fridays were always busy days in the café. Patty wasn't sure if the menu for that day was the draw or if it was just a day people liked to get out for some food made by someone else. Certainly, people tended to linger over their meals more on those days and chat with friends.

Whatever the reason, it was all Patty could do to keep up with the demand. She bustled back and forth preparing more of each menu item based on anticipated demand, serving, refilling coffee mugs and water glasses, and collecting payments.

At one point, early afternoon, she emerged from the kitchen with both hands full of hot, plated foods, to find a tall stranger refilling coffee mugs and chatting with her customers. Patty froze for just a moment. She couldn't stop longer, people were waiting for their food while it was still hot.

She served the booth full of hungry diners and turned her attention to the stranger. She was an older woman with hair piled high on her head, a brash shade of red that could only come from a bottle, no matter the age. Before Patty could get to her, the stranger approached Patty, handing her the money she'd collected from the customers now leaving the café. Patty stood there with a fist full of money and her mouth hanging open, not sure what to make of this woman but there was no time now.

"Here, you take the cash and go get the food for the corner booth. I got this," the stranger said, looking at Patty with her calm, collected slate blue eyes, before heading to the end booth with the coffee and decaf carafes.

Still in mild shock, Patty returned to the kitchen to fill more plates and they worked together seamlessly until time to close.

"Nice little place you got here," the stranger said, patting the seat next to her. "Sit here, rest a spell, you surely earned it."

"Thanks," Patty said, uncertain if sarcasm rang through her tone. *Inviting me to sit in my own place! Who the hell ... ?* "Who are you?"

"My name's Carole Gibbs, but you can call me Care," she said shrugging dramatically with her full body. "Most people do. I can't explain it, 'cause, Sugah, I don't."

Patty's brow wrinkled as she puzzled out what this 'Care' person was saying. *She doesn't? Doesn't what? Oh I get it, she doesn't care.* "Where did you come from?" she asked.

"Oh, that's a long story and we'll have plenty of time to talk tomorrow. What time do we open in the morning?"

Patty's eyes widened at Care's use of 'we'. Carefully emphasizing the first person pronoun, she replied, "I open at 7:00."

"Seven, huh? I don't do seven. Okay, I'll see you tomorrow at eight."

"Wait, I don't even have a 'Help Wanted' sign out."

"Maybe not, but you surely do need the help and I can do the job. I'll turn the sign to 'CLOSED' on my way out."

TEN

Finally finished for the day, Patty carried slices of leftover three cheese pizza with strips of roasted red peppers and sliced olives upstairs for their dinner, where she found Jon once again at work at their table. "You're not going to believe the weirdo who came in today," she told him.

"Hmm," he mumbled without looking up.

"Somehow, I don't think I have your full attention," she said, giving up for now and heading back to their bedroom to change clothes and get comfortable for the evening.

When she returned wearing sweats and a shirt that threatened, *Don't make me use my Teacher Voice*, Jon had packed up his materials, clearing space on the table.

"Still working on city corruption?" she asked.

"No, actually I've put that story on hold while I follow another trail."

"What?"

"It's too soon to say anything just yet," he said. "Let me see where it goes before we discuss it. What were you saying when you came up? Some weirdo?"

Patty busied herself getting dinner on the table while she answered. They had taken to eating much earlier these days since she had to get up before six

93

each morning to get food prep and everything else ready downstairs. Jon was being a pretty good sport about it. "I said you wouldn't believe the weird lady who came into the café this afternoon."

"Not one of your regulars, a new customer, then. Isn't that a good thing?"

"She started out as a customer, but then she just sorta took over." Patty shook her head at the memory. "She's an older lady, maybe mid-sixties or so. It's hard to say. She has this bottle red hair that doesn't occur in nature that she wears piled up on her head, like the B-52's. Remember them?"

"Yeah, they were retro way back then. Okay, I'm getting a picture. What'd she do to make her seem weird?"

"I was coming out of the kitchen with the plates for the people in the number four booth and found her refilling mugs for number one. By the time I got them served, she had collected payment from number three and handed it off to me." Patty paused, eyes focused inward for a moment while she collected her thoughts. "For the rest of the afternoon, she took over the waitress duties and I got to concentrate on cooking. But that's not the best part."

Jon chuckled. "It gets better?"

"Yeah, at close of business, she asked what time do 'we' open tomorrow morning. When I told her, she said she 'didn't do seven' she'd be in at eight. Jon, she just hired herself. Like I didn't even get a vote in it."

"Is she some sort of threat? Do you want me to hang around downstairs tomorrow at eight?" Jon asked, straightening, his tone a mixture of humor and concern.

"No." Patty paused. She smiled, noticing for the first time the shirt Jon was wearing which cautioned, *Never question your wife's choices, you're one of them.* "First of all, I don't know if she'll even show up tomorrow. She may be a crazy for all I know. She didn't seem scary, just a little strange."

"You're right, she sure sounds weird."

"I'll tell you what's weird," Patty said surprise leavening her tone. "What's weird was how smoothly everything went this afternoon with her help. I could get used to that." A smile slowly transformed her face as the muscles in the back of her neck relaxed.

O O O

The next morning Patty started her morning preparations like every other morning since she'd opened the café. But she found herself glancing at the clock much more frequently. The few regular early customers came in, business as usual. At eight o'clock on the dot. Carole, 'Care', appeared, just as the last of the morning guests was departing. She followed Patty through to the kitchen.

Patty looked her over while Care explored the kitchen, peering at the prep set ups and even into the walk-in fridge. Patty estimated her height at around 5' 7" or 8", she was so slim that she might appear taller than her actual height. She looked to be about 140 lean and stringy pounds. Her brash red hair was piled on her head, just like yesterday, but her eyes looked more blue than gray today, to match her powder blue eye shadow. Her triangle shaped face had a pointy chin and was well lined, covered with heavy foundation, powder and blush. Her lipstick a garish red.

"Tell me about yourself," Patty coaxed.

"I guess that'd be easier than filling out a full bio for a job application," Care said, pulling in one of the chairs from the two-top table in the dining area and settling herself. She took a deep breath. "I'm from Newnan, Georgia, in case you didn't catch the accent." She looked around and lowered her voice. "I've worked diners all my life. I like this better, Sugah. You've got a real nice set up here."

"Thank you," Patty said, nodding for her to continue.

"Anyway, my husband worked as a long haul trucker and all those years, it was fine, him being gone most of the time. Then after one trip, he just didn't come home. I called the truck company to report him missing and they told me he wasn't missing, he was still working for them. I tracked him to his last job, out of San Diego, and came out here to retrace his trail. Then I started to hear about a woman traveling with him." Care paused, huffing out a big breath. "Honey, I'm not sure he's worth the trouble. If another woman wants him, she can have him." She shook it off. "None of that matters. You need some help here and I can do the job."

"That's probably true," Patty said. "But I don't know that I can afford to hire you."

"I tell you whut," Care drawled. "Let's try it for a couple of days and then we can talk about hiring me."

They worked together for the rest of the busy weekend. It wasn't perfect, their paths crossed a couple of times during the busiest moments, but for the most part it went smoothly. And the guests all loved Care. Patty watched her interacting with them and saw how warmly they responded to her. And that was strange because she was downright caustic with them. Most seemed to recognize it was all in good fun and laughed along with her rather than taking offense. Others just sat back, enjoying the show.

Care suggested a couple of minor changes in the service set up which made sense to Patty and things did run more smoothly. *Amazing what having someone around with experience adds.*

Patty didn't have a Café du Jour polo shirt to fit Care, but Care had said it wouldn't work with her coloring anyway, patting her red hair. "I don't mind wearing the khaki skirts or trousers and these shoes always worked for me, but I'll wear my own shirts."

Patty looked down at Care's shoes. They were khaki tan or almost flesh colored, closed toes, as required by the Health Department, with at least an inch of foam padding and lots of excellent arch support. Patty, her own tired feet aching, gazed at them longingly. *I hope she stays long enough for me to find out where she gets those shoes. I want a pair.*

For the first couple of days, Care wore polo collared shirts with attractive floral prints. But when she came in for work on Friday, she was sporting a message t-shirt that proudly declared, *The BOOBS are real. It's the SMILE that's fake,* over her mostly flat chest. Patty had to laugh and the customers loved it. There was no doubt about it, Care's flamboyant style was a big draw for the café.

By the end of that first week, Patty happily hired Care to work from eight to two, four days a week, from

Thursday through Sunday, when the café was busiest. Just twenty-four hours a week. What a difference it made.

Care was satisfied with the work schedule but surprised at the $15/hour pay rate. "That's a lot more than I'm used to," she said.

When Patty had discussed it with Jon the previous evening, he'd said, "You know your business is small enough you don't have to meet the new minimum wage rule."

"Yeah, maybe not, but I have to." Patty said. "Look, either I support the new minimum wage or I don't. I can't support it for other employers and not pay it myself. I'm limiting the number of hours she works and I won't need to provide health coverage since she's already on MediCare. Thank heavens the same payroll service through the bank that handles payroll for your paper, will handle all the required withholding and reporting for me. I don't need all those bureaucratic headaches."

O O O

A couple of days later, Patty came upstairs at the end of the day to find Jon stretched out, fully relaxed, lounging on the sofa, on the phone with their twenty three year old son, JJ. "Here, let me pass you off to your mom," he said, handing the phone to Patty.

"Hello, Sweetie, how's it going with you?" Patty wasn't really worried about JJ starting his career, not even in a crime ridden area of LA. He usually rose to the occasion. But her mom instincts kicked in anyway.

"Getting' settled in," JJ said. "I'm 'bout ready for

my first classroom assignment. My room is rundown but okay, the students seem pretty energetic, and the admin people have been mostly absent so far. Boy, it sure is different here from when I was in fifth grade."

"I'm sure it is," Patty said, remembering the suburban neighborhood schools JJ had attended. He'd won a slot in California's APLE, Assumption Program of Loans for Education. It was a highly competitive incentive program that would pay off his college student debt in exchange for a promise to teach in select inner city schools for five years after graduation. Patty'd been nervous about where he might end up teaching when he'd pursued the APLE program but JJ was determined and had won a place in the program. It turned out to be good thing he'd applied when he did. The program had since stopped accepting new applications.

"Tell her about the conflict resolution bit," Jon shouted loud enough for JJ to hear.

"He's not even on the phone and he's still directing the call," Patty said, turning her back to shut Jon out and focus her attention on her son's voice. "What conflict resolution thing? Are there problems already?"

"Not for me," JJ said, laughing. "At least I haven't gotten in any conflicts so far. Cross your fingers. Dad's talking about this really exciting new program. The school's looking for volunteers to try it with their classrooms. If it works, maybe they'll expand it to others."

"And you volunteered?" Patty asked.

"Yeah, I would've wanted to try it without any incentives. I'll send you a copy of the materials I got

99

from the Peace Alliance on it."

"Peace Alliance? That sounds interesting. How's it work?" the teacher still inside Patty asked.

"Basically, I'll be using social and emotional learning, communication techniques, mindfulness, and meditation to avoid bullying and truancy, and to give these kids a solid foundation to resolve conflicts before sending them off to middle school."

"What a great idea, give them the tools the earlier the better. I can't wait to look over those materials, don't forget to send them."

"I won't, Mom. When I was putting together my lesson plans, I came across this wonderful quote from Brother David Steindl-Rast, 'It is not happiness that makes us grateful, but gratefulness that makes us happy.' It sounds like something you would say."

"Yeah, I like it. It's a good reminder." Patty's smile split her face and made her eyes wet. It had been a toss-up whether JJ would follow in his father's footsteps or Patty's, and she'd been surprised when he'd chosen to teach elementary school instead of high school, but teachers like him were just what public schools needed. *Jon and I did something right with him.* Patty let her gaze drift across the room to Jon. He'd been a great father. Whether it was natural or his journalist training, he'd always been observant of any little shift in JJ's demeanor or behavior and JJ had always been responsive to his father's listening skills, resolving many teen problems before they grew past a manageable level.

○ ○ ○

After dinner, Jon followed Patty to the kitchen as she cleared the table. "I want to ask you a question about my new story," he said.

"Sure, what's it about?"

"I need a female perspective," he replied.

"Well, I still got the creds," she joked.

"Yes, you do," he said reaching out to pat her butt as she passed, but missing as Patty playfully swiveled her hips out of his reach.

"Okay," he began. "The piece is about sexual harassment in the office of the city manager."

"Whoa," she said. "That's big."

"Wait for the details." Jon cleared his throat, his eyes glittering as the tale unfolded. "The thing is that the city manager has hired a very young, very attractive woman as his new executive assistant into his already fully staffed office."

"So she's unnecessary?"

Jon waggled his eyebrows suggestively. "Unnecessary to the office perhaps but he seems to find her all too necessary personally. It's generally accepted, based on their public displays of affection around the office, they're sleeping together." He paused, shrugging expressively. "He's divorced and she's unmarried, that's not the problem."

"He's sleeping with a staff person who reports to him. Isn't that the definition of sexual harassment?"

"Yes, but that isn't what has people all riled up. The fact that the city manager is sleeping with a staff member, who is less than half his age by the way, isn't the problem."

Patty came around to sit at the counter top with Jon to focus on his story. "Then what, pray tell, is the

101

problem?"

"The problem is that he hired her in the first place. Our city, like most cities in California, has budget problems. Some 70 to 80% of the annual budget goes for staff salaries and benefits and for retiree's benefits and health coverage, leaving very little money for everything else. Hiring an additional, and unnecessary employee, commits the city to her salary and benefits not just for the term of her employment but for the rest of her life."

"Oh."

"Yes, 'oh' indeed."

"As new as we are here, are you sure you want to cover a story like this? How is this going to affect our lives here?"

"I haven't decided yet." Jon stood up and stretched, frowning. "For now at least, my job as a reporter is to research and report the facts, not to tell the reader what to think or how to feel about it. And it's not even ready to print yet, I still have to do more investigating. Let's not cross that bridge until we get to it."

ELEVEN

On a Friday morning, like any other, Jon sat at the two-top, lingering over his coffee. They'd put the paper to bed last night, it was out this morning and he was feeling free to go in to work a little late. Carrot red hair up in the usual do and smart mouth in rare form, Care was working the booths and, kitchen work caught up for the moment, Patty was enjoying a quiet moment with Jon.

The door opened and Alec Harrison entered. He walked straight to Jon's table but didn't sit. Patty checked her watch, he was a little earlier than most Fridays. He usually came in Friday mornings to share coffee and time with Jon, insisting on having his own pecan sticky bun, not sharing that.

"Aren't you sitting?" Jon asked. "Are you passing on the sticky buns this morning?"

Alec looked longingly at Jon's nearly empty plate and shook his head. "Not today. I got a call I thought you might want to go out on with me. You got the time?"

"Sure," Jon said, inhaling the last bite of his sweet treat and brushing the crumbs from his chin. "What's up?'

Alec opened his mouth to reply but then clamped it shut. "No, I think I'll wait 'til you see it for yourself and get your first impression. Okay?"

"Sure." Jon raised his eyebrows, gave Patty a quick peck on the top of her head and followed his friend to the door.

He got into Alec's official police vehicle and they drove out of town, heading inland. He wondered where they were going and why but decided not to ask since Alec was being so mysterious about this call. "You could have taken a sticky bun to go," he told Alec.

Alec smiled, brushing his long fingers along his perfectly shaved ebony chin, but shook his head. "It's not a good idea for the chief of police to be seen stuffing his face while driving. Sets a poor example."

They drove to the very edge of the city limits, arriving at a small farm just past the city line. Alec pulled over to the side of the road and stopped the vehicle but didn't get out.

"Isn't this outside your jurisdiction?" Jon asked.

"Yup," Alec replied, nodding. He tossed his chin toward the farmhouse. "Wanda pointed that out when they called in this morning. They said they'd called the county sheriff's office first but that they'd told them it sounded more like a city problem."

"What makes it a city problem? What's going on here?" Jon asked.

Alec took a deep breath and slowly opened the car door, saying, "Let's go take a look."

Jon followed his friend down the unpaved gravel driveway and around the aging farmhouse to where a small group of people were standing, talking. They all fell silent, turning to see the new arrivals.

"Which one of you is the homeowner here?" Alec asked.

"I am," a tall gangly man in dirty jeans and a plain gray sweatshirt said, raising his hand. His hair a dirty brown to match the stubble on his weathered face and the ground under their feet, he looked to be about 40 years old, but it was hard to tell his age for certain. "Name's McDowell, Jerry McDowell. My wife and I bought this place three years ago. I tell you we ain't never seen anything like this."

When he mentioned his wife he turned to her and opened his right arm, including her in their discussion. She moved closer, nodded once and said, "My name's Joyce. I'm the one who saw it first looking out that window up there," turning to point to an upstairs window on the east facing side of their home.

Jon began to fidget. *What the hell? What's this all about? Let's get to it already.* He glanced around at the others gathered at the edge of the field, staring silently at them.

As though reading Jon's mind, Alec rubbed his hands together and said, "Let's take a look. Can we use that ladder over there?"

"Sure, but you can see it better from inside. Wanna go in and take a look from that window?" Joyce said, inviting them in with a toss of her head.

"Okay, ma'am, let's do that first," Alec said, nodding Jon to follow. They followed the home owners to the side door and up the stairs to the front room. Jon took in the warm, inviting kitchen, and the rest of the rooms they passed. The furnishings were worn but clean and neatly kept.

The view out the window was of their sixty acres planted with a crop Jon didn't immediately recognize. It looked lush and vibrant, green as far as the eye could see.

"That's our alfalfa," Jerry said with pride.

"And that's the problem," Joyce added, pointing to a bare patch just off center to the right.

So they've got a bare patch in their field, Jon thought. *How's that a police matter?* He leaned out the window a little to see it more clearly. *It's not a bare patch, it's some sort of design.*

"A crop circle!" Joyce said. "A crop circle in our field. Just sprung up overnight. It wasn't there yesterday, I would've noticed."

"Wait a minute, let's not get ahead of ourselves," Alec said, holding out his hands and slowly shaking his head before the discussion went any further.

"We're not saying aliens done it or nothin'," Jerry said. "It could've been vandals or somethin'. That's why we called you."

"And we'll investigate," Alec reassured him. "Has anyone walked out there this morning?" He watched as Joyce turned to look at Jerry.

"I did," Jerry admitted. "Joyce called me up here to see it and I went out there to see what's what before I thought to call you guys. So yeah, I walked out there. I turned around and came right back, though."

"Okay," Alec said. "Let's go see what we've got. Jon, you coming?"

"Like I'd miss this."

They first walked back to the police vehicle to get some evidence protecting booties, the official police camera and some evidence bags. They trudged through the green field toward where they thought the crop circle to be. "It all looks really different from ground level, doesn't it? And, I'm afraid we're going to mess up any evidence out here wandering around trying to find our way to the crime scene," Alec said.

"Crime?" Jon asked. "I know they destroyed some of his crops, and that's his income stream. I get it, but is this kind of thing some sort of crime?"

"And now you understand why the county boys thought this was a city matter. Pass the buck."

"Humph, I get it," Jon muttered taking a sharp turn to avoid tripping, sniffing the fresh green aroma and wondering that green has a smell. "I'm a city boy, I don't know how to navigate these fields without doing more damage."

Arriving at the edge of the bare spot, Alec stopped short. Jon barely missed bumping into him.

"Wow, look at that," Jon said, gazing around, marveling at the silence, hearing only the light breeze dancing through the alfalfa. "Who knew it'd be so neat?" The two men stood in place, turning to stare at the entirety of the scene in front of them. From this perspective they couldn't make out the design, but they could see how pristine the bending of the alfalfa had been. No foot prints, no tire marks, no broken stalks, no damage of any kind apparent, just the disturbance in the field, each stalk bent over as though of its own accord.

They took pictures, measurements and made notes, each of them muttering to themselves, for almost an hour. Alec found no evidence of humans in this area of the field. Finally ready to give up, he stretched his long back and looked around one last time. "I don't see anything more we're going to get out here. Do you?"

"No." Jon shook his head. "Did you see any

indication anyone has been out here, how this was done?"

"Not yet." Alec nodded toward the farm house. "Okay, let's head back and take interviews from the ... umm ..., let's call them witnesses."

Jon chuckled. "Do you want me just to eavesdrop or can I ask some questions of my own?"

"Go ahead and ask your questions, but follow my lead. If I tell you to back off, you back off. Understood?" He didn't wait for an answer, making it clear this was an order, not a request.

Alec and Jon separated the handful of spectators who had waited and were still standing around, into two groups. They recorded the witness names, took their initial statements, and asked a few follow up questions.

Alec trekked out to their car and came back with a roll of yellow 'CRIME SCENE DO NOT CROSS' tape which he strung loosely across the edge of the field. Finished, they thanked everyone for their time and promised the homeowners they could return to their fields as soon as the crime scene people had been out to collect any evidence.

As they walked back to the police car, one particularly cranky old man called after them, "We'll let you know iffn' we hear from ET."

They remained silent as they got into the car, started it up, and made a 'u' turn to head back to town. "Well, that was fun," Jon said with a particularly flat affect.

Alec started laughing and then couldn't stop, tears leaking from his eyes and coursing through the light layer of dust that had accumulated on his face.

"Oh, Lordy," he said. "I can't wait to hear what Wanda has to say about this!"

"You know she'll be waiting to hear all about it, too."

"Yeah, what do you say we stop by the café and get lunch first? I need some time and a cold drink before facing her. I can make a call for the crime scene crew on the way."

"Sounds good," Jon said. "Can we tell Patty or do I need to keep this quiet? The paper isn't due out for almost a week so I can't publish anything right away even if you say I can."

"You might as well," Alec said sighing. "I'll be surprised if Wanda isn't at the café, surrounded by the whole town, already talking about it."

○ ○ ○

When it got to be almost 2:00, closing time, Patty crossed the café to turn over the "OPEN" sign and lock the door. That's when she noticed Trevor, Alec's son, sitting quietly by himself in the last booth. "Hi, Trevor. I almost missed you there. I'm about to close up for the day, is there anything I can get you before you go?"

"I was hanging around to talk to you, if you have time?" he began nervously.

Reminded of her old high school students staying after class to ask her a question, she joined him in the booth. "Sure," she said. "What do you need?"

"Need?" Trevor repeated, his voice tight, stressed. "Yeah," the lanky teen said, seizing on her word. "Need. I'm hoping my need can meet a need you have."

Patty leaned back against the booth. *Okay*, she thought, *this's going to be good.* "I'm listening."

Trevor leaned forward, using his big hands to present his case. "School's out for a while and I'm looking for a job. You seem pretty busy here, I'm hoping you might hire me. See, my need meeting your need."

Patty smiled, almost chuckling. She had to give him credit, he'd clearly given this pitch some thought. "What would I be hiring you to do? I do the cooking and Care handles the guests. What would you bring to the table?"

Encouraged, Trevor became more animated. His face lit up, his dimples deepened and he began gesturing with his hands. "I bet you could use help cleaning up. I could wash dishes, sweep floors, whatever you need."

Patty's brow furrowed as she considered this. An hour or so after closing did sound good. "Would you be interested in one hour a day, Wednesday through Sunday, to start?"

"Would I?" he asked, almost shouting in his excitement. "Yeah. When can I start?"

"Let's give it a try, starting tomorrow at 2:00."

"Two's perfect," he said, getting up to leave. "With that schedule, I can keep working even after school's back in session. I won't even have to miss track workouts. They're mostly in the mornings." He stopped just short of the door and turned back to Patty to ask a final question. "Can I maybe hang around the kitchen some, learn some of your cooking?"

"Are you interested in learning to cook?" Patty asked him, surprised.

"Yeah, with Moms gone, just Pops and me," he said. "I figure I can either learn how to cook or learn how to live without eating."

Patty followed him to the door, chuckling. *Looks like I'm going to get to use my teaching skills after all.*

"Moms didn't cook all that much when she was around."

TWELVE

Patty was in the kitchen, starting the prep work for tomorrow's menu, when she heard Jon and Alec return from their call.

"You in the kitchen?" Jon called. "Can we come back and get some late lunch?"

"Sure," Patty replied. "I left some out for you when I packed up leftovers for the food bank. What would you like?"

"Whatever you got sounds good to me," Alec said, smiling as he took his first real visual tour of the cafe's kitchen.

Patty shooed them out. "There's no chairs in here. You go sit and I'll bring it out to you." She put two servings of roasted red pepper and olive pizza each on two plates and took them into the dining area. "What'll you have to drink?"

"After that call," Jon said. "I'll go upstairs and get myself a cold beer. You?" he asked Alec.

"No, I'm still on duty," Alec replied, shaking his head. Turning to Patty he asked, "Any iced tea left?"

"I'll provide the pizza and iced tea if you'll tell me what this mysterious call was all about."

"Don't start without me," Jon shouted from the top of the stairs.

Patty disappeared back into the kitchen to get Alec's iced tea and some of the cookies for herself. By the time she got back, Jon was coming down the stairs with his beer and Alec was returning from the restroom, drying his face and hands on a paper towel.

"Okay, spill. What's this mysterious call all about?" Patty asked Alec.

Alec didn't reply. He looked to Jon who only shook his head. "You go first," Jon said. "Tell her the facts, just the facts, Joe Friday, and I'll provide color commentary." He took a deep drink of his beer and reached for his pizza.

Alec told her how the call had been passed from the county to the city and about the couple and their farm, with contributions from the peanut gallery, in the form of Jon's barely suppressed amusement. Talking around eating his pizza and drinking his iced tea, Alec finally worked his way around to saying, "There appears to be some sort of crop circle in their alfalfa."

Patty leaned forward, a smile twitching her lips. "Is this for real?" she asked. "I've read about crop circles around the world. I never gave them any serious consideration."

"They looked pretty real to me," Jon said.

"What did it look like?' Patty asked. "Was it just a small circle in the middle of the field or some sort of design?"

Jon and Alec exchanged a questioning look until Alec nodded to Jon to go first. "Well, from the upstairs window, I couldn't see much of anything. It just looked like a blurry patch in the middle of a whole lot of green."

Alec nodded.

"Then once we got out into the field, into the middle of it, all I saw were wide paths of smashed down alfalfa right next to big bunches of still upright plants,"

Jon said, using his hands to describe the scene.

"Right," Alec said. "Once we were waist deep in the middle of it, it was hard to discern any pattern. Our perspective was all wrong for that."

"Do you think you can send a helicopter up for a better look?" Patty asked.

"The city doesn't have a helicopter and I don't see myself explaining to the city council why I want to spend money for time on the county chopper for this." Alec turned to Jon. "Does the paper own a drone?"

Jon made a face. "At this point, I'm lucky to afford the printing press."

Alec sighed audibly. "I guess for now we'll have to settle for having the crime scene folks take measurements and draw the design for us. The point is, all we saw was a complicated design carved into the field. We didn't see any evidence of how it was made."

"That'll have to do until we hear further from ET," Jon said.

"I know you're a journalist, my friend," Alec said sternly, all traces of humor erased by the arching of one eyebrow. "But don't go feeding the beast. I dispatched my crime scene unit just now before I came in. We'll see what they find."

"What are you thinking?" Patty asked, her eyebrows practically meeting in the middle in her confusion. "Aliens?"

"More likely vandals, high schools pranks," Jon suggested, looking around for cookies. "One of the other farmers, one I interviewed, said circles like these have been cropping up out there - yes, he really said 'cropping up' - in one field or another for years, for decades. But no one ever took them seriously, reported them or anything."

"Hmmm," Alec said. "Give me his name. I'll need to follow up on that. Anyway, as you can see, the investigation is just beginning. It's too soon to say anything about it."

"I can't wait to see how much more we have by the deadline for next week's paper." Jon rubbed his hands together with glee.

Alec's gaze fell to the table. He sighed deeply before asking Jon, "You're going to make me sorry I took you out there, aren't you?"

Jon chuckled. "No, I won't. I promise I won't publish anything to inflame the masses until you get more evidence."

Alec looked up to the ceiling as if seeing the sky above, "Just don't say aliens and get everyone all stirred up."

"There's more than one kind of alien, you know," Patty said, casually resting her chin on her fist.

Alec's head snapped around to her, his eyes wide with surprise. "Lordy don't let it be immigrant aliens, legal or illegal," he said. "We don't need anything to fan that particular flame. There's enough trouble over illegals passing through here without adding to it."

Patty cleared their plates, taking them to the kitchen where she grabbed some lemon cookies for them, and another one for herself.

When she rejoined them, Jon and Alec had their heads together, merrily dissecting their new shared story. *Jon's so much more relaxed here, and even more so on Fridays after he's put his paper to bed for the week,* Patty thought. *Moving here was a good*

115

choice. Now if my little café will just do well.

When they were through, Patty walked Alec to the door. "My last customer today was your son. Did you know he was going to ask me for a job?" she asked Alec.

Patty watched Alec's face as his demeanor shifted at the mention of his son. It transported Patty back to a time in her young life when she'd spent the summer with her grandparents.

Her grandfather raised homing pigeons and during her visit he had a mated pair sitting on the nest, waiting for their eggs to hatch. That summer, Patty learned that pigeons take turns on the nest until their eggs hatch. But the male of this pair became fidgety after only a few minutes each time it was his turn. Her grandfather was concerned the female wasn't getting enough of a break to eat and rest. Then, the day the eggs hatched, everything changed. Suddenly the male bird couldn't spend enough time with his offspring. His love for his babies had been clear to Patty in his actions, if not on his little beaky face.

Now Alec's face, his whole body language, contradictorily both melted, the muscles in his face relaxing, and strengthened, his posture going even straighter than usual, at the mention of his son. Seeing his love for his son, how proud he was, made him much more handsome to Patty's eye.

"Yes, I knew in general," he said. "I didn't know he'd talk to you today. How'd it go?"

"He made a good pitch." Patty turned to Jon. "I told him to come back tomorrow and we'd give it a trial run." She turned back to Alec, "But I'm planning on hiring him for one hour a day, five days a week. Is that good with you?"

"Sure, I'm glad to see him take an interest and a little extra spending money would do him good." He shrugged his broad shoulders under his miraculously still creased uniform shirt. "He's seventeen now, it's time and he seems ready."

"In fact," Patty said, "he seems more mature than most of the students I remember at that age."

"That's his mother's doing," Alec said. "When I was gone, she told him he had to be the man of the house and I guess he grew into the responsibility."

"I seem to recall," Jon said, smiling. "My first job didn't bring in much money but it took up some of the time I would've been spending money. So it worked out pretty well."

"From your lips to God's ears," Alec said.

○ ○ ○

There wasn't much talk about the crop circles in the café over the weekend. Most of the town hadn't heard about them yet.

By Monday, a few were buzzing with the news. Wanda came in for lunch with Doris and they had their own, very strong, opinions on the subject. Wanda was energized by the investigation, all the activity within the police department, and all the possibilities for mischief. Doris, on the other hand, didn't give much credit to the very idea of crop circles. "They can't be real," she said. "If there were anything to them, we would have heard it all before now and from somewhere much more important than our little town."

"Then, how do you explain them?" Wanda asked.

"I don't know," Doris said, shaking her head in firm denial and self-consciously straightening her t-shirt proclaiming, *Aging has slowed me down but it hasn't shut me up.* "It's not my job to explain them. I don't want to hear any of this."

"You just wait," Wanda said, leaning back in the booth, opening her arms, and waving her hands expressively. "You just wait, this will turn out to be the comic relief opportunity of the year. Defenders and deniers fighting over every unconfirmed rumor, the police running after every supposed lead. This is going to be fun."

And it was for a couple more days. But by Saturday, some people were looking for someone to blame. There were those who suspected the circles in farmer McDowell's alfalfa field were nothing more than high school high jinx. A small, but very vocal, contingent had landed solidly on the theory that illegal immigrants moving through the area had left the circles behind, insisting that the circles were the result of their camps.

Patty didn't take a stand. But she did enjoy the increase to the lunch business at her café. More and more people showed up each day to discuss the origin of the circles over lunch, many lingering to talk just the way Patty had hoped. The breakfast diners discussed it as well, but it was mostly the same small group of people, no new customers came in that early.

Friday's edition of the Valley Gazette featured full coverage of the circles. True to his promise to police chief, Jon hadn't included any speculation about the origins of the mysterious crop circles. Instead, he'd focused on the specific facts, the measurements, the intricacy of the design as well as he could from the drawings, the interviews with the witnesses, and the progress of the investigation to date.

O O O

It was almost 2:00, time to close. Patty came out of the kitchen to find the café nearly empty. She joined Care sitting in the number one booth with Patty's own best friends, Doris and Wanda. Care had positioned herself next to Wanda, facing the number six booth across the dining room. Patty checked out the two guys at that booth before sitting on the other side, next to Doris. One of the two guys was Robert, Doris' son, the man who'd sold them the Valley Gazette.

Patty stole the opportunity to study Robert for a moment. He was dressed well in a linen sports jacket over a polo shirt and khakis. His deeply tanned face going a long way to mask the ruddy complexion of a heavy drinker. When she'd met him, she'd sized him up to a couple of inches shorter than Jon's 6'1", maybe 5'11", and about 200 very soft pounds, no doubt from too many years sitting behind a desk or enjoying too many business lunches.

Sixty-one years old, his thick silver hair was combed straight back from his forehead, which was expanding as his hairline receded. His pale blue/gray eyes jerked around under his unruly eyebrows. Patty realized for the first time how perfectly the term 'shifty' describes someone whose eyes are constantly on the move, maybe looking for a way out. His eyes seemed to avoid landing on his mother.

But Patty didn't know the second, younger man. "Who's the hunk?" she asked.

"Hunk, indeed," Care drawled. "I know he's way out of my age range, but I can look, can't I?"

Patty turned again to check out the very attractive stranger as surreptitiously as she could, subconsciously comparing him to Robert Shepard. What she saw was a man not much younger than her own 46 years, looking to be about six feet tall, maybe 200 or so firm pounds, arranged into broad shoulders, a V shaped torso, and strong thighs.

That was all well and good, but most arresting was his face. Under short, thick medium brown hair, almost blond from summer sun, she found a triangular face with a full but neatly kept beard and moustache, and the most startling blue eyes she'd ever seen. "Aquamarine," she said, musing on his eyes.

"More blue topaz, if you ask me. Very striking indeed," Care said, nodding and smiling. "Especially set off by his dark eye lashes and brows."

"Right, blue topaz it is. Who is he?" Patty asked. "Is he new in town, passing through? This is the first time I've seen him in here."

"No," Wanda said flatly, her distaste clear in her tone. "He's not new. He's been around. I guess he's been avoiding this place up to now."

"Why?" Patty asked at the same time Care said, "My, my, my. How has he escaped my attention until now?"

"That's Chris Woods," Wanda said.

"Wait," Patty said, quickly covering her mouth

and dropping her voice to barely above a whisper. "THE Chris Woods? The guy who thought he'd make a better police chief than Alec? No wonder he doesn't come here often." She turned to Care to explain. "Alec is a good friend and he comes in to eat or take out several times a week."

"I know," Care replied. "You think I'd missed that tall dark drink of handsome? I may be old, but my eyes still work just fine. I know who Alec Harrison is."

Patty turned to Doris who had remained suspiciously quiet throughout the discussion. "Is he some good friend of Robert's?"

"I wouldn't say friend," Doris replied. "Lately, they spend time with their heads together over something but I can't figure out what they'd have in common."

Seeing the two men look around, ready to go, Care got up to give them their bill and collect their payment.

"Look out," Wanda warned, staring at Chris Woods. "His good looks draw people in until they get to know him."

You think maybe that beard hides a weak chin? Patty wondered.

121

THIRTEEN

Around ten o'clock on the following Tuesday, Patty came into the café carrying plates filled with a wedge of frittata and a couple of scones, to find Jon escorting a new stranger to the number five booth. Surprised to see him choosing to sit other than at his usual place at the two-top on the east wall, she took mugs and both coffee carafes to the booth. Care didn't work on Tuesdays so she was busy handling both cooking and waitress duties.

Jon ordered some coffee and a blueberry scone, he'd already had a wedge of the western frittata earlier. The stranger ordered just water, no ice. She had an accent but didn't speak enough words for Patty to identify it.

The stranger was tiny, by Patty's estimate no more than 4'9" tall and maybe 90 pounds, dripping wet. She wore her dull, straggly, un-styled short brown hair in a longish bowl cut with short bangs, ending well above her unshaped eyebrows. Patty could barely see the woman's dull green eyes behind her heavy, dark rimmed eyeglasses which seemed huge on her tiny face. Her dull and uneven skin was heavily lined under her deeply furrowed brow.

When Patty returned to take their plates and offer refills, the stranger barely glanced up, intensely involved in her conversation with Jon, reluctant to be distracted. They finished and Jon led the woman from the café. Patty crossed to the window to watch as Jon walked her away, toward the town center.

A few moments later when Jon returned, he walked directly to the kitchen to see Patty. "And now it begins," he said.

"What? What begins? Who was that weird little woman?" she asked.

"That was Doctor Linda Rasmussen, world renowned botanist from Germany," Jon said reading from the business card in his hand.

"German, that's her accent. She didn't speak enough for me to place it." She huffed a sigh. "So what's she doing here?"

"Apparently AP picked up my story on our crop circles and it was carried in Germany, where she picked up on it," Jon said. "It triggered the alarm she has set up on her computer to alert her any time crop circles are reported anywhere around the world."

"And now it begins? The influx of crop circle groupies? You really think so?" Patty stopped working the dough, her face slack in disbelief.

"Oh yeah. When AP first carried it I got some good-natured ribbing from some of my old journalist friends. You know, saying not only had I escaped the rat race, I'd joined the lunatic fringe where crop circles are reported as legitimate news."

"I'm sorry, honey," Patty said. "You didn't say anything, I didn't know."

"What was I supposed to say? What were you going to do about it? I can't go crying to my mama any time the big boys give me a little grief." Jon shook it off. "The point is, if Dr. Rasmussen has picked up the story, others will as well." He blew out a breath. "I'm going to run back to the newspaper office for a bit to check her out online. I have better search programs on the office computer and I want to know who I'm dealing with. Is she a serious scientist or just some nutcase?"

○ ○ ○

"Jon?" Patty called. "Dinner's on the table, where are you?"

"Back here," Jon called from their bedroom. "I got caught up and lost track of time. I'll be right out."

Over dinner, Jon reported what he'd found online about the stranger come to town. "Oh, she's a serious scientist alright," Jon said as he helped himself to a second slice of shrimp and banana pepper pizza. "In fact, she's so serious, she's gotten into several disputes with others she doesn't think are serious enough."

"Okay, I can see that," Patty said. "I didn't see any social graces in her." She shook her head, her entire body posture drooping. "That isn't fair. The whole time she was in the café, I was judging her by her appearance instead of getting to know her. And that's on me. No excuses." She shook her head again and blew out a breath. "I only spent a few moments with her. What else did you find?"

"I printed out some of the articles she's had published, some in some pretty well respected scientific journals by the way. I'll show them to you later. But the most interesting article was from 1976 when she was just ten years old."

"Wait," Patty said, holding up her hand. "She

124

was publishing in science journals when she was ten?"

"No, that article was about her, not by her. When she was ten years old," Jon said, pulling out some printouts to read from. "She was spending the summer with her grandparents in Weiheim, Bavaria. Crop circles were discovered, not on their farm but on a neighbor's farm and her young mind was entranced. She's been studying them all over the planet ever since."

"As a botanist? How'd that work out?"

"Her biography on Wikipedia says that when she was still in high school she was already considering possible explanations and that she settled on nature, natural phenomena, as the most promising field of study, so she studied botany."

"Wow," Patty said, blowing out a breath. "Who would've thought a serious, really serious, scientist would be interested in crop circles. Of all things."

"But that's still not the best," Jon said, patting his mouth with his napkin and getting up. "You gotta see this video I found on YouTube for yourself. Wait, I'll get my laptop."

When he returned, Patty was clearing the table and getting some of the Angel Food cake for their dessert.

"Okay, give me a minute to pull it up again." He tapped around for a moment and then lit up as he announced. "Here it is, wait 'til you see this."

They watched Linda Rasmussen delivering a presentation. She was standing behind a podium in what looked like a hotel conference room. "Where is this? When is this?" Patty asked.

"It's the 2009 Annual Conference of the

International Scientific Circular Research. Her presentation was titled 'Botanical Evidence for the Enigma of Crop Circles'. Whoever posted this edited it to the final minutes of her presentation and what followed. Here comes the good part."

On the video, Dr. Rasmussen finished up to polite, if unenthusiastic, applause and then a voice from the audience shouted "Bullshit!" Patty's eyes grew large. She turned to see Jon's reaction.

"Keep watching," he said, pointing to the screen.

On the video, Dr. Rasmussen stretched to her full 4'9" and arched her thick eyebrows. "Yes, Mister Hartford, you have a dissenting opinion to share?" Her already thin lips disappeared as she pressed them together and her jaw line firmed.

"Notice Doctor Rasmussen called him Mister Hartford," Jon said. "This is it, here it comes."

"I said 'bullshit' and that's what I have to say to all your so-called scientific 'proof' about these silly circles," Mr. Hartford said, standing up. "It doesn't matter how many slides, charts and graphs you produce to support your nonsense. This is all bullshit and you should be ashamed. All these circles are nothing more than hoaxes. And you - all of you - are giving them legitimacy." He turned to the crowd, pointing to this one or that.

"I would be glad to review any scientific evidence you can provide to back up your hoax theories," Dr. Rasmussen said, coming out from behind the podium to face her accuser. "But since I know all your so-called facts proving the circles hoaxes are based on late night pub talk, I can't imagine you have anything worthwhile. You know, you may want to consider actually doing some research of your own rather than just putting down the hard work, valid work, of your betters."

On screen, she turned her attention to the audience at large. Seeing several men and one particularly angry woman jumping up, reaching for the denier among them. "I don't doubt some of them are actually hoaxes," she continued. "But that doesn't mean they're all hoaxes and if even one is not a hoax, it has tremendous implications for all mankind, even you."

The video ended as a man wearing an official's badge over his nice suit approached Dr. Rasmussen, hands out, patting the air to defuse the situation. Watching, Patty thought that Dr. Rasmussen did not appear at all placated. She looked fighting mad. At the same time, two security guards took hold of the protesting Mr. Hartford, rescuing him from the angry crowd, and dragged him kicking and screaming, from the room.

"The news reports after the conference said they try to screen the attendees to keep the deniers out but every year a few troublemakers manage to gain access." Jon closed out the video and turned his attention to his cake.

"Oh my God," Patty said. "I had no idea this was so big. Are there are enough, I guess I'll call them 'believers' to fill up an annual conference?"

"Apparently," Jon said, nodding his head. "I can't wait to ask her for a full interview for next week's paper, now that I know enough to ask semi-intelligent questions."

Over the next days, the townspeople divided themselves into groups. Some blamed this as well as other problems on illegal immigrants. Some insisted the circles were all hoaxes. Others enthusiastically accepted the idea and went further to speculate on their alien creation. And a few, like Patty, were intrigued and curious. For the most part, the people and their discussions remained civil, more good-natured debate than arguments like the video of Dr. Rasmussen.

Care continued to be great with the guests, navigating easily between the believers and the deniers, keeping everyone laughing and ensuring the discussions remained cordial.

Trevor began working his one hour five days a week. Patty couldn't be happier with him. He was a conscientious worker, seeming mature beyond his years, and needing little to no training or supervision. Suddenly she had more time and, more importantly, more energy for the parts of the business she liked most, cooking and spending time with the guests.

Patty emerged from the kitchen Thursday afternoon to find Jon and Alec sitting at the two top, watching the room. It was near the end of the day and few diners remained. Alec stood to offer her his chair. "No," Patty said. "I won't be here long. I just wanted to see who was left." They all looked toward the door at the newcomer, Trevor, reporting for work. Patty smiled to see him coming in, her workday lightened. Alec nodded to him, a father's pride warming his eyes. Jon chuckled at his t-shirt which claimed, *I'm so hot, I'm responsible for global warming!*

"Anything special you need me to do today, Boss?" Trevor asked Patty.

"Just the regular today. When you get the place all cleaned up, I'll be making pecan sticky buns for tomorrow, if you're interested."

"You bet! I'll go get started on the dishes until these last few people clear out."

"You sure know how to motivate my son," Alec said, grinning at Patty. "And the food at our place has certainly gotten better since he's been working here with you." He looked over to Jon. "I'll follow up on what we were discussing and get back to you. That may be a good direction to take this inquiry." He said his goodbyes, picked up his official hat and left.

"Follow up?" Patty asked Jon.

"Just to see if he can eliminate the hoax accusations spinning around the circles."

"Accusation?" Patty asked. "That sounds ominous. What's changed?"

"Apparently some townspeople aren't satisfied just saying the circles are a hoax. They've identified some high school students to accuse."

FOURTEEN

The following Wednesday was a busy day at the café. Care was working the booths and Patty had just come out from the kitchen, laden with full plates, when she saw Alec introducing a stranger to Jon, sitting at the two top on the east wall.

Care beat her to them and escorted them to the number four booth in the corner where the three of them could spread out. Looking at them, heads together in serious discussion, Patty stole a brief glance at the new guy and then looked at him again. She made the reluctant decision not to interrupt, not to join in. This looked more like a work meeting than a social occasion.

Care brought their orders in for Patty to fill and plate. "Who's the new guy?" she asked Care.

"Wish I knew, Sugah," Care practically purred. "Isn't he purty?"

Patty thought back to what she'd seen of him. It was just a quick assessment but the impression she'd gotten was of a good looking guy about her husband's age, not as tall, with a compact but muscular body. He wore his dark hair long enough to be pulled into a ponytail, a look she usually didn't like. But she was willing to make an exception for him. She hadn't been close enough to see the color of his eyes but she had noticed a rugged, squarish face carrying a flat, very serious affect.

"So you don't know him either, huh?" Care asked, smoothing the front of her t-shirt - *Are you on meds?* When Care turned to see the handsome stranger better, Patty saw, *Should you be?* written in fancy script on the back. "That must mean he's new to town," Care added.

"I wonder what he has to discuss with the chief of police and the publisher of the local newspaper," Patty mused.

"No, you don't," Care teased. "I bet he's here about those circles and that's what you think, too. I'll see what I can hear when I deliver their meals."

Patty froze, turning on her employee. "Care! Don't you dare! Surely there's some sort of privacy owed to our guests."

Care burst into laughter. "Oh Sugah, our guests are always the best sources of gossip. This may not be a diner, but you must know how much local news gets exchanged in your café." She grinned mischievously. "I saw a few strands of gray in his hair and stubble on his face and I don't even care. I could just eat him up." Grinning and shaking her head, she returned to the dining room.

O O O

By closing time, each of the other booths had emptied, filled, and emptied again, but the threesome in the number four corner booth still sat together, talking.

Shift over, Care left. Shift beginning, Trevor

arrived. As Patty met him at the door and turned toward the kitchen with him, Alec stretched and looked around the dining room, noticing everyone else had left. "Hey Patty, come over here and join us, if you have the time," he called.

"Sure," Patty replied. "Trevor knows what to do. He doesn't need me hovering over him."

Jon scooted over, patting the seat next to him. He glanced at his watch, appearing surprised by the passage of time.

The stranger jumped up and held out his hand to Patty. "Spenser Elliott, ma'am. Please call me Spense."

"Patty," Jon said. "Spense has come to town about our crop circles."

Did his eyes actually twinkle? Patty thought, eyes helplessly cast to her shoes. *I thought that was just in hokey movies when they want to make the lead actor seem charming.*

"Are you responsible for that delicious pizza I just ate? And that Dutch apple pie, too? How is this entire town not overweight?" When he smiled at Patty, this time she was sure his clear blue eyes *did* twinkle! *It wasn't just my imagination!*

Shameless, Patty's heart fluttered as she reached to pat her now long gone locks. It was unusual for her to find herself speechless.

"I guess I need to get out of here and get myself checked in at the local hotel before they give my room away." Spenser took Patty's hand saying, "Best meal I've had in, well just about ever, ma'am. Thank you."

Watching him go, Patty sighed. "He another botanist or what?" she asked, her eyes never leaving his broad back until on the other side of the door.

"No," Alec replied. "I'm not exactly sure how to describe him. He's some sort of a conspiracy theory investigator or myth buster, or something. It's not clear which side he's on. I took a quick look into him online before Wanda sent him back. And then I brought him over here. It's your husband he wanted to meet. I'll look into him further as soon as I get back to the office."

"Yeah, I'll see if I can find anything on him from other news sources," Jon offered. "So far, we know he's a retired MP, like Alec here."

"Not exactly," Alec said. "He was Army, I'm Marine."

"What's the difference?" Patty asked.

"There's no real difference in the actual MP training, that's pretty standard across all services. But of course, Marine boot camp is more rigorous."

"That was pretty interesting," Jon said. "What he said about his experiences with the feds. Did you ever have anything like that?"

Alec turned to Patty to explain, "People are always confused about the differences between MP's and the feds, like CID, Criminal Investigation Division, or NCIS."

"Yeah," Patty said, nodding. "We've all seen NCIS on tv. What is the difference?"

"Mostly red tape and bureaucracy, as far as I'm concerned," Alec said with a rueful smile.

"That's what Spense was saying," Jon said. "So what is the difference?"

"MP's function more like city cops, with some occasional special details," Alec explained. "But CID is a federal agent position, just like the FBI. They deal with high profile crimes and most CID agents specialize in one area, end up being detachment commanders."

"But then Spense had some sort of problem with them when they tried to recruit him?" Jon asked.

Alec nodded. "I'll look into it, see if any of my old contacts ever heard of him. Whatever. It sure left him with a sour taste in his mouth about all feds."

"What was that bit about the four reasons?" Jon asked Alec.

"What?" Alec started, absently scratching his chin. "Oh, that. That's a theory, also across all services, developed now that the military is all volunteer. Let me see if I can still get it right. There are four reasons for a man to join the service. One is legacy."

"Legacy?" Jon interrupted. "What's that?

"They're following a family tradition, father's uncles, older brothers, nowadays, mothers and sisters, too." He shrugged his broad shoulders. "The second is patriotism."

"Okay, I get that one," Jon said. "They want to serve their country."

"Right," Alec confirmed. "The third is they need a job. Everyone can understand that one." He took in a deep breath, his face all angles and dark shadows. "And the fourth is they're looking for an opportunity to kill their fellow human beings." Alec paused as Jon and Patty just stared at him.

Patty, who'd been nodding along as Alec listed the first three reasons, was brought up short at the final one. "Whoa, really wasn't expecting that last one."

"Yeah," Alec said, nodding. "Numbers two and three are usually pretty much okay. Number ones are sometimes a big pain in the ass. But it's the number fours that'll run an MP out of the job. Looks like it did for Spense and me both."

The three of them sat in silence for a while, adjusting to this new information. "I guess I'll get back to work in the kitchen while you guys dig into his privacy."

O O O

Over the next week, the café saw increased business as townies and strangers alike, divided on real vs. hoax crop circles, came in to discuss their differing positions. Patty noticed that the addition of Spense Elliott to the clientele also brought in more female guests. Lately the yoga ladies had been coming in after class and on other days as well. Ladies representing a range of ages and other demographics were suddenly flocking to her café.

"I swear that boy smells just like chocolate chip cookies hot out of the oven," Care drawled as she joined Doris, Wanda, and Patty, all watching the female commotion swirling around him.

"Girl, that's his pheronomes working their magic on you," Wanda snapped with a big smile. "And I notice some of the fellas seem pretty interested, too."

"They're just jealous," Doris said.

"Not all of them," Wanda said with a quirk of her eyebrow.

"I don't know what it is," Wanda said. "He's no better looking than other guys, but something about him is simply irresistible. Maybe it's those cowboy boots of his. Or his southern accent, which is just charming on him."

135

"I thought it was his eyes," Doris said. "But then I decided it was his smile."

"I think it's both," Patty said. "The intensity, the way he uses his eyes and smile to focus his attention on you. I felt like I was back in high school when he turned his beam on me. And I'm old enough to know better."

"We all are, Sugah," Care said. "But that doesn't mean we're immune to his charms."

"Charisma," Doris said. "That's the word I've been trying to remember. That boy has charisma."

"I only hope he uses it for good and not for evil," Wanda said, straight faced.

All four women ended up laughing anyway.

○ ○ ○

With all the increased business, Patty had begun to wonder if the café could afford to hire another waitress. She could use the extra help but she was worried that the surge might be temporary, might fade once the interest in the crop circles inevitably died down.

On the other hand, she'd had a couple of inquiries about renting the yoga room for times when it wasn't in use. If even one of those came through it would go a long way towards balancing the budget, with or without the boost from the crop circles.

With these thoughts on her mind, but still undecided about hiring someone, Patty decided to browse the campus 'Help Wanted/Help Available' board after her weekly ceramics class.

She stood a couple of feet away from the board

in the afternoon sunshine, watching the students milling around it, reading the postings. She held her own "Help Wanted" flyer in her hand, still making up her mind about posting it.

As she watched, one student in particular caught her attention. The student was a young woman, about the same age as most of the students at the board. She wasn't pushing but she managed to make her way to several postings, each of which she compared against the printout in her hand, probably a class schedule.

She appeared to be maybe 5' 7" tall, with a very slight figure. Her skin was the color of tea with milk in it. Her cheekbones were high, drawing Patty's attention to her dark, almond shaped eyes.

Patty made her way closer to her. "What kind of work are you looking for?" she asked her.

Startled, the young woman looked around. "Are you asking me?" she asked in a soft, lilting almost musical voice.

Patty smiled to hear the lyrical quality of her voice which was only slightly accented. "Yes," she replied. "My name is Patty Townsend. I haven't decided yet if I'm hiring right now. But I'm curious. What type of work are you seeking?"

"My name is Jamala Dirie," the young woman replied, bowing her head slightly. "The type of work is not as important to me as the hours. The hours must fit into my class schedule. Getting a nursing degree so I can work to support my family is all that matters." Raising her eyes to meet Patty's, she asked. "What kind of work would you have, if you decide to hire?"

Patty considered Jamala. She was soft spoken

137

but firm. She was polite without being submissive. "I might be looking for a waitress for my café. I'd like to find someone to work for twenty to twenty-four hours a week. The hours could be flexible, depending on your class schedule. Would you be willing to come to my café to discuss it?"

Jamala brightened. "Yes madam, I would." Looking at her watch, she added, "I could come tomorrow right after noon, if that is convenient for you?"

"That would be perfect. You'll be able to see what would be required of you and meet the other employees." Patty beamed a warm smile at her. "I think this could work. You'll fit right in." *As a counterpoint to Care's strong personality,* she thought but didn't add out loud. She gave Jamala the one copy of the flyer she'd brought. "Here's the address, do you think you can find it?"

"Yes, madam," Jamala replied with her own small smile. "I will be there."

FIFTEEN

The next day, a Thursday, Patty worked with Care to keep the guests happy, neither of them getting much of a break all morning. Shortly after the lunch rush had eased somewhat, she looked up to see Jamala enter the café dining room. Like the day before on campus, Jamala was wearing sandals, a white skirt that fell well below her knees, and a loose fitting top. The young woman paused in the doorway for a moment before finding Patty and crossing to her.

"Thank you for coming," Patty said as she led Jamala into the kitchen to discuss her potential employment.

"Thank you for your interest in me," Jamala replied, looking around, her eyes widening.

"Well, as you can see," Patty said. "We're not a big operation."

"But you seem to be very busy, with many customers."

Patty smiled to herself, enjoying the musical quality of Jamala's voice. "Yes, so far we're doing pretty well." She explained the set up to her and collected enough personal information from her to make the decision to hire her. After comparing her class schedule to the days she would most be needed at the café, Patty offered Jamala 24 hours a week, six hours a day Saturday through Tuesday. This would mean both Care and Jamala would work the weekends when the café was the busiest, giving Patty a little more time to enjoy the guests lingering over their weekend meals. And it would add some coverage for Monday and Tuesday. Wednesday would now be the only day she was solely responsible for her café.

○ ○ ○

After the café was closed, after the prep work for the next day's menu was finished, Patty took some leftover bacon brie frittata and devil's food cake upstairs for dinner. She was surprised to find Alec at the table with Jon. She had known Jon was upstairs but didn't realize Alec was up there with him.

"This is a pleasant surprise," she said, putting the leftovers on the kitchen counter top. "Trevor just left a little while ago. Did he know you were up here?"

Alec looked up, surprise straightening his posture. "No, I didn't realize it was this late." He stood up and began hurriedly packing up his tablet computer and papers. "I better get home before he calls Wanda on me." He turned to Jon. "This is pretty good progress. Let's do a little more and then get together again."

"Right, I think I have a couple more leads to follow, then we can compare results." Jon followed him downstairs to lock up behind him.

"Leads?" Patty asked when he'd returned.

"Yeah," Jon said, packing up his own laptop and printouts. "We started out discussing what we'd found out about the new guy, Spense, and then got off track, discussing hoax accusations."

"So, he's a denier?"

"No. As far as I can tell he doesn't have any position on crop circles, Area 51, UFO's, or any of it, really. His thing seems to be investigating big government cover ups. He's the ultimate 'just the facts' guy," Jon said, scratching his afternoon stubble. "Pretty fascinating, actually."

"Yeah, fascinating," Patty said with a sigh.

"Not you, too?" Jon asked. "You think I haven't noticed all the female commotion around him?"

"Yeah," she said, shaking her head. "I'm not sure what it is about him. He seems more attractive than the parts should add up to. But somehow he is."

Patty took the warmed leftovers out of the microwave and brought them to the table.

"Man, I love this one," Jon said, inhaling deeply rubbing his hands together. "I didn't think I'd like it when you first put it on the menu, but I should have trusted your instincts. It's great."

"I wasn't sure there'd be any leftover for us. I admit I panicked a little when I saw Alec up here. There's not enough for three." Putting their drinks on the table, she asked, "What was that about leads as he was leaving? You guys investigating Spense? Is he shady or something?"

"No, it was reading some of what he's written about studying hoaxes that gave Alec an idea how to look into the allegations that our crop circles are teenage pranks."

"It'd be good to be able to rule that out, to rule out anything, really."

"Yeah, particularly since Chris Woods and that rat, Robert Shepard, are spreading the theory that Trevor's behind it."

141

"Trevor?" Patty's body jerked straight up. Something was threatening one of her cubs. "That's absurd. He's a good kid. I don't believe he'd have anything to do with vandalism."

"Spoken just like a mom," Jon teased, his dark eyes glittering. "But I don't think just your faith in him is going to be enough. You remember he got in trouble at school right after his mother left town? He was suspended. Now, Alec tells me he's on the school's unofficial troublemaker list."

"And as his dad," Patty sighed, calming minutely. "I suppose Alec won't be seen as able to defend him objectively. I may understand it, but I don't like it."

"Me either." Jon pushed his empty plate away and looked toward the kitchen. "Isn't this devil's food cake day? Any of that left?"

When Patty had brought the one remaining slice of cake to the table with a scoop of coffee ice cream and two forks, Jon asked, "Hey, did that student you were thinking about hiring show up this afternoon?" Jon watched Patty nod, her mouth too full to reply. "How'd that go?"

Patty finished her bite of cake and said, "Yes, she came in and I hired her already. I liked her and her story moved me."

"What story?" Jon asked, journalist antenna twitching.

"She's nineteen years old but seems more mature, a refugee from Somaliland, a nursing student, and the mother of a nineteen month old son she obviously lives for, scheduling her classes and work around his care. Her father was killed in some ongoing

142

conflict in their country, I'm not clear whether it was political or religious, or both. Only her mother came to America with her. They didn't even realize she was pregnant 'til after they got here."

Jon put down his fork and leaned in, now more absorbed by the story than the cake. "Hmm, I'll look into the history there. Go on."

"They originally lived within the refugee community north of San Diego but Jamala wanted to move closer to the college to start her nursing classes. Her mother watches the baby during the day." Patty paused, tilting her head in thought. "Isn't that odd? I don't think I caught the baby's name. I'll have to ask when she comes to work on Saturday."

"Saturday? Don't you already have Care working on Saturday?"

"Yes but if Jamala works four days, Saturday through Tuesday, it'll cover the cafe's busiest days and fit in with her class schedule. As an old teacher myself, I couldn't help responding to her drive to learn. Plus it frees me up to enjoy the weekend, at least part of it."

"Okay, I'll meet her Saturday. What about the baby's father? Where's he?"

"I don't know. She didn't mention him and I decided if it made her uncomfortable, it could wait." Patty reached over to steal the last bite of cake that Jon had forgotten in his pursuit of Jamala's story. She hadn't orchestrated the distraction but she wasn't above taking advantage of it.

○ ○ ○

Saturday morning Jamala reported to work on

time at eight. She had followed Patty's advice and gotten some well soled closed toe shoes but she was still wearing her lovely loose fitting top and skirt. Patty would provide a Café Du Jour apron, but she worried Jamala's pretty blouse might not still be lovely by the end of the shift.

Care greeted her at the door and took charge of her training. Patty relaxed watching them together. Care's usually acerbic manner was pure southern charm with her young protégé`, treating her like a beloved granddaughter.

When one of the regulars playfully teased Care about her shirt's message, *Sometimes I have to remind myself it's not worth the jail time.* Care had snapped back at him, "Why bless your heart Sugah, you're definitely not worth the jail time."

Jamala's startled face betrayed her shock at Care's response. Patty laughed softly, amused at this slice of life at her café.

By the time Jon came down for his breakfast the early regulars had been in and left, served by Jamala under Care's vigilant eye. Jon ordered a carrot raisin muffin and a slice of sun dried tomato/herb frittata. When Jamala brought it to him, he took the opportunity to introduce himself as Patty's husband and chat with her briefly.

Alec came in and joined Jon at the two top. He rubbed his hands together in anticipation as he ordered a wedge of the ham and asparagus quiche. "I have to ask Patty what she puts into this to make it taste so bright and fresh."

"She adds a little fresh mustard flower," Jon replied around a mouth full of muffin. "Don't change the subject. What'd you find out about our new friend?"

"He comes up legit. He's not a favorite among government types because of his constant questioning of what they do and do not know, or release."

"No, he wouldn't be."

"But other than that, no marks against him I could find." Alec paused to accept his breakfast from Jamala, smiling at her. Tossing his chin at her retreating back, he asked Jon, "Who's the new girl?"

"Patty's latest hire. This is her first shift. So far, so good."

"Okay." Alec turned to his meal. "What'd you come up with on the high schoolers?"

"Not much. I've heard about a little get together that night no one wants to talk about, certainly not to you or any of your people. It could provide alibis but since it might involve some other criminal activity, no one wants to say who was there."

"Criminal activity?" Alec tilted his head curiously.

"The rumor is some pot and a beach bon fire but that's all I've gotten so far. I'll keep on it."

"Okay, that's a lead I can follow, too." Alec nodded and tapped a note into his phone. "Maybe some of my guys have heard something. I'm surprised you already have a line into the teen community here."

"I don't, not really. One of their grandparents repeated something to my pressman, Henry. He told me and I tracked the kid down from there. I will say, investigating something this vague, trying to disprove a negative, is a slow go."

"In the meantime," Alec said, nodding. "The crime scene crew finished their drawings of the design."

"And?" Jon asked. "Don't keep me waiting."

"At first glance it looks like a series of six concentric circles but they're off center just enough to be odd," Alec said. "That's when the CAD system came in handy. When they converted it to a 3-D model, it turned into a short, stout cone shape, sorta like a rounded pyramid."

"You use a CAD system?" Jon asked.

"Oh yeah," Alec responded. "That's something I came to rely on as an MP. It's not always possible to protect a crime scene in an active military zone. So I insisted on one for the department here."

"Cheaper than a drone," Jon said.

"Much," Alec said. "And my crime scene people love it. By the way, they did report they found only one item in the field of unexplained human origin."

Jon perked up, leaning forward.

"Don't get too excited," Alec continued with a smirk. "It turned out not to be anything." He paused to shake his head. "They uncovered an old weathered chewing tobacco canister. Jerry McDowell initially denied it was his but as soon as his wife walked away, he admitted he still uses the stuff. He thinks she doesn't know."

"The wife always knows," Jon said, sighing.

Their discussion stopped as someone new opened the door, gazed around the café until finding Linda Rasmussen sitting at the number five booth and headed toward her.

"Now, who's this guy?" Alec asked, his dark eyes narrowing.

"Seems to know our resident botanist slash crop circle expert," Jon replied, his eyes never leaving the pair in booth five.

Alec, who was accustomed to quickly sizing up a potential threat, witness, or victim, saw a man in his late twenties or early thirties, with rust colored hair worn short but long enough to curl naturally and a pale pink complexion obscured by many, many freckles. "I make him about six foot even and around 190 rangy pounds. He looks like he could be a swimmer with those shoulders and ropy muscles."

"How'd you get all that?" Jon marveled.

"Years of practice," Alec replied, returning his attention to the remains of his breakfast. "His eyes are so pale blue, they're almost like ice. And his skin wouldn't have any color at all if it weren't for all those freckles,"

"Clearly they know each other."

SIXTEEN

The following Friday morning, as he did on many Friday mornings, Jon slept in. When he eventually got up, he took a shower, put on chinos and a message t-shirt with an old grammar lesson, *You're nuts. Your nuts. Know the difference.* and headed downstairs for breakfast.

Entering the cafe's dining room, he found his usual Friday morning breakfast partner, Alec, sitting at the big number four booth with Spense and the new guy, the redhead. *What's his name?* Jon thought. *Have I forgotten or did I not hear it yet?*

Alec waved him over and he joined them. Alec leaned back, out of the line of sight of the two others who were canted forward in discussion, and shook his head at Jon, subtly distancing of himself from whatever the others were saying.

"Pardon me, Eddie," he said. "I don't believe you've met Jon." When Eddie had reluctantly pulled his attention from Spense, Alec introduced the two men. "Eddie, Jon is the publisher of our weekly newspaper and the husband of Patty, the nice lady you just met who runs this café. Jon, this is Eddie Alexander. He's an electrical engineer with an interest in crop circles."

Speaking in a soft voice with a slight upper class British accent, Eddie said, "Pleased to meet you, sir."

Jon stuck his hand out to shake but just then

148

Care delivered his late breakfast of spinach and feta quiche.

Jon began eating as Eddie returned his attention to Spense, saying, "I've been collecting data about the ultra and infra sound and the RFs emitted from some of the formations, topics on my regular lecture circuit. At present, I'm converting crop glyph pictures, agriglyphs if you will, into sound. After I've entered the data for this one, we can see if it matches any previous events."

"What documentation do you have of the emissions versus a control group?" Spense asked.

Alec leaned back and over Spense's head, arched his eyebrows at Jon. Jon shook his head in response to Alec's unspoken question. All this scientific evidence was going over both their heads.

Eddie pulled his tablet computer out of his backpack and began searching for the file he wanted. "I have it here. You can see the controls, my methodology. Okay, here it is. Take a look at these charts. I've taken numerous readings within each phenomena and at various points outside of them."

When Linda Rasmussen appeared at their booth, Eddie greeted her warmly, scooting over to make room for her to sit. Alec and Jon made their excuses and left, but not before hearing her say, "I've just come from the field. The stems are not broken, not a one of them. They're bent at a ninety degree angle at the first node."

"I have no idea what that means, but they're certainly all excited by it," Alec said. "I'm going to head back to the station. You?"

"No, I may not go into the office at all today," Jon

replied. "Henry gets the print edition out and Carl already has the electronic version up online."

"Carl's that student intern who worked on the paper as a class project?" Alec asked.

"Right. I hired him as a contractor and so far, it's working out well for both of us." He looked around the busy dining room. "Care's working today. I think I'm going to see if Patty has any time for me."

Alec left and Jon wandered back toward the kitchen, almost bumping into Patty coming out with three full plates. "Need help with those?" he asked.

"No, I got it." Her eyes took a quick trip around the dining room, as Care relieved her of the plates. "In fact, I think things are well enough under control to take a short break. You got time for me?"

"You're reading my mind again. I was just about to ask you to sit a spell with me," Jon said, heading to the two-top table few customers ever used.

"What's up?" Patty asked. "Something you want to talk about?"

"Not really. I'm just enjoying my morning, thinking about how well everything's going and I want to revel in it while I can." Care came by to refill Jon's coffee, bringing a cup for Patty and leaving without interrupting. "Anything up with you?"

"Yes, well no, not really," Patty said. "I've just been thinking about something."

"Words to strike fear deep in the hearts of husbands everywhere, ever since Lucy first uttered them to Ricky Ricardo."

Patty smiled, relaxing. She leaned back against the chair and shook her head. "It's nothing scary. This isn't an episode of 'I Love Lucy' and I'm no Lucille Ball."

150

Jon reached across to hold her hand. "I know it, sweetheart and believe me I'm thankful for it every day."

Patty smiled at him, reassured. "I've been wondering if it's time to add a row of tables down the center, like we talked about."

Jon too leaned back, looking at the bustling dining area. "There's plenty of business to justify them."

"But what if it all goes away once the crop circle excitement dies down?"

"They won't be built in," Jon mused. "It'll be easy enough to take them out if they aren't needed. Are you thinking round or square?"

"Hmm, they both have good points," Patty said, sizing up the space under discussion. "I could make an argument for either shape. The square ones would be easier to pull together for a large group but the round ones take up less room and would be easier to work around? Other thoughts?"

"How often do you get groups needing a bigger seating? Is that really an issue? I think the flow around them is more important."

"That makes sense. I'll think about it. But right now, I see Wanda and Doris coming in for lunch and I want to join them. The pizzas and the stuffed potatoes are in the oven. I have two double batches of lemon cookies on the counter cooling. I want to hear what they have to say about the latest crop circle groupie in town."

Jon waved her off toward her friends as he got up to leave. "Go. Enjoy. I'm gonna walk the streets to see if I can drum up some man on the street stuff on the circles for next week's edition."

Patty greeted her friends already seated in the number two booth. "Welcome, ladies. Room for one more?"

"For you? Always," Doris said, scooting over to make room and in the process twisting her t-shirt which reminded all, *Youth is a gift of nature. Age is a work of art,* printed over the famous portrait of Whistlers' Mother.

"Pretty good crowd this morning," Wanda said, today wearing a shirt that accurately presented her true nature, *I may be a bad influence, but I'm fun as hell.* "Must be the corn chowder, or maybe the stroganoff stuffed potatoes drawing them in."

"Right," Patty replied, smiling at Wanda's usual sarcastic tone. "The crop circles, the kooky botanist, the handsome myth buster, and the new red headed Brit couldn't have anything to do with it. What's the word on the new guy? Anyone know anything?"

"Born in the UK, trained as an electrical engineer, served in the Royal Air Force which is when he first got interested in UFO's, then swerved into crop circle research after his first personal sighting," Wanda recited flatly. "Other than that I got nothing."

Patty and Doris gaped at her, mouths hanging open. "Nothing? That's a lot. Looking at him I wouldn't have thought he was old enough for all of that," Doris said.

"He's twenty nine years old, born January 6, 1988."

Patty lowered her voice and leaned toward Wanda. "Isn't all of this some sort of breach of confidentialty? Should you be sharing it with us?"

Wanda looked at her and shook her head sadly.

"Girl, this is all public knowledge. I didn't get any of it off a secure police site. Look at Google or Wikipedia for yourself."

Following this revelation, Doris and Wanda continued to speculate on Linda Rasmussen, Eddie Alexander, and Spense Elliott. Patty already knew most of the info about Dr. Rasmussen from Jon's research but Wanda pulled out her tablet to add her birth date, April fourth and her age, fifty-one. She reported that Spense had been born on June twenty-seventh and he was now forty-seven.

Patty would've liked to pay attention to this discussion, she was sure it was interesting, but all of what mental power she had was consumed by her own problems. She'd probably decide to put in three or four round tables, the increased business certainly justified it, at least for now.

What she really needed was to find another renter to help pay for Care's, Trevor's, and now Jamala's employment, now totaling $795 a week, plus the required withholding. Business has been up, but Patty still wanted a little more rental income as a cushion.

O O O

On Sunday with both Care and Jamala working, the dining room was in good hands, and Patty was busy in the kitchen. She put the stuffed potatoes and the pizzas into the oven she had just taken the frittatas and quiches out of, and got the soup started. Two red velvet cakes had been completed and were waiting in the walk-in fridge since last night. Patty looked around the kitchen. Everything was ready. She could take the morning to enjoy breakfast with Jon, with a little eavesdropping on the conversations in the cafe's busy dining room for entertainment.

She found Jon and Alec seated at the middle of the three new round tables, delivered just after closing yesterday, and joined them. Looking around the dining room, Patty calculated the effect of the added tables. Not yet crowded but it felt busier, noisier. Jon had a wedge of the sausage and cream cheese frittata and Alec had a similar serving of the Quiche Lorraine. Both had cinnamon rolls waiting for their dessert. Patty had brought a cinnamon roll and a cup of hot Chai tea for herself.

From this strategically placed table, they could overhear the conversation between Dr. Rasmussen, Spense, and Eddie, as well as the comments from the locals at nearby tables who were probably here as much for the show as for the food.

"The plant stems within the circle appear to have been subjected to a short but intense burst of heat, softening them sufficiently to drop to the ground at a 90° angle, where they've re-hardened into their new shape without damaging the plant," Dr. Rasmussen said.

"You mean these plants could still produce viable alfalfa?" Spense asked.

"Yes," Dr. Rasmussen replied. "But their growth will be affected by at what stage the event occurred."

"I plan to use microwave and ultrasound waves to see if the effect can be reproduced," Eddie added.

"Wait, back up a minute," Spense said to Eddie, holding his hand up like a traffic cop, a conversation traffic cop. "What were you saying earlier about a link between UFO sightings and crop circles?"

"That is, well for me there's a link because it was when I was investigating a UFO incident for the military when I saw my first crop circle." Eddie shrugged his broad shoulders. "So I tend to see a link in the frequency the two events occur in the same areas but there's no evidence yet whether there is a causal relationship."

"You documented all this for 'Project Blue Book', right?" Dr. Rasmussen asked Eddie. She turned to Spense and asked, "Weren't you involved in the US version of 'Project Blue Book'?"

"Not exactly," Spense replied, leaning back, away from Eddie, distancing himself. "I worked on a military project 'Scientific Study of Unidentified Flying Objects' and some of my report ended up in the big 'Project Blue Book' final edition. It was how the government tried to control the release of that information that drove me out of the service."

Jon looked up to see a casually dressed couple approaching Patty, asking if she had a moment to talk. She excused herself and left with them, the three of them heading for the empty yoga studio space.

O O O

That evening, over dinner, Patty told Jon, "Chris and Pat want to rent the yoga space for their ballroom dance classes. The rent they'd pay would be good but there might be issues with Nathalie's yoga classes. They'll have to work out a schedule that'd meet both of their requirements."

155

"That shouldn't be too difficult," Jon said. "Nathalie was there first so I know you'll want to give her priority."

"Yeah," Patty said, slouching into her seat and giving in to how tired she felt. "I think the scheduling will go okay, but they want to make some changes to the space for their classes. Mirrors and things. I texted Nathalie to set up a three-way meeting so we can work out the details."

"Were you still at the table when Spense said government cover ups were why he left military service?" Jon asked.

"Yes, I heard that part but I missed any follow up discussion," Patty said, willing to be distracted from worries about changes to the yoga/dance studio.

"There wasn't any follow up. I'm looking forward to asking him the next chance I get."

SEVENTEEN

On a Thursday afternoon shortly after the café closed for the day, Patty took a platter of leftover cranberry/orange scones to the yoga studio for the meeting with Nathalie, Chris, and Pat.

Afterward, she returned to the cafe's kitchen to finish the work for the next morning before heading upstairs with dinner for Jon and herself. She found Jon closing down his laptop and collecting his work for Friday's publishing date.

"All done?" Patty asked him.

"Yeah," he replied. "This week's issue is almost all about the circles. We have an interview with Eddie Alexander and some really good man in the street stuff that turned out to be more than just filler."

"Great, I know you always enjoyed getting those first person response stories."

"I never really bought into the whole 'if it bleeds, it leads' mentality. Now that I'm in charge I can publish the stories I like. So far, I haven't seen any evidence that people won't buy a paper that doesn't print all the bad news available."

"It's good to know our new neighbors care about more than crime and violence," Patty said as she brought their re-heated dinners to the table.

"That's not to say I won't carry the ugly stuff when it pertains, just not only crime and violence." Jon

157

flipped his napkin onto his lap and smiled as he sniffed deeply of the aroma, with just a hint of nutmeg coming off his bowl of cream of broccoli soup, remembering Patty had picked up the idea of using nutmeg on their trip to France. "Hey wasn't that meeting today, with the new people who want to use the studio space - what're their names again? How'd that go?"

Patty nodded. Feeling particularly tired this evening, she'd served herself just a bowl of soup. She leaned back in her chair and sighed. "Their names are Chris and Pat."

"Wait, which is which?" Jon asked.

"What?" Patty asked, her brows contorted in response to the interruption to her train of thought. "Oh no. You're not going to start up your obsession about unisex names, are you?"

"It's not an obsession," Jon said, pulling his arms across his chest defensively. "I just find it interesting. What were their parents thinking? Why didn't they plan ahead?"

Patty shook her head, used to this from her husband of more than twenty-five years. "Since they're married and share a last name, it's even more confusing. It's Christopher and Patricia. Should be easy to remember, I'm Patty, she's Pat. Our meeting went well, actually. The days and times Chris and Pat want won't interfere with Nathalie's classes and everyone seemed willing to work together on the schedule."

"And yet you seem down," Jon observed. "What's wrong?"

"Nothing," Patty said straightening up and trying to shake off whatever was bothering her. "I don't know what feels off. Chris and Pat want to put in a wall of mirrors for their dance students and some lockers for them to use for their personal items during class. Nathalie loved both ideas, her people could use both the mirrors and the lockers during her classes as well."

"And the problem is?" Jon invited.

"I don't know," Patty said slowly, shaking her head. "They agreed to split the costs and the new rental income will really help cover the monthly loan payments so I can make payroll. Maybe I'm just tired. It seems somehow daunting to start one more new thing."

"You'll," Jon started to say, stopping himself suddenly. His wife Patty was a strong, competent woman. Her café was far more successful than either of them had expected. She didn't need him to solve this for her. She needed a husband who would listen to her while she worked it out for herself. "What do you think is getting you down?"

Patty reached over and ruffled his wavy hair, gray strands and all. "I don't know. Let me sleep on it overnight and we'll see tomorrow. Cake and ice cream?" she offered as she got up to take her only half eaten bowl of soup to the sink.

"Devil's Food?" he asked. "You have to ask?"

A smile warmed Patty's eyes and voice. "I'll split it with you, if you're having some."

○ ○ ○

The following morning, Patty got up and headed down to the cafe's kitchen. As she worked, setting the pecan sticky buns out to rise before putting them in the oven, getting the frittatas and the quiches ready for the oven, and chopping onions and slicing celery for the soup, she enjoyed the peace and quiet of working alone in the kitchen. She put on an old Smokey Robinson CD she'd almost worn out and hummed softly to herself. *This is good,* she thought. *My café is exactly what I want it to be.*

She served the few early morning regulars that came in until Care reported for her shift at eight, wearing a shirt that admitted, *Some days I'm just one tent away from a full circus.* Patty smiled at the sentiment. *Maybe that's all that's wrong with me,* she thought. *Maybe adding another renter sounded good until the idea of construction came up. It'll all be fine as soon as I cash their first rent check.*

By the time Jon came down for breakfast, Patty was ready for a break. Emerging from the kitchen, she found him sitting with Alec, talking over their empty plates and coffee. She pulled over a chair and joined them just as two strangers entered the café and paused to look around.

The guy looked to be a little older than Jon, closer to Alec's age, heavier but only slightly taller than either of their 6'1" heights. He had the appearance of a guy who had once been athletic but had softened with age. His light brown hair, parted on the left, fell over his brow, giving him a boyish charm, in spite of the fact his hairline was receding.

The woman with him was older, probably in her late sixties, around the same height as Patty's 5'2". She had broad shoulders, a deep chest and well-muscled arms and legs, but was thickening around the middle. Her gray/blond hair was shoulder length, worn straight and simple. When her eyes found the *Stressed is Desserts Spelled Backwards* sign, she brightened and made a beeline for the treats on display below it.

The threesome crowded in at the two top watched the stranger's eyes search the café diners. Spotting Alec's uniform, he headed for their table. "Are you Chief Harrison?" he asked, looking at a note in his hand to confirm the name. "When I checked in at the hotel, I asked for directions to the newspaper office or the police station but the desk clerk told me you'd more likely be here. Is this the right place?" He looked around at all the diners, most outright staring back at him.

Alec stood up to face him. "Yes, I'm Chief Harrison, and this," he said, turning to Jon, "is Jon, the publisher of the Valley Gazette." Alec pivoted to introduce Patty, but Nate was already focused on Jon, the real object of his search.

"That's perfect," the stranger said, smiling in relief. "You're the guy I'm looking for."

Patty got up, offering him her seat. "It's time for me to get back to work anyway," she said.

"And you are?" Alec inquired.

"Oh, sorry. My name's Nathan Phillips, Nate. I used to work for a big city paper. I left to publish a true crime book on a story I'd covered and when I was ready to come back, the paper was no longer publishing. Bought out. You know how it goes." He shook his head and waved his hands, figuratively erasing the previous topic. "Anyway, I'm looking to see if there's a story here, in these crop circles, to turn into my next book."

"Hmm," Alec said. "And who's the lady with you?"

Nate reluctantly pried his attention from Jon and

turned back to Alec. "Her name's Barbara Woodward. I don't really know much about her except she's a licensed pilot who'd heard about the crop circles and was willing to give me a lift here." He once again turned his focus to Jon. "So what can you tell me?"

Jon looked at Alec, who stood stone faced, giving no indication what his thoughts were on sharing info with this new guy before looking into him. Rather than giving him anything, Jon offered, "I can introduce you to some of the crop circle experts who're here studying them."

Nate took in the café as they crossed the room. "Circles, circles, everywhere," he muttered.

"What's that?" Jon asked.

"Crop circles, round tables. That roundabout in the middle of town. What is it with this town?" Nate asked.

Jon saw the new round tables with fresh eyes. "Oh," he said. "Those were chosen for the ease of movement, nothing to do with the crop circles."

"Just saying," Nate said, arching a single eyebrow at Jon. "It's like some sorta theme here."

As they passed, Jon heard Care discussing the pizza and cookies of the day with Barbara Woodward. "Just give me some of those cookies for now," the female pilot said. "After I've had some of them, I can decide what else I want."

"You're my kind of person," Care said. "An eat dessert first kinda gal."

o o o

On Sunday afternoon, just after closing, Patty

welcomed the employees of the café and several friends for an after-hours birthday celebration. As the guest of honor, Jamala sat at the center of the big corner booth. Several party guests joined her in that booth with overflow guests filling the nearby booths and tables. Patty purposely chose to sit farther away, at the middle table, so she could go to and from the kitchen as needed. Jon, Alec and Trevor joined her.

For her party, Patty had made Jamala's favorite three cheese, roasted red peppers, and olives pizza and mushroom and onions stuffed potatoes, both vegetarian, and a big cheesecake topped with fresh strawberries.

Jon nudged Patty as Jamala began opening her presents. "It looks like several people stole your idea of getting her a t-shirt," he said.

"Yeah", Patty said softly. "I like Jamala but she's so private, I didn't really know what to get her. Then I had the bright idea to give her a message shirt with a nursing theme so she could protect her nice blouses." She frowned. "So far there haven't been any spills that didn't come out in the laundry. How long can that last?"

"What's with the frown? Second thoughts?" he asked.

"Not exactly," Patty said. "I worry that she'll feel we're all rushing her Americanization." She glanced over to watch Jamala opening the next gift. She let a sigh slip out. "I don't want her to think we're ganging up on her."

Jon patted her hand. "Don't worry so much. It'll all be alright in the end."

Patty read Jon's shirt, chosen with the nursing theme in mind, *A semi-colon is not a medical condition.*

She searched the group for other shirts. Of course Alec bucked the trend in a sharply creased plain khaki t-shirt. Patty herself was still wearing her Café Du Jour shirt but Wanda sported a shirt saying, *My people skills are fine. It's my tolerance to idiots that needs work.* Doris's shirt explained, *The more you weigh, the harder you are to kidnap. Stay safe - eat lots of cake.* That's good, Patty thought. *Only a few people are wearing messages.*

Jamala, appearing uncomfortable at being the center of attention, looked often to her new friend, Trevor. Seeing this, Alec asked his son if there was a budding relationship.

"Nah, Pops," Trevor replied. "I see her more as my little sis. She's older than me but I feel like a big bro around her. She's had kinda rough time."

"That so?" Alec prompted.

"Yeah, when it gets quiet here and I'm cleaning up, she talks to me, told me some of it, sure makes me appreciate how easy I've had it."

Alec was surprised at the troubled look on his son's face. Since school let out for the summer, Trevor spent more time at the café, watching Patty and learning how to cook. He appreciated the change in his son, from surly teen to caring young man, was largely due to his time working at the café. "Anything you feel comfortable telling me?" he asked.

"Not here, not now." Trevor shook his head. "Too many people. Maybe later, after we get home." He turned back to watch the gift opening activities.

Jamala opened Wanda's gift next, finding a t-shirt – *Nurses, we can't fix stupid, but we can sedate it.* She stared at it, brows creased, in silence until Care explained why it was funny.

This exchange did nothing to allay Patty's concern that all these message shirts might overwhelm Jamala. Her English was excellent, not the problem. But funny didn't always translate for someone whose early life had been very different.

Then Jamala accepted the package from Doris and found another shirt, this one read, *Nurse - the first person you see after saying, "Watch this!"* This time it was Doris who explained it to her. Jamala laughed her soft musical laugh and her smile finally reached her dark eyes.

The last gift she opened was from Trevor, another shirt. When she read the message - *Cute enough to stop your heart, smart enough to restart it*, no translation was needed. Beaming a big smile, Jamala waved across the room to thank him.

After the gift opening was finished, guests stood and began to mill around, saying their good-byes and leaving. "These should provide you with some choices of what to wear to work so you don't mess up your good clothes," Patty said, accepting Jamala's thank you.

"And wear to class, as well," Care added. "So you'll fit in with the other students."

Patty cringed, exactly what she didn't want said.

"I've seen some t-shirts I liked since I got my pilot's license," Barbara said. "I didn't buy 'em because I didn't think I'd ever wear them. Guess who'll be online shopping tonight," she added with a wink.

"What is it with all the t-shirts in this town anyway?" Spense asked Jon.

"I don't know," Jon said. "I never thought about it. Do you think it has something to do with being so close to campus?"

"I think it's Care," Alec said. "The shirts really multiplied after she started wearing them."

"Oh, it's Care alright," Patty said with a soft laugh. "Or maybe," she suggested, "it's because we're not in a formal classroom or a stuffy office. Wearing my shirts makes me feel young again. I'm glad my café is a casual place where people can feel comfortable wearing who they are right on their shirts."

"Whatever," Spense said. "I have some shirts that'd fit right in with this group. I'll have to see what I packed for this trip."

Doris turned to Patty. "You know those pillows I make for sale to support the food bank? You think I could make up some message t-shirt pillows and sell them here? Maybe some of the profits could go to the food bank."

"No," Patty replied. "Well, yes of course you can sell them here. But all of the profits will go to the food bank."

EIGHTEEN

Trevor sat in the family car in front of the café, anxiously tapping his hand against the steering wheel. He'd returned from taking Jamala and all the packages home some time ago. His mind still troubled by his visit to Jamala's home, he wasn't ready to go in just yet.

A sharp slap on the car's roof startled him out of his thoughts. "Let's get going, son," Alec called out as he and Jon passed by, returned from their evening run. "You're wasting daylight."

Trevor shook off the dark memories, pasted on a smile, and followed them upstairs. "Anything I can do to help clean up, Boss?" he asked, looking around the tidy upstairs kitchen.

"No," she replied. "I think everything's as good as it's going to be. Did you get Jamala home okay? Did you get to meet the baby?"

"The baby? You met the baby?" Jon asked as he and Alec stretched, cooling off after their run. "Tell us all about it," he said, looking around the kitchen. "Wait, what's for dinner?"

"Okay, you guys go clean up. I'll warm up some dinner for us." She turned to Trevor. "Don't start yet. We all want to hear every last detail."

Once everyone was seated and serving themselves from the pot of beer and cheddar chowder soup and the platter of chili and cheese stuffed potatoes, Trevor started. "I drove her to their place."

"Wait, where do they live? What's it like?" Alec asked.

"Ever the cop, gotta have all the deets," Trevor said. "A small apartment in a big complex, off campus." He paused for other questions, milking the delay. "Her mom was sitting out on the patio when we drove up. I got out to help Jamala with all the gifts and stuff but her mom gave me such an evil look I stayed outside while Jamala took everything in."

He paused there so long, Patty finally said, "And . . . go on."

"Her mother had on one of those scarf things. What's that called?"

"Hajib," Patty answered. "I asked about them when I visited the IRC in San Diego. It's a headscarf some Muslim women wear for modesty around adult men who aren't family. I was surprised to learn older women wear them more often than younger girls. I thought they'd want to protect the modesty of their young girls more. Whatever. So Jamala doesn't wear one but her mother does. Interesting."

Trevor huffed a slow breath and looked around the table. "Her mother, sitting there all small, like some sorta gnome, just glared at me, really angry like, then she goes, 'All the men in my daughter's life have brought her only sorrow and sadness. Will you add to her grief?' Her eyes were like really boring into my skull. I didn't know what to say. I'm just glad she decided to stay home with the baby instead of coming to the party. What a downer."

"Go on," Jon urged.

"Well, just then Jamala came back outside and

spoke kinda harsh to her mother in, well I guess it was Arabic. Her mother got up, handed the baby to Jamala and went inside. Jamala told me she was sorry for what her mother had said to me. She sat down and the baby crawled up onto her lap. Baby! Wait till you see him! I know Jamala is small but holding that kid makes her look way tiny. He must be almost three feet long."

"Tell us about him," Patty said, leaning in. "His name is Max? Is that right?"

"Yeah, she calls him Max 'cause she wants him to be fully American but his name is really Maxamed. She said it means 'Worthy' in Somali."

"Is that what you were talking about earlier, what you said you'd tell me later?" Alec asked.

Trevor didn't answer right away. Finally, he said simply, "Her father's death was a big deal in her early life."

"Okay," Jon said, fork down, leaning in, totally absorbed in the story. "Start there, tell us about that."

"Yeah," Trevor began. "Well one day I said her English was really good and she goes 'It should be, it was the language used at my school'." He turned to ask Alec, "Somaliland used to be British or something?"

"Right." Alec scratched at his chin and added, "I think it was British Somaliland until sometime in the early 1900's."

"Were you ever stationed there?" Jon asked Alec.

"North Africa, yes. But not actually Somaliland," Alec replied. "Well, that explains her English."

"Yeah, she said her family spoke Arabic at home but English was mostly used in schools, government offices, businesses and stuff. That's probably why her

English is so formal-like."

"What happened to her father?" Patty asked. "She said he died in the conflict. What side? How'd that happen?"

"She said he wasn't on either side. She said he wanted his only child to go to school, even though she's a girl, even though they were Sunni Muslim. You know, like most of their neighbors. And he wasn't even involved in the conflict, just one of those innocent bystanders you hear about."

"Oh, that's sad," Patty said, eyes distant, food forgotten.

Unbidden, Trevor's thoughts revisited the angry, accusing stare of Jamala's mother. *Not sad, just really, really angry,* he thought.

"Sad, yes," Alec said. "Were there any brothers or uncles nearby?" he asked his son. When Trevor had shaken his head 'no', he continued. "Being two women alone with no male family members around in a Muslim country wouldn't be a good thing."

"That sounds medieval," Patty said. "What's the problem?"

"Sorta is, at least not far from it," Alec said. "It isn't just that no man in the house means no one is working, bringing in income. Apparently two women alone just historically, culturally, isn't done."

"Jamala told me something about an arranged marriage, wouldn't that lift some of the social stigma?" Patty asked.

Trevor recalled the part about a distant uncle on her father's side arranging a marriage for little Jamala. It'd sounded like a good deal when Jamala had first said it but then came the part about marrying at twelve or thirteen years old.

Watching Trevor stare silently into his bowl of soup instead of answering, Patty continued, "I know Jamala's mother put off the wedding until she finished school. Jamala told me that much, and how her father had been determined she be educated."

"There's no husband in the picture now, what happened to him?" Jon asked.

Trevor sighed. He stole a minute's delay by pausing to take a spoonful of his soup. He shook his head, remembering what she'd told him. "After they'd been married for a little while he told her they were moving to America."

"She got no voice in this decision?" Patty asked.

"No, she was probably in favor of it, but he didn't ask her, just told her."

Trevor sat, transfixed by the memory of Jamala telling him her story. He thought about the explanation the move was for business reasons. The husband's family has an import/export business that his older brothers will eventually run. As the younger son, he was being sent to America to learn about business and marketing, to see if they could expand here sometime in the future.

"He divorced her in some sort of sherry ceremony or something, before they got here," he said.

"Sharia law," Alec said, nodding. "I remember that part from the cultural training before assignment to a Muslim country. Under Sharia law, a woman can buy her way out of a marriage if she has the financial resources, which is almost never the case. But a man can divorce his wife for any reason, or no reason at all, simply by repudiating her, repeating it three times before witnesses." He frowned. "Wait, wait, wait," he said, correcting himself. "That's not right. That's not actually Sharia law anymore, it's more the accepted tradition, accepted practice in many areas."

"Whatever," Trevor said. "That's what she said happened. When they landed here, they were all set up in the same community. Jamala and her mother moved to a different neighborhood but they still saw him and his friends too often for comfort so Jamala wanted to move away. Then she came up pregnant."

"Oh my God!" Patty gasped. "All alone, in a new place, not much help. Poor girl."

Trevor sighed again but this time he found a reason to smile. "She says her one goal in life is to raise her son to be a better man than his father."

"Good for her," Patty said, her smile joining Trevor's. "And now I see the significance of his name, 'Worthy', indeed." Patty said, nodding. "I was already impressed by her drive to become a nurse before I heard all this."

"She told me she was inspired to become a nurse by a British nurse she met in the camp."

NINETEEN

Monday morning, Patty came down early to start the prep work to find Trevor waiting outside the door. He'd picked up knife skills pretty quickly and was enthusiastic with yeast doughs, but he still struggled to use a gentle touch with the scones. She enjoyed their time together, reminding her of when JJ was young. Except, of course, JJ had never been interested in learning how to cook. Trevor soaked it all up like a thirsty desert plant.

"Hey Boss," Trevor greeted her with one of his trademark dimpled smiles. "What you got for me to do this morning?"

"Same old, same old," Patty replied, heading to the kitchen. "Lots of rinsing, chopping and slicing. Have you been practicing what you're learning at home?"

"Yes," he said, pride clear in his smile. "I made your Wild Mushroom Medley soup last week and it turned out just right."

"Good for you."

"Yeah, with no woman in the house, our meals for sure hit bottom." Trevor pushed up his sleeves and dumped some vegetables into the sink to wash before chopping. "Dad's pretty serious about keeping the place clean, to military standards, but all those years in the marines, he never had to cook."

"But you guys are getting along better, aren't

173

you?" she asked. Remembering how her teen students had opened up more when their hands were otherwise occupied, she forced herself not to look at him.

"Yeah," he said after a brief pause. "Mostly. He's really nothing like Mom, but he's there."

Patty sighed softly, thinking of how Trevor must have struggled with his mother leaving so suddenly. "How so?" she asked.

"You know," Trevor continued. "When Mom left, I couldn't believe it. I couldn't believe she'd leave me like that. Leave him, sure. But why leave me too? It had always been the two of us against the world. It was like that had all been a lie."

Patty turned to look him in the eye, waiting for him to look up from chopping the onions. "Lucky for me you found your way into my kitchen. I miss my son and I miss teaching and you fill in quite nicely." Teaching Trevor how to cook fulfilled Patty's drive to work with eager young minds, the one thing she missed about her old life.

Trevor grabbed a paper towel to wipe his eyes. "These darn onions always make me cry."

Patty turned back to her work, hiding a smile.

o o o

Later that afternoon, just before closing, Doris came in with several bags bulging with her pillows for Patty to sell for the food bank. She had some familiar ones, like the ones that were printed with bunny or cat faces with ears made out of gray velvet extending out from the body of the pillow and some new ones with funny messages. One had a cartoon picture of a neon pink flamingo on a soft pink background over the words, *Thigh gaps are for flamingos*, and another that reported, *A recent study has found that women who carry around a little extra weight live longer than the men who mention it*, in a bright red florid font.

They worked together to arrange them on the open shelves under the coffee carafes and the desserts display, Doris bustling around despite her bulk. Patty artfully placed a couple on the seats in the booths so people would notice them and get the idea.

"Didn't you tell me you volunteer at the library teaching English or something?" she asked.

"Sort of," Doris corrected. "It's the Literacy Services program that's housed within the library and we teach a lot more than English."

"That's right," Patty said, motioning her friend to join her at the two top for some coffee and date/nut cookies. "That's the part I want to ask about. If someone's English skills are okay, can they still get help with, oh say, the citizenship test?"

"Honey," Doris said, shaking her head sadly, "poker's not your game. And don't try undercover work. You are not subtle."

Patty had to laugh. It was true, she could be a little too direct when she had a goal she cared about. "Alright, you've seen through me. Jamala's English is good, more proper than a lot of American born citizens speak including me, but I'd like to help her get her citizenship. She's so busy with her family, her classes, her hours here, it may not be a priority."

"I'd think she be a delight to tutor. Her English is so good and she's obviously bright and goal driven. Does she know you're asking?"

"Not yet," Patty answered quickly, shaking her head emphatically. "I didn't want to say anything until I knew what I was talking about. Max was born here so he's already a citizen, and you're right with very little help, Jamala should be able to pass the test. I haven't met her mother. I don't know how she'd do."

"Surely the International Rescue Committee provides classes, support, all that?" Doris asked.

"I'm sure they do," Patty said, searching for an excuse. "But Jamala's so busy, I'd hate to see her have to travel back to the refugee community to get their help." *There,* she thought, *that's sounds like a believable reason to keep her away from her ex and his friends.*

"I'll pick up a flyer," Doris offered, "and any other info I can find, and drop it off for her the next time I'm in. Okay?"

"Perfect. I'll make sure to talk to her about all this before then," Patty said, running her hands through her cropped hair. "I don't want to be one more person in her life taking decisions away from her."

o o o

Jon and Nate approached the booth where Dr. Rasmussen, Spense and Eddie were lingering over coffee and dessert. "There's been a lot of interest here in town about what you guys are finding," Jon started.

"Yes?" Dr. Rasmussen asked.

"Yes. We were thinking," Jon said, pointing to Nate, including him. "It might be a good idea to set up a panel discussion. It'd be an opportunity for you to speak to the community about what you're finding and for them to ask questions. Is that something you'd be willing to do?"

While Dr. Rasmussen and Eddie exchanged a look and a mutual shrug, Spense spoke up, "Where? When? What would be the ground rules?"

"We haven't gotten that far yet," Jon said. "I was thinking we could set up right here. Maybe on a weekend day after closing so more townspeople could come." He looked to Nate. "I guess one of us could moderate it."

Nate shook his head, absently brushing back the hair that habitually fell over his right eye. "I don't know about you but I'll be too busy taking notes to emcee it."

"Yeah, you're probably right. Me too," Jon said. "Maybe we could see if Alec would moderate it. Would that do?"

Nodding, Eddie said, "You understand we aren't yet ready to make a definitive statement. The audience would have to understand that before we could begin." After Jon nodded, he continued, "We could each make brief opening statements."

In her clipped German accent, Dr. Rasmussen. added, "I'd like to have questions submitted ahead of time in writing in order to research my responses."

"At least to start," Spense amended. "Maybe we could have a little give and take at some point."

"Okay, this is all good," Jon said. "I'll check with Alec and set a date. I'll get back to you as soon as we have something a little more firm."

o o o

Patty emerged from the kitchen and, finding the few remaining customers this late in the day well cared for, joined Doris, Wanda, and Barbara in the number one booth. Care accepted payment from one last group of customers and, pulling up a chair, joined the conversation, saying to Barbara, "I guess your online shopping went well."

Barbara looked down at her new t-shirt. It showed an old red bi-wing plane like Snoopy the Red Baron flew, on a field of sky blue interrupted by a few fluffy white clouds, trailing a banner which read *For most people, the sky is the limit. For a pilot, the sky is home.* "Yes," she said. "Isn't it great? I ordered four new shirts. Two came in and one is expected tomorrow but the fourth is on back order." She smiled. "I like this one best."

Doris smiled broadly and asked, "Doesn't your husband mind all your gallivanting around?" nodding pointedly at the wedding ring on Barbara's left hand.

Barbara quickly looked down at her left hand and covered the ring in question with her right hand. "Um, I'm not actually married any longer. I'm a widow. I just haven't taken off the ring yet," she said softly.

Doris reached across the table to cover Barbara's hands with her own. "I've been widowed myself for more than thirty years," she told her. "Was it recent?"

Barbara nodded 'yes' then looked around the table, asking the others wordlessly.

"Don't look at me," Wanda declared. "I was married once. Kicked the son of a bitch to the curb and never looked back."

"You haven't been above a one night stand,

here and there," her best friend Doris, teased.

"Yeah, but as I get older those get fewer and farther between," Wanda fired back with a smirk.

"In my experience," Care spoke into the ensuing silence. "Women who don't remarry, don't for one of two reasons."

"Do tell," Wanda coaxed, an expectant smile cracking her dark face.

Care pointed one finger, "Either you got lucky with the first husband and you know no one else will ever measure up." She looked around the table to nodding heads. "Or, the first marriage was so bad you're not interested in trying again."

Patty watched the reactions of the others, all older, ladies. "Don't look at me," she said. "My marriage is still in progress." She turned to Barbara, "So, will you be re-marrying?"

"Oh dear," Barbara replied, shaking her head and waving her hands in front of her. "It's too soon. My David only passed last year. No, it was the year before." Her eyes widening in surprise at the time passing.

"That's not all that soon, if you ask me," Wanda said with characteristic bluntness, looking over her reading glasses at Barbara.

"Well," Barbara said. "It was a very good marriage for a very long time. But after David got sick, I spent twenty-four hours a day taking care of a man who no longer knew who I was." She sat up straight and shook herself. "Wow, I don't think I've ever said that out loud to anyone."

"My Robert wasn't the same after his stroke," Doris said. "But he wasn't totally dependent until

B K Robinson

almost the end."

Care leaned toward Barbara. "I can surely see how that kinda thing could change your feelings about marriage," she said.

"Thank you," Barbara said. "You know, when I first took up flying, I wanted to be free, to soar, to find my wings again. Now, I fly more to avoid going home. I can't tell you how empty the place feels." She blew out a breath through pursed lips. "That place was our happy home for so ...," she said, closing her eyes, "so ... many happy years. But now that old place, I swear it echoes, it sighs, and shudders and I just can't bear to be there."

She cast her eyes to the table. Her usually animated, smiling face went slack, revealing lines and wrinkles. "And I'm not sure the kids understand. They're upset at losing their father and they act like I'm not grieving properly."

"As if there's one right way to grieve Sugah," Care said, her voice as soft and soothing as honey.

I guess Care's name is right for her after all, Patty thought. *No wonder Care, Doris, Wanda and I are such tight friends and that Barbara fits in so naturally with us.*

TWENTY

In the end, in spite of their well-reasoned plan, the panel was set for Wednesday afternoon at 2:30, in time for Jon to cover it for this week's edition. Alec had said it might not be proper for a sitting chief of police to moderate the panel, but Wanda, a civilian employee, had immediately volunteered her services. Patty had laughed when she'd heard, saying Wanda wouldn't be shy about directing the discussion.

Jon paced near the doorway into the studio, looking over the crowd. And it was a crowd. They had decided, since there weren't any classes Wednesday afternoon, they could set up in the studio instead of the café. They'd set up Wanda and the three panel members at a table at the south side of the room, backed by the newly built in oak lockers, and filled the rest of the space with rows of chairs. Jon imagined he could still smell the distinct mix of oak sawdust, turpentine, and lemon oil furniture polish of the fresh construction.

They used the chairs already in the studio, brought in all the chairs from the café, and Doris lent them folding chairs from the church's basement meeting rooms. They set them up in neat rows facing the panel, with a single center aisle. The soft afternoon sunlight, streaming in through the eastside windows, shone on the new mirrors on the west wall without

181

glare, but perhaps made the room a little too warm with all these bodies.

The studio was standing room only when Benjamin Rodriquez stationed himself at the door, looking sharp in his Valley Center Fire Department uniform. He'd been a good customer at the café since Patty had shared the first day's leftovers with the neighboring fire station. But he was here this afternoon in his capacity as a firefighter. He counted heads and checked that number against the room capacity set by the VCFD and posted near the door. No more people would be admitted unless some left.

Jon and Nate positioned themselves on the outside edge of the crowd, near the back so they could see the panelists and watch the crowd. Jon spotted Care's bright red beehive hairdo first, then found Patty, Doris, and Barbara sitting with her. At 2:35, Wanda placed two fingers between her lips and let out a piercing whistle, silencing the murmuring crowd. She was dressed conservatively, for her, wearing navy chinos and a simple white polo shirt.

"Welcome everyone," she said. "Today we're going to hear about our new crop circles from these honored guests and then you'll get an opportunity to ask your questions. The index cards on the chairs are for you to write down any questions and pass them up to the panel." She looked around the crowd, her dark brown eyes twinkling gaily. "Everybody find some cards to use?" After a brief pause, she continued, "Let's start with Dr. Linda Rasmussen. I'll let her tell you about herself."

Dr. Rasmussen rose to polite applause. Today she wore a loose fitting pair of pleated khaki trousers and a matching shirt that looked as though they might have been purchased in the big boy's section at Target. Seeing how short she was in her sensible shoes, Wanda motioned her to the front of the table where she could be seen better.

"Good afternoon, everyone. My name is Dr. Linda Rasmussen. My home is Munich, Germany but I spend most of my time traveling around the world, studying the crop circles. My education is in botany and I study the effects of the phenomena on the crops, on the plants themselves."

She went on to describe the effects she had documented at different sites on four continents but she was quickly losing her audience. One piece of new information she offered was about sending samples to the Burke/Levengood/Talbott laboratories here in the US for analysis. But by then, the audience had lost interest in all her scientific mumbo jumbo.

"Thank you, Dr. R," Wanda said, gently ushering her back to her seat. "I'm sure we'll hear more later when we get to questions. Next, we'll hear from Eddie Alexander."

Eddie made his way, all knees and elbows, to the front of the table, to polite applause. Pink rose to his cheeks, threatening to obscure his freckles. He was dressed casually in light brown cords and a t-shirt showing various geometric crop circle designs. He told the crowd he was from Warminster, UK and about his early interest in UFO's. He explained to the audience about his use of special computer programs to convert the collected ultra/infra and radio frequencies into visual representations. Before very long the crowd became fidgety, lulled by his soft, melodic voice.

"Thank you, Eddie," Wanda said soon after noticing the crowd's attention wandering, motioning him back to his seat. "And now," she said, smiling broadly, "let's hear from Spenser Elliott."

Spense made his way to the front of the table to more enthusiastic applause, particularly from the females in the audience. His long hair wasn't pulled back today and hung, freshly washed, loosely around his face. He wore rumpled and faded jeans and a navy blue t-shirt - *The NSA has read this shirt'* with *'(no we haven't - NSA),* in smaller, but bright red, print below. "Thank you, Wanda," he said in that 'aw shucks' manner of his that melted female hearts and overcame the staunchest resistance and good sense. "I know I speak for everyone when I thank you for pulling this panel together and keeping us on track." He beamed a smile at her, eyes twinkling, then turned to the crowded rows of chairs.

He told them a little about his history, including some earlier debunking of hoaxes, before saying, "The important thing for you to understand is that science doesn't come up with an answer and then look for evidence. The way science works is these good people," he said, pushing back his unruly hair and turning to Dr. Rasmussen and Eddie, "collect their evidence, botanical, electronic, and biophysical, then study what they've found."

"And that seems to me like the perfect point to start taking questions," Wanda said as Spense returned to his spot behind the table. She sorted through the questions she'd received and selected one for Dr. Rasmussen about the testing on the plants.

Jon noted that Dr. Rasmussen's initial response

was far too technical for most of the audience. Although he saw several people from some of the neighboring farms nod or shake their heads as they listened. At least they seemed to grasp the import of the effect on their crops. And he saw Jay Stone in the crowd, who had a nearby avocado ranch, although Jon still didn't understand what made it a ranch instead of an avocado farm, or what interest he'd have in crop circles, or what crop circles have to do with avocado trees.

"Earlier I mentioned the BLT lab in Michigan, founded by William C. Levengood," Dr. R said. "Although Levengood, a leading biophysicist, has since passed, the BLT lab still collects samples from crop circles all around the world. Theirs is the most complete catalog of botanical records in existence. Their information is without question. I have sent them samples from the crop circle here and from several of the surrounding farms for analysis."

Again sensing little interest from the audience, Wanda pulled another card from the stack. "This one is for Eddie Alexander and it's been repeated by several people. What do these circle look like, what do they mean?"

Eddie rose to answer, but remained behind the table. "I can't tell you what they mean, but I've entered the measurements data into my software and I can describe them for you." He began using his hands to suggest the shape, or rather shapes, as he described them "At first they appear to be simple concentric circles but from a better perspective, you can tell that they're slightly off center. Once I entered them into my CAD program and shifted them, they exhibited another

185

shape with a third dimension. Either a cone shape or a funnel."

"But what do they mean?" someone from the back of the room called."

"Again," Eddie said, "I don't pretend to be able to interpret them. But if anyone is interested in seeing them for yourself, they appear to be quite similar to the," here he paused to refer to his notes, "Cissbury – that's C-i-s-s-b-u-r-y – Rings found in England, near Sussex, in 1995, which you can look up online."

Several members of the audience quickly made a note of that as Wanda pulled the next question. "This one is for each member of the panel. The question is simply, 'Are our circles real or faked?' So, Dr. R, what do you say?"

"Real or faked?" Dr. Rasmussen repeated. "It's far too soon to say. We are still gathering data, once all the data is in we will have an answer. So far, I can tell you, all the indications are that this is a genuine crop circle event. Of course I cannot make any definitive pronouncement until all the results are collected, including those from the BLT lab."

"Yes," Eddie spoke up. "I can tell you from the data I've collected these circles look like the real thing. Unless or until, more information comes in to prove differently. The emissions I've collected ..."

"I heard they were a hoax, made by some of our more troubled youth, not ET," shouted a middle aged man sitting close to the front, no doubt meaning Alec's son, Trevor, but not saying his name. Jon didn't recognize him but he did recognize Robert Shepard sitting next to him nodding along, encouraging him. He saw his face clearly reflected in the studio's newly installed mirrors.

"Ah yes, deniers," Spense said. "There will always be deniers. There are people who still say the world's flat, that the moon landing was faked."

"Provocative word choice," Nate whispered.

"Yes, it was," Jon said, nodding as he watched the audience, seeing several individual members of the crowd stiffen or murmur at Spence's use of the term 'deniers'.

"There are people in my country who deny the Holocaust happened," Dr. Rasmussen added.

"In mine, too," Eddie said. "As recently as 1996, we had a major libel case brought by a Holocaust denier." He looked to the audience, spreading his arms, palms up, in appeal. "Even if these circles are eventually proven to be genuine, we're not saying they were made by extraterrestrials."

"Right," Dr. Rasmussen immediately chimed in. "That's why I research the effect the phenomena has on the plants, to verify the event and to further my search for a natural explanation." Her emphasis on the word 'natural' loud and clear.

"Exactly," Eddie added. "And my own studies into the sound, light, and physical impact both on the effected plants within the circles and on those immediately surrounding them for comparison are designed to understand the scientific phenomena, not explain the origins."

"I still say this is too far out to be real," a second man, slouching in his seat on the other side of the crowd, said.

"The crime scene crew reported there was no evidence of recent human presence in that particular section of the field and the investigation has pictures from postings on social media proving many of those originally suspected as hoaxers were somewhere else that night," Spense said, his deep blue eyes boring into that second speaker. "Remember, we have to be just as careful about deniers as we are about true believers."

"That so-called evidence could all be faked, just like the circles," another voice said. "If his son has been cleared, why aren't we hearing about it?" Even from this oblique angle, Jon recognized Chris Woods sitting next to this speaker. He looked around the room, searching for his friend Alec but failed to find his distinctively military presence anywhere.

Now Wanda waded into the discussion, her no nonsense tone putting an end to chatter from the audience. "There can be no official report from the police department until the investigation is closed. What Spense is saying, what has been printed in Mr. Townsend's paper, are the progress reports released as different avenues are pursued and eliminated."

She stared down each of the three who had spoken out about hoaxes. "Now, returning to the questions submitted on cards. This one asks about other crop circles found years ago, why those reports weren't investigated like these?" She paused, looking up, shaking her head. "I don't remember hearing about any previous circles around here and I wanna hear more about this my own self. Who submitted this question?"

Her eyes roamed over the crowd, landing on a woman sitting near the front who had raised her hand. She was probably middle aged but her well tanned face and strongly muscled arms gave her a vigorous appearance. "What can you tell us about them?" Wanda asked.

"I never saw them myself," the woman said. "But my father told me they used to get 'em in one field or another around here every few summers."

"Were they reported? Investigated?" Spense and Dr. Rasmussen asked simultaneously.

"They were reported and the sheriff's office came out but nothing else was ever done," she said. "The newspaper wouldn't even cover it."

Jon's interest was piqued by why the paper hadn't covered the story but the buzzing of his silenced phone distracted him. It was unusual enough for Henry to send a text message, but this message read, 'Come quick. I need you at the newspaper. Now.'

Jon leaned into Nate, seated next to him and whispered, "I gotta go. Share anything you get?"

"Sure," Nate responded without pulling his eyes from the discussion.

Blowing out a breath, Jon got up and left as unobtrusively as he could. Not that anyone was paying attention to anything but the discussion about the area's previous crop circles.

As he was exiting, Jon passed an attractive stranger waiting for someone to leave so she could enter. Even in a quick glance, he took in her best features. She was a slim and trim 5'5" tall, probably about 120 pilate toned pounds in an emerald green dress. Her hair was bottle blond but professionally done streaky to look natural, in an expensive looking cut with lots of layers. Her blue eyes were widely set in her heart shaped face and made up to minimize how small and deeply set they were. Her skin was either perfect or very well made up. *Sizing up a pretty lady is an excellent use of my journalist's skills,* he thought.

Jon nodded to her in greeting as she glided into the back of the room and headed for Jon's now vacant seat next to Nate.

TWENTY-ONE

Jon rushed into the newspaper offices, enjoying the scent of industrial lubricant familiar from every news operation he'd ever known, to find Henry leaning over, half his upper body disappearing into the old printing press. "What's up?" he asked.

"You know I like to run the ad supplement on Wednesday so there's less push getting the paper out each week?" Henry asked, straightening up, rubbing his big rough hands off on his already badly stained denim jumpsuit.

Jon was used to Henry speaking at a snail's pace but this was new. Usually he used so few words that no matter how slowly he spoke, he still got to the point pretty quickly. "Yes," he replied, while thinking, *get to it already.*

"Well," Henry said. "When I started that ad run this afternoon, I heard a hitch in the rhythm. She didn't sound right. I shut her down as fast as I could, started looking for the problem."

"A hitch in the rhythm?" Jon asked, shaking his head. "Okay, what'd you find?"

"So far I've found this here belt ripped loose and something that looks like it maybe used to be a paperclip stuck in here where it shouldn't be."

"A paperclip?" Jon asked, his entire face furrowing. "How? We're pretty strict about keeping

191

anything loose far away from the machinery. You taught me that."

Henry silently shook his head.

"I know I haven't brought anything like that in here," Jon said. "And even more, I'm sure you didn't. You're more obsessive about it than I am. Has anyone else been around here?" he asked, looking around as though he might see traces left by a visitor.

Henry leaned back, crossing his arms, his mouth turned down as he searched his memory. "You know, now that you mention it, Robert Shepherd came around late Monday, bringing that Chris Woods fella with him."

"What'd they want?" Jon asked. "Why would either of them be in the print room?"

"Let me think," Henry said, scratching his head of curly grey hair. "I was in your office, on one of those Skype calls with Carl, when I heard someone talking. I headed to the front door to see who was there and what they wanted. You know, like for any visitor. But by the time I got to them, they'd already come in here."

"I guess Robert's as familiar with this place as we are," Jon said, running his hand through his short, wavy hair, unconsciously mirroring Henry.

"Uh huh," Henry nodded. "Robert said he wanted to make sure he hadn't left something behind in the desk. I thought it was hinky. You know I don't trust him. But he pushed right by me and I didn't think you'd want me to be rude."

Jon's gaze drifted toward his office. "Did he find anything left behind?" He shook his head firmly. "I know he didn't. I cleaned out that office before I moved in."

"No sir. I followed him in because I didn't like the

idea of him being alone in there with your stuff. But thinking back on it now, I remember Chris Woods saying he'd wait here." Henry nodded, affirming his memory.

"You left him alone here so Robert wouldn't be alone in my office." Jon said, nodding along as he recapped Henry's story.

"I'm sorry, Mr. Townsend," Henry said, looking to his feet. "I made a mistake. This's all my fault." He gazed around the print room where he'd spent most of his adult life.

"That's not what I meant, Henry," Jon said, reaching a hand toward Henry's shoulder. "No one expects you to be in two places at once and how were you supposed to know they might be up to no good?"

"Those two?" Henry said, slowly shaking his head and screwing up his mouth like he'd tasted something foul. "Who'd expect anything else?"

Jon looked at his watch. "I guess I'd better call the maintenance folks and get them out here to take a look at it so they can give me an estimate. And then I'll have to call the insurance carriers and file a report. Do you remember what time they were here?"

"Not 'xactly, but they'll be a record of that Skype call with Carl," Henry said, turning toward the office and the computer in there.

"Right," Jon said. "Let's talk to Carl before getting the insurance people involved. I'll need to have as much detail as I can about what happened before I file that report."

Once in the office, Jon used the mouse to wake up the computer. He chose the Skype icon and called up the history, quickly finding the call Monday afternoon. He sighed, shrugging his broad shoulders and muttering, "Better safe than sorry," and clicked the redial button.

Carl's smiling face quickly appeared on the screen. "Oh, hi Jon. I was expecting Henry to call back to finish our Monday call. I didn't expect you to join us. It was just a routine call, nothing requiring the boss's attention."

"This isn't about that," Henry said. "Or rather it's about that call but not about what we were talking about."

Jon sighed as Carl's brow creased. "That didn't clear up anything," Jon said. "Let me try." He sat down and faced Carl's image on the screen. "Carl, we're trying to clear up something that happened here during the time of that call. The call record says it was Monday about 1:30. Does that sound right to you?"

"Yes," Carl said. "About then. I wasn't really keeping track. And then the call was interrupted by those two guys who came in. So I moved on to other business until Henry was free again."

"So you saw the two guys who came in?" Jon asked, eyebrows rising along with his hopes.

"Yeah, sure," Carl said. "The older guy who came in the office with Henry and the younger guy who stayed on the printing room floor. Is this about them?"

"Yes, it is," Jon said carefully, not wanting to lead Carl or put words in his mouth. "Did you watch what he was doing while they were here?"

"I sure did," Carl said. "He looked suspicious to me, shifty, if you know what I mean."

"Good," Jon said, looking up at Henry and winking. "Now we're getting somewhere. What'd he do? Did he mess with anything in my desk?"

"Oh, you mean the older guy," Carl said, shaking his head, pushing his thick glasses back up his nose. "No, I was watching the young guy. He's the one caught my eye."

Jon slumped in the chair, he shook his head, his hopes dashed. *Oh well, too much to hope for.*

Henry leaned into the camera range. "What was it about the younger guy that worried you?" he asked.

"It was the furtive way he kept looking around, like he was checking to see if anyone was watching, and then he pulled something out of his pocket and ducked down out of sight. When he stood up again, he pulled something else out of his other pocket to wipe off his hands." Carl shook his head. "It just didn't look right to me."

Jon and Henry looked at each other and then both turned to see the line of sight from the camera imbedded in the computer to the printing room floor. Sure enough, it led directly to where Henry had found the mangled paperclip and the damaged drive belt.

"That's great," Jon said to Carl. "That's exactly what we need. Can I get you to tell the police chief all this? He may want you to pick out the younger guy from a photo lineup. Okay?"

"Well, sure," Carl said. "It's all true. I guess I don't mind repeating it." He paused, an emerging question screwing up his expression. "But wouldn't he rather see the video?"

"Video?" Jon asked, eyebrows rising again.

"Yeah," Carl replied. "I've gotten in the habit of documenting all my work calls. I'm an independent contractor, not an employee, so I record everything to back up my billing. I got the whole call. I haven't looked at it so I don't know how well he'll show up in the background, but you're welcome to a copy." He looked down for a minute as his fingers flew over his keyboard faster than Jon could hope to follow. "Wait a minute, I'm sending you a video file now."

Jon's inbox chimed. "Okay Carl, thank you. I'll take a look at this and let you know if we need you for anything more."

They disconnected and Jon cued up the video.

Henry laid his big knuckled workingman's hand on Jon's shoulder. "Damn me, I guess all this new technology is a pretty good thing after all."

"Sure looks like it now," Jon said through his widening smile. The ringing of his phone interrupted before he could get the file open. He checked the caller ID, tempted to let it go to voicemail, but since it was Alec, he answered. "Just the man I want to talk to," he said.

"Wanda came back after the panel discussion and reported on all of it to me," Alec said. "Then Nate came over to introduce Kylie Weber to me. Like I didn't already know who she was, haven't I been watching her on the tv nightly news? But when you didn't show up I got curious. Wait. What was that part about wanting to talk to me?"

"Yeah," Jon replied. "I think I may need to report a crime. Can you come over to the newspaper office, check out the scene of the crime?"

"What crime? Anybody hurt?" Alec asked, the rustle of paper and clothing sounding loud to Jon's ears over the phone as his friend got ready to leave his office, heading his way.

"No one hurt," Jon said. "Property damage. I think maybe sabotage."

"Sabotage? At the newspaper?" Alec asked. "Are you kidding? No. Of course you're not. I'm on my way. See you in a minute."

Almost as soon as Jon ended the call, his phone rang again. He hit the 'accept' button and said, "So quick? You can't come after all?"

"What?" Patty asked. "Are you expecting me somewhere? I was calling to find out why you aren't home yet."

"Oh hi, honey," Jon said, his voice and posture relaxing. "I didn't realize it was you. I thought it might be Alec calling back."

"You guys planning your evening run?" Patty asked. "Want some dinner after that?"

"Uh, no," Jon said, then hesitated. "Something happened here at the office. Alec is coming over to take a report and I'll probably have to take a pass on my run tonight."

"Really? Something happened at the paper? Is everyone alright?"

"Yeah, everything's okay. It looks like Henry caught it in time, before any real damage was done."

"Should I come over?" Patty asked.

"Nah, there's nothing you can do here," Jon said. "I think I hear Alec coming in already. I gotta go. I'll tell you all about it when I get home."

"Yeah," Patty said to the already dead phone.

Jon joined Alec and Henry in the print room.

"Hey Jon, Henry tells me you found some mechanical problems with the printing press," Alec said, turning to Jon, his dark policeman's eyes continually scanning the room, missing nothing. "What makes you think it might be sabotage?"

"We didn't at first," Jon said, leading Alec to the place at the press where Henry had found the problem. "When Henry turned it on this afternoon, he thought it didn't sound right. After he'd quickly turned it off, he found this twisted paperclip."

"Couldn't that have been an accident?" Alec asked.

"Sure," Jon said. "Except we're both pretty obsessive about keeping stray items away from the press."

"Still," Alec said.

"Yes, to be fair, it could've been an accident." Jon looked at Henry, who reluctantly nodded. "And then he found this damaged drive belt." Jon accepted the belt from Henry and passed it over to Alec who donned his reading glasses to examine the edges.

"Edges look a little too clean to be a tear," Alec said, looking up at Jon. "I'll ask the Crime Scene Unit to look at these edges under a scope, see if it was cut." Alec patted his pockets until he found an evidence bag and dropped the belt into it. "But still, why did you make the leap to an act of sabotage?"

Jon nodded to Henry to continue with the story. "Monday afternoon, R ..." Henry began.

"A couple of guys," Jon interrupted, deciding they shouldn't tell Alec who the guys were until he'd heard the whole story. That way, there'd be no question of jumping to conclusions.

"Uh right," Henry continued. "A couple of guys came in on Monday. One distracted me in the office." He turned, gesturing to it. "While the other one stayed out here in the print room, mostly standing right there, where I found the damage."

"Circumstantial, at best," Alec said, shaking his head. "Who'd want to stop the press? Why?"

"Well, I can't tell you why," Jon said. "But I've got a bit of video to show you that'll clear up the who part for you."

Alec watched the video file in silence, his face freezing, betraying no reaction to seeing one of his officers on the video. Maybe someone who knew him really well might catch a small twitch. When the video clip finished, he straightened up and blew out a breath. Without meeting Jon's eyes, he said, "Send me a copy of that video file."

Jon nodded.

Alec nodded to himself and returned to the printing room, pulling out his phone. "I'll call CSU to go over the scene, collect any physical evidence they can find."

"They're mostly going to find evidence of me," Henry said. "I was all over the big girl today, looking for what was wrong with her."

"They'll have to take elimination prints from you," Alec said.

While Alec punched the speed dial number into his phone, Jon turned to Henry. "You got that damaged clip out. If we replace the drive belt, can we get it up and running before we need it for Friday's run?"

Henry blew out a breath slowly and shook his grey head. "I don't know. I can't be sure I found everything that's wrong. Starting her up before we're sure could make everything worse."

"Okay. Good point," Jon huffed out a big breath

through pursed lips. "Okay, you give it a good look for anything else and I'll find the number for the company that services it. Maybe they can come out early tomorrow and give her a clean bill of health." He shook his head again. "I wonder how much that's going to cost. Every time I think the paper is doing well, getting a little closer to running in the black, something else comes up."

Henry's mouth turned up in a little smile. "What was it that little Roseanne Roseannedanna used to say on *Saturday Night Live*? 'If it's not one thing, it's another.' Truer words, huh?"

Jon smiled, remembering those old Gilda Radner skits when he was younger, more care free, an employee of the paper, not the one responsible for paying for things like this.

TWENTY-TWO

The following morning Alec stood up, bringing his discussion with Jon to a close, and led him out of his office. "I'm set up for the interview in here," he said, pointing to a door marked 'Chief's Private Conference Room' as they passed.

"You sure I can't stay?" Jon asked. "I'd love to be a fly on the wall during that discussion."

"I know you would," Alec replied, ushering Jon out through the reception area, past Wanda's desk. "I probably would too if I were in your place but no way. Even if you weren't the fourth estate, you're an interested party here and I can't have you in the room."

"How about ..." Jon began, pausing just before the exit.

"No, we don't have any one way mirrors like they do on tv and even if we did, it's still 'no'. Not gonna happen." Alec shooed Jon to the door. "See now, this's why journalists and cops can never be friends." Alec turned to Wanda. "Make sure he actually leaves, no hanging around."

"Alright." Jon threw up his hands. "I'm going."

Alec returned to his conference room and rechecked a few details. He took his regular seat at the head of the table and checked the laptop he'd set up in the middle of the broad oak expanse next to the two evidence bags containing the drive belt and the damaged paperclip. Each sat atop analysis report printouts from his crime scene unit. Mostly they had only found evidence of Henry but Chris Woods, the suspect, wouldn't know that. The fact of the evidence and the reports should be enough to put the fear of justice in him.

At precisely five minutes after their nine o'clock appointment time, someone knocked on the door. "Come," Alec responded.

Chris strolled in, familiar confident smirk on his face and in his eyes. "You need me for something?"

The chief noticed his detective had once again resisted calling him by his title. He smiled, motioning him in. "Close the door behind you."

Chris' vibrant blue eyes finally landed on the evidence bags. If he noticed his boss's smile hadn't reached his eyes, he didn't show it.

The chief nodded his head toward a chair and his suspect sat down.

"What's all this?" Chris asked. "You got some evidence of a crime?"

"Anything you want to say in your own defense before we begin?" Alec asked.

"My defense?" Chris said, mouth twisting. "I don't know what the hell you're talking about."

"These," Alec said pushing the evidence bags toward him, "Do these look familiar to you?"

Chris silently shook his head.

Alec knew his subordinate officer had been on the other side of the table in too many of these interviews. He hadn't expected him to say anything. Not right away. He reached over to the laptop and stroked the touch pad, bringing the screen back to life.

He watched he suspect's eyes as he recognized the scene Alec had cued up, a still from the video clip showing himself standing by the big printing press, wiping his hands.

Alec watched the blood drain from Chris' face, saw the smirk fade in his eyes, saw his jaw clamp closed. He waited until the other man turned his eyes to him. "Want your rep here?" Alec asked, arching his left eyebrow.

Chris froze, only his eyes moved, darting all around the room.

Alec sighed. Someone else might have gotten satisfaction from seeing this thorn in his side brought down like this. But Alec didn't. He couldn't feel any gratification having a fellow officer go wrong.

Chris looked down at his hands, his mouth working but no words came out.

"I'm placing you on administrative leave until this investigation is complete," Alec said, standing up. "We'll schedule a follow up after you speak with your union rep. I'll take your gun and your shield now."

Without meeting his eyes, Chris removed his gun from its holster and took the embossed shield folder from his breast pocket. Hands trembling, he placed them on the table, as far away from the laptop and the evidence bags as he could.

"I ...," Chris said, his usual cocky posture folded in on itself, his head hanging.

Alec returned to his seat and waited. But no more words followed.

"I didn't think ...," Chris tried again, sputtering to a stop.

"You didn't think you'd get caught. You didn't

think there'd be any evidence. You didn't think about how this might affect the paper. You didn't think about anyone but yourself," Alec said, empathy softening his tone in spite of his harsh words.

Chris shook himself, bravado straightening his spine for one more try. "You got nothing."

Alec picked up the interoffice phone line and punched in four digits. "Wanda, have an officer come in to escort Mr. Woods from the station. He doesn't get to return to his desk, speak to anyone, or make any calls. Thank you."

The two men waited in an uncomfortable silence until shortly the door opened and a young female uniformed officer, one of the latest hires, stuck her head in. Alec nodded to her and Chris started to say something but wisely shook his head and left without breaking his silence.

Once Chris was gone, Alec returned to his office where he found Wanda waiting for him. "That was smart," he said to her, "picking someone new who didn't have any longstanding relationship with him, good or bad." He nodded. "Good job."

"You okay?" she asked him.

"Yeah, sure," he said, sounding more tired than usual this early in the workday. "All part of the job. Find the bad guys and take them off the street." He sank into his desk chair. "It's a sorry day when it's one of our own." His sad dark eyes met Wanda's and he shook his head.

"He's been nothing but trouble ever since you got the chief's job," Wanda said.

"Oh hell, he wasn't that good a cop before then," Alec said, his sad smile once again failing to reach his eyes. "Back to work."

"Same old, same old," Wanda responded on her way out the door.

o o o

Jon returned to the café to find Nate splitting a wedge of caramelized onion quiche with Kylie Weber, heads together, laughing over their coffee. Wondering how he'd failed to recognize the familiar tv personality until Alec had mentioned her name, he wandered into the kitchen to see if Patty had time for him.

"What's up?" Patty asked him. "Do you know anything yet about," she paused to look around the kitchen area, making sure there was no one near to overhear them, "the interview?"

"No," he said. "Alec wouldn't let me stay. I know he had the evidence bags and printouts of the reports and he had the video cued up to a particularly incriminating spot. So it should be airtight but you never know with these things."

"Leaving you at loose ends, huh?" she teased.

"Yeah," Jon said. "I went over to the paper but the maintenance people have already come and gone. Henry has everything there in hand. I don't know what to do with myself."

"Go out front," Patty urged. "Talk to people. That's what you do, isn't it?"

"Yeah, but I don't feel like talking to anyone when all that's on my mind is the one thing I'm not supposed to talk about yet. And besides everyone's out with Barbara taking flyovers of the crop circles, except Nate, who's all busy with Kylie."

"Oh my God," Patty said through a great big smile. "You sound just like JJ when he was a kid and didn't want to do his chores." She turned back to her work. "What do you mean Nate's busy with Kylie? What's up with that?"

"I don't know," Jon said. "I just saw them sharing breakfast. They looked way too cozy for two people who just met."

"Hmmm," Patty said, wiping her hands on her apron and peeking around the doorway to see for herself. "Do you think they knew each other before here?"

"Maybe," Jon said, turning toward the café. "I'll go find out."

"I knew all he needed was a distraction," Patty muttered to herself. "He can resist anything but a good story. Curiosity always gets the better of him."

Jon got to their booth just as Kylie was getting up to leave. "Pretty lady," he said to Nate, watching her go.

"Yeah, and smart, too," Nate replied as Care refilled his coffee cup and left. "And she's ambitious, but I'm afraid she may be getting near her sell-by date."

Whoa, Jon Thought. *Good thing Patty didn't hear him use that sexist phrase!* "Yeah?" Jon asked. "She still looks pretty good on the nightly news."

"Yeah. Local," Nate said. "But she really wants to make the leap to a national network and if she doesn't get that chance soon, it'll be too late, they won't be interested in her. That's why she's here, covering the circles, hoping to get noticed."

"You seem to know her pretty well," Jon said.

A smile lit Nate's face. "We hooked up years ago

in Santa Barbara when I was making my big move from the paper for my first book. Even then she was too ambitious to stick around. When another story broke, she took off after it and I got left in the dust."

"Do I hear some regrets there for you?" Jon asked. Years of interviewing people had taught him to listen for what was not said as well as what was said, listen between the lines, and ask the right follow up questions.

"I don't know," Nate said with a shrug. "It was great fun while it lasted but I get the feeling whoever ends up with little Miss Kylie will always come in second to a new story."

"Speaking of new stories," Jon began, "how come you're sitting here when Barbara's offering flyovers of the crop circles?"

"Kylie and I went out with her early this morning," Nate said. "We got some great footage with the dew still glistening in the morning sunlight. Should make a good cover photo for my next book. Did you get any shots for the paper?"

"I didn't," Jon said. "But Carl, my tech guy was really excited about getting to see them. He got some good pics for the paper. Way more than we need." Jon shook his head, smiling as he remembered the young tech expert's enthusiasm. He still didn't know if Carl was more excited about seeing the crop circles or about going up in the small private plane. "Patty's supposed to go up with her later this afternoon, after the café closes, with Doris and Wanda."

"That'll be a fun group," Nate said, laughing and using his napkin to dab at the coffee that had dribbled down his chin.

○ ○ ○

After he left the police station for the day, Alec stopped by the café to check in with Jon. He found him in the kitchen listening to Patty's excited tales of her flight over the fields with her friends. Alec paused in the doorway, watching Jon laugh along with his wife, smiling to see his friend in better spirits.

After he'd watched for a while, he cleared his throat and interrupted. Jon and Patty barraged him with questions about his interview with Chris Woods and he told them only that the interview had taken place. "This is just a courtesy call, I can't answer any questions about an ongoing investigation." Jon tolerated that response better than Patty did.

"I just wish I could see some way out of this that doesn't end in a 'he said/he said' situation," Jon said, shaking his head sadly.

Patty looked from Jon's face to Alec's. Alec nodded once but his mouth remained firmly closed. Patty turned to her husband's troubled face. "He said. He said?" she asked.

"You know," Jon explained. "Chris blames Robert and Robert blames Chris. Each giving the other enough for a jury to find reasonable doubt."

"Oh crap," Patty said.

"Exactly," Alec agreed.

TWENTY-THREE

Friday morning, paper out right on time in spite of the scare over the big printing press, Jon slept in and came down to the café for a late breakfast. Just like always. Patty's café was full of happy diners regaling each other with their own tales of flying over the fields to view the crop circles. Jon listened for a bit, while enjoying his breakfast, then got to work collecting some stories for next week's edition.

One farmer talked more about seeing his own fields from the air than about the strange circles in the McDowell alfalfa fields. Another avoided meeting Jon's eyes as he told him about his grandfather's stories of circles in their own fields years ago. A townie held firm on her belief that crop circles were about as believable as ET and UFO's. And finally, one local businessman said he didn't care if they were real or not, who had or hadn't made them, the interest in them had been good for his bottom line.

Everyone was excited by their experiences, but it didn't seem to Jon that many had changed their minds about the circles. Those who'd thought they were a real, if unexplained, phenomena, still thought so. Those who'd believed they were a hoax, if not done by local teens, then maybe made by illegals passing through the area, held to their beliefs just as dearly. He'd quickly ended the interview with the lady who

209

started a rant on illegals, "I don't need to fan that particular flame," he muttered to Care, passing her as he left the ranter's table.

Notably absent this morning were Robert Shepard and Chris Woods. Jon shook off a shiver traveling up his spine, thinking about the story not under discussion at the café, the story few people in town knew about. Finished with breakfast, notebook full of juicy quotes for next week's issue, Jon headed over to the newspaper office.

Not long after Jon left, Patty finally found time for a break. Emerging from the kitchen, she joined Care, Wanda, and Doris, sitting with Barbara, who had her own stories to tell about all the different passenger experiences from two days of flyovers. Some had been nervous. Others had been almost reverent. All had taken many photos, of the circles, of their own properties, of other local landmarks, and even some selfies with Barbara or in the plane.

"I'm as bad as anyone else," Patty admitted. "I took pictures of the circles, the surrounding area, our café here, and even one of all of us before we got into the plane. This is such a beautiful area and seeing it from a bird's eye view was simply breathtaking."

"I'm new to the area, too," Care said. "I had no idea the farms and rolling hills nestled up against those mountains could be so pretty. Bless my heart," she said, patting her mostly flat chest over her heart, covered by today's t-shirt, declaring *Pleasing everyone is impossible. Pissing off everyone is a piece of cake*.

"Well, I've lived here all my life," Wanda responded. "And I still found it exciting. From that perspective, I could really see the three dimensional aspect of the shape. I'm thinking about making at least one of my pics into a t-shirt. The circle design was amazing. I just don't know how well the pictures will capture it."

"I'd buy that shirt," Care said, tapping her order pad against the table top.

Patty perked up. "Did I tell you about our latest assignment in ceramics class?" she asked. "In class this week all anyone could talk about was their flyovers and the circles so Claudia gave us an assignment to each make a ceramic piece expressing what we saw."

"Those'll be terrific," Barbara said. "I hope there'll be an exhibit so we can buy one or two. I'll want my own to remember the circles."

"Oh, the circles," Patty said, straightening and gesturing wildly with her hands. "I was so distracted by the beauty of the area, the excitement of the flight, I completely forgot about the circles. They look just like that old crop circle Eddie told us about."

"It's the event of the year," Doris said, grandmotherly perm bobbing. "Better than the county fair and the Fourth of July all rolled into one."

"I almost envy your life," Care said to Barbara. "Flying around everywhere. New places, new faces. Makes me think how much of my life I wasted in one little diner, in one small town." Care saw Barbara's eyes widen and fly to Patty.

"Oh my God," Care said. "Not here. I've only been here a short time. This place is great." She reached over for Patty's hand. "You know I love it here."

"No worries," Patty said. "This place is not a diner." Care, Doris and Wanda all chimed in on the word "diner", knowing how strongly Patty felt about it, coaxing a smile from her.

"And it's been great for our little food bank," Doris said. "Ever since I started leaving some of my pillows here, they've become our hottest selling item. We're getting more clothing donations and the small income from the sale of the pillows means we can purchase food items we need that aren't donated."

"I don't think I've ever seen anything like those t-shirt pillows before," Barbara said. "Wherever did you get the idea?"

"Our church collects donated clothing to distribute to whoever needs it," Doris explained. "But some of the donated t-shirts were too worn or too stained to be wearable. I couldn't bring myself to throw them all away so if the message part of the shirt is still okay, I cut it out and make a pillow to sell."

"What I love," Wanda said, shaking her head with a smile, "is that some of the pillows have been bought by the very people who donated that shirt in the first place. I guess some people carry sentimental attachments to some of their old shirts, old sayings."

"Not to change the topic," Doris said. "I brought you that information I promised on tutoring for Jamala. Did you get a chance to talk to her about it?"

"Yes, I did." Patty stopped, frowning. "I think she was interested but she was more concerned about her class and work schedule. I don't think it's a priority for her right now."

"That's okay," Doris said with a shrug of her shoulders. "If she misses the next learner orientation, there'll be another one in a few months. But her busy schedule doesn't have to be a problem. They'll find a tutor who can work around her schedule. I promise."

"I'll give her the materials," Patty said, taking them from Doris. "And I'll mention the bit about working around her schedule, but I don't want to push her on it."

"No, that's right," Care said, nodding. "It has to be something she wants. She has to commit to it in order for it to work." Seeing Spense motioning with his empty coffee cup, Care left the group, grabbed the refill carafe and headed to the big booth where he, Eddie, and Dr. Rasmussen were talking to Nate and Kylie.

"Sit here, Care," Nate invited. "Listen to this."

Care sat down at the table across from their booth. "I was saying," Eddie repeated. "Hoaxers try to deceive, confuse, and muddy research waters, in the same way computer virus writers seek attention and to contaminate the data."

"At the same time," Spense picked up the topic, shaking his handsome head. "Governments confuse and misinform people through their control of popular media."

"Exactly," Nate replied, nodding along. "While Hollywood tries to manipulate the truth and credibility of scientific evidence and facts, film goers just get all the more intrigued."

"Some crop circles are hoaxed," Dr. Rasmussen admitted, nodding reluctantly. "Some are not. We research those that are not. One of our primary aims is to help people communicate and share ideas about these events without censorship and without prejudice."

Care waved over Patty, Barbara, Wanda, and Doris who joined her to hear their own private version of a presentation on the circles from the experts.

"There's a site, cropcircleresearch.com," Eddie told Spense. "You sign up and it'll automatically send updates with news of all the latest crop circles or any relevant news. That's how Dr. R and I heard of the circles here."

"In my own experience," Spense said. "I've seen the military, particularly the military in the UK, endanger lives and safety in order to investigate and monitor crop formations and yet they continue to deny they have any involvement."

"What do you think, Spense?" Care asked.

"I don't have an opinion, I keep an open mind to any and all unexplained phenomena," Spense drawled. "There's more we don't understand than there is that we do. I just don't like it when governments try to cover things up. What do they got to hide?"

"No one, well few of us," Eddie said, casting a meaningful look at Dr. Rasmussen. "Are suggesting these are the work of extra-terrestrial beings or anything quite so far out. We just don't know where they come from and we won't know if we deny them without studying them."

"We have to admit," Dr. Rasmussen said, stabbing her index finger into the air. "There are those few, a very few, who want to believe these formations are the work of extraterrestrials without any proof. And that's just as detrimental to our research as outright denial."

"I've always been interested in the emissions from the circles," Eddie said. "Wondering about the why and how of them. Now that I've recently been taught the skill of remote viewing, I intend to start another avenue of research using that new skill."

214

Spense leaned in toward Nate and whispered, "Just when I was starting to like the guy."

○ ○ ○

Following his second interview with Chris Woods, this one accompanied by a union rep, Alec invited Robert Shepard in for a meeting. He'd set the interview up in an interrogation room so it would be recorded.

When Shepard showed up, Wanda called a uniformed officer to escort him to Interrogation Room One and buzzed Alec to notify him of his arrival. Alec gave him a few minutes to stew, then entered the room without knocking. He looked around the room, his face reflecting surprise at finding only Shepard present. "Are we waiting for your attorney?"

"Attorney?" Robert asked, arching his thick silvery eyebrows on his deeply tanned face. "I'm certain I won't need an attorney to handle whatever this might be about."

"You have a right to an attorney and one will be appointed for you if you cannot afford one," Alec recited.

"I assure you I can afford the best attorneys money can buy," Robert said, straightening his spine and shooting his cuffs under his expensive cashmere sports jacket. "The Miranda warning? Really? Am I under arrest?"

"This is an interview," Alec replied. "It's being recorded and I want to be clear you're agreeing to answer questions without your attorney."

Shepard rolled his eyes and waved his hand,

dismissing the offer. "No attorney. I look forward to answering your questions," he said with a politician's oily smile, extending his right hand to Alec as he passed by on his way to his chair.

Alec's eyebrows lowered in disgust at Robert's smile. He turned away, fiddling unnecessarily with the evidence and his notebook to avoid the proffered handshake. He laid out the evidence bags and CSU reports in silence and checked that his laptop was positioned out of Shepard's line of sight before refreshing the screen.

He settled himself into the interviewer's chair, set slightly higher than the suspect's chair, which was affixed to the floor, and smiled at Shepard with his mouth only.

"What's this all about?" Robert asked. "If you don't mind me asking."

Keep trying charm, see how far that'll get you in here, Alec thought, noting his deft use of silence had prompted Shepard to speak first.

"This," Alec said with a little dramatic pause, "is all about a criminal act of sabotage perpetrated at the newspaper. Anything you know about that you'd like to share?"

"No, nothing," Robert responded with another well lubricated smile. "Why I haven't had any dealings with the paper since I sold it to Mr. Townsend coming up on a year ago now. You should be talking to him about this. I'm certain it has nothing to do with me." He braced his hands against the table, as though to stand and leave.

Alec raised one finger and shook his head. "We're not done yet." He pushed the evidence bags across the table toward Shepard and asked, "Recognize these?"

"Yes, of course I do," Robert replied calmly. "I ran that paper for years. I'd recognize one of those drive belts anywhere. And I bet anyone would know that used to be a common paperclip." He shook his head and leaned back into his chair, making himself comfortable in spite of the circumstances.

Alec nodded his head. "Exactly right," he said. He turned the laptop screen toward Shepard and asked, "And how about this? Do you recognize this?"

Robert's pearly smile froze in place for only a microsecond, but Alec caught it.

"Why that's a picture of me in my old office at the paper," Robert replied, his smile widening. "From the scene around me, I take it that was taken last week when I went in to look for my fountain pen. You see it was a gift from my father, so it's not only very expensive, it's important to me. When I misplaced it, I searched everywhere, even my old office, in the mistaken hope I might have left it there." He resumed his comfortable posture in the uncomfortable chair, his confidence having returned at providing a feasible explanation for his visit to his old office.

Alec forwarded the screen to the next picture in his prearranged sequence. "Any reason why Chris Woods went with you?" he asked.

"I believe we had just finished breakfast at the café and, since this was merely a quick stop, he tagged along with me before we continued to the golf course," Robert replied, calm smile resettling on his face.

Alec watched him carefully. His training and all his years of experience had taught him to trust his gut.

He understood his so-called gut instincts were actually his body reacting to things he'd seen or heard that his brain hadn't yet fully processed. He'd found, time after time, his gut was usually right. And he believed it now. Shepard's calm demeanor didn't seem forced but Alec's gut told him it still felt off somehow, more a role he played rather than genuine.

"And can you tell me what he's doing here?" Alec asked, advancing the video one more scene. He gave Shepard the long slow blink that had been such a powerful weapon used against a lengthy line of suspects over the years.

Robert leaned forward to see the screen more clearly. "Why no, I can't," he said, leaning back in his chair once again, examining his manicured nails. "It looks like he may be doing something at the big press but I was busy in the office, looking for my pen you know. I wasn't keeping track of what Chris might, or might not, be doing."

Alec leaned back in his chair, crossing his muscular arms across his chest and swiveling his chair as he studied the man across from him. He believed Shepard not only knew what Woods had been doing but that he had directed him to do it, keeping his own hands clean. But he had no proof and as long as Shepard didn't crack, didn't implicate himself in any way, he didn't have a case against him. *Better let him go for now and hope to get more from Woods before talking with Shepard again*, he thought.

Alec took his time closing down the laptop, stacking the evidence bags and reports, allowing the continued silence to work on Robert Shepard, who fidgeted uncomfortably in his chair but didn't break his silence.

"You're free to go, for now," Alec said, opening the door. "Shall I contact you or your attorney for follow up interviews?"

"Oh, I feel certain there's nothing here I can't handle on my own," Robert said, smug smile pasted on his overly tan face as he passed Alec in the doorway and left the police station.

"Entitled SOB," Alec whispered. "I remember dealing with your type from some of the legacy officers I investigated over the years. Think because their daddies and their daddy's daddies before them served, they're entitled to special consideration." Alec stood up and collected his things to return to his office. "Not on my watch. Not them. Not you."

TWENTY-FOUR

Alec sat at his desk, his back to his office's one window, signing some of the seemingly endless stack of paperwork necessary to run their police department. He looked up to find Wanda leaning against his open doorway. "What's up?" he asked her.

"It's almost time for Woods' next interview," she said, her mouth set in a hard line. "Are you sure you need to be the one doing this? One of the other detectives couldn't handle it?"

Alec blew out a breath. "No. It has to be me. It's bad enough to have this happen here. I don't want it to poison the whole department. For better or worse, the others know him too well not to be affected by it."

"You're the boss," Wanda said, shaking her head sadly. She might disagree with his decision, with his choice, but she accepted it. "You want them back in Interrogation Room One again?"

Alec nodded and returned his attention to the slowly dwindling stack of paperwork.

"I'll send them back as soon as they get here," she said, her voice fading as she disappeared down the hall.

A short while later, Alec sat at the interrogation room table, official recorder running, facing an unhappy Chris Woods and his union rep. "So that's your story?" he asked, eyes steady. "You were working at the behest of Robert Shepard?"

Woods looked to his rep who nodded he could answer. "Yes, exactly," he said. "Robert asked me to mess with the printing press to disrupt the paper's production. He really doesn't want to see the paper have any success now that he no longer owns it."

"Interesting," Alec said, reaching for the laptop where selected portions of his interview with Shepard were cued up. He stroked the touch pad, wakening the screen to a single still showing Robert Shepard at the same table in the same interrogation room they now occupied. He'd picked a shot of Shepard's smarmiest smile. "Mr. Shepard here says he had no idea what you might have been doing in the other room, he was there to look for his pen." This was close enough to what he'd actually said to hold up if the two conspirators compared notes, but he'd put an inflammatory slant on it to provoke Woods into talking. "He gave you up in a second."

And it worked. Blood rushed to Woods' face. He lurched forward in his chair. "You're not going to be happy until you've ended my whole family are you?" he demanded, voice cracking.

Woods shook off his rep's hand, ignoring his pleas, "Don't answer. There's no question there. Don't respond until I tell you."

"You killed my brother," Woods growled. "You stole his wife, then you killed him."

"Shut up!" his rep shouted. "Not another word."

"Ended? What?" Alec asked into the sudden silence, his mouth dropping open. "I didn't remember you had a brother. He's dead?"

"Yes, he's dead," Woods fumed. "And his death

killed my mother. Then my father died not six years later. You've killed my whole family. I'm all that's left and now you want to put an end to me as well."

Alec pushed himself away from the table, away from Chris Woods, a member of his detective squad, who was all but foaming at the mouth. He turned to the union rep. "I'm going to give you the room for a moment so you can get your client under control. Call for me when you're ready to resume."

Alec left the room in a daze, walking to his office on autopilot and plopping himself down into his chair. He swiveled it around to gaze sightlessly out the window. Under other circumstances, he might have pushed this advantage, but he was too stunned to continue the interview right now. What was this all about? Is this why Woods has been such a problem ever since I came back to town? Why he's opposed me at every turn. "And here I thought he was a run of the mill racist. He's a total nutjob," he muttered to the indifferent trees outside.

Eventually Wanda buzzed him to report they were ready for him to return and he strode back down the hall. Woods, fully under the control of his rep, never spoke another word. Alec and the rep worked out a tentative deal. In exchange for not pursuing any prosecution, Woods would agree to leave the force without benefits, no public disclosure from either side, and he'd immediately seek treatment for anger management. Additionally, he agreed to return to town to testify against Robert Shepard, when and if asked.

Alec wasn't happy about any of this but he was satisfied with the agreement. He didn't want to drag his department through the courts and he saw clearly now that Woods needed help. Now, he'd have to sell this to Jon, the victim.

After they left, Alec remained in the room. He cued up the video of this interview session to where Woods had lost control and studied it again.

Alec looked up to find Wanda standing in the doorway watching the video. They watched together until the video got to Woods' accusation. Wanda staggered into the room, pushing the door closed behind her, and fell into a chair at the table. Her face slack, her mouth falling open. "That old story?" she breathed. "He's bringing up that old story again?"

"What old story?" Alec asked, looking at her with surprise, curiosity sparkling in his dark eyes. "You know what he's going on about?"

"You don't remember any of this?" she asked.

"Remember it?" Alec replied, hands out, palms up. "I don't think I even knew he had a brother, much less that he'd died. And Woods somehow holds me responsible for it? Are you kidding me?"

"Okay, let's begin at the beginning," Wanda said, settling into her chair more comfortably. "Do you remember who Darla was dating before you two got together?"

"Darla? My wife, uh ex-wife? What's she got to do with any of this?"

"I'm telling you all of this from distant memory," Wanda said. "I may not be able to get all of it exactly right." She repositioned herself, gazing around the room as though gathering what facts she could from her memory. "Word was Kurt Woods, Chris' older brother, thought she was his soul mate." Her mouth curled up and her tone dropped down in mockery at the term. "But then she kicked him to the curb while he was off at university." She shook her head at the memory.

"Alls I know is she approached me, asked me out," Alec filled in. "I seem to remember hearing she'd been dating someone else, someone who was away at college. That guy was Chris Woods' older brother? I didn't even know him and she sure seemed available enough when she came on to me. How'd I miss all this?" Alec asked.

"Huh," Wanda huffed. "I'll tell you how you missed the connection," she said. "Kurt Woods was older, already off to college so you never knew him and his younger brother Chris was too young, still in middle school. No wonder you didn't know them." She sat in silence for a moment, finally asking, "Didn't that seem more than a little strange? The school's prettiest blue eyed blonde coming on to one of the school's few black athletes?"

"Hey, I was young," Alec said in his own defense. "She wanted me. I responded like any other red blooded male." He paused, his eyes closing as he remembered what came next. "Then she told me she was pregnant and we needed to get married in a big hurry."

"Wait," Wanda said, sitting up straighter. "Trevor's way too young to be the product of that pregnancy."

Alec pressed his lips together in disgust, snorting a breath through his nose. "She told me, right after we were married, she told me she'd had a miscarriage. But now I wonder if she was ever pregnant in the first place. I'm not sure I believed it even back then."

Wanda silently shook her head, eyes closed.

"It was right after then that I left for the marines. It didn't take long for us to decide we got along better when I was gone. The rest, as they say, is history."

"How come she didn't bring Trevor and go with you, live at the base?"

"That was just Darla being Darla," Alec said. "She brought Trevor once when he was really young but she didn't like life on a military base and quickly ran back here, back home." Alec slumped back. "But how does the story of me and Darla end up with Woods accusing me of killing his brother?"

"Ah yes, that," Wanda said. "It was the talk of the town at the time. As well as I remember it, he was supposed to be so upset over her marriage to you that he left university and volunteered for military service."

"Oh," Alec said. "I get it. He died overseas."

"Nothing so meaningful," Wanda intoned, her head wagging. "He was killed in a training accident before he ever got deployed, ever got overseas."

"Ooh," Alec commiserated at the unnecessary loss of a young life.

"Yes," Wanda nodded. "And this is the one thing Chris got right. His death did just about kill their mother. She died less than a year later."

"And that's why I've never heard any of this. I was long gone by then." Alec looked up suddenly. "Darla never said a word about any of this. I wonder who I was married to all those years." Alec jerked up. "You know, I never understood that woman. I didn't understand her when she asked me out or when she tricked me into marrying her, much less when she left without a word." He blew out a breath. "And at the time,

I really didn't care to know."

"Understood." Wanda dragged herself to her feet to leave.

"Wait," Alec said. "One more thing. What was that last bit about his father's death?"

"I don't see how anyone could connect that to the whole Kurt and Darla tragedy," Wanda said. "The man had cancer. He held out until Chris finished the two year criminology program at Valley Community College, then died."

"Damn," Alec said. "That's a lot of tragedy for a young man to handle. No wonder he's so screwed up now, a really angry man."

Wanda returned to her desk at reception and Alec returned to his own office.

O O O

"Someone to see you, Boss," Henry said the following afternoon. Jon looked up from the story he was drafting on his computer for next week's edition to find Robert Shepard standing at the doorway with Henry. He sighed loudly but nodded him in. Henry backed away slowly.

Jon leaned back, straining his chair, watching in silence as Robert strolled around the office space, touching one surface or another and then brushing his fingers off as though soiled. He ended up next to the visitor's chair, examining it closely before lowering his expensive pants onto it.

"What ...," Jon started. *I'll be damned if I'll ask what I can do for him,* Jon thought. *Forget courtesy!* He searched his mind for some neutral greeting that wouldn't grate, settling on, "Haven't seen you in here for a while," thinking, *at least not in person, just on video*.

Robert ventured forth what he considered his most charming smile. It failed to disarm Jon. "I heard there was some problem with the big printing press," he said.

"Oh, you heard that, did you?' Jon replied.

"Yes," Robert confirmed. "I was thinking, you have coverage for that sort of thing, don't you? You picked up the policy I carried and my father before me carried. Right?"

"Yes. And I've maintained the service contract as well."

"Good," Robert nodded. "Well, like I said, I was thinking, that old machine served me well for many years before you bought this business. So anyway, I was thinking maybe I could pay the deductible for that repair, as a gesture of my goodwill."

"Are you admitting you played a role in the sabotage?" Jon asked, leaning forward.

"Of course not," Robert said, himself leaning back, distancing himself from Jon and his question. "I would never say anything like that. I'm merely suggesting that a great deal of the normal wear and tear on that old machine occurred while I was in charge so I might be willing to pay that small portion toward its repair."

Jon stood up, ending the discussion. "That's certainly an interesting offer," he said. "I'll have to think it over."

Robert blinked twice in response, making Jon think the older man hadn't expected to be dismissed, certainly not from his old office. Robert slowly levered himself out of the visitor's chair and again attempted a disarming smile, which Jon ignored.

Jon joined Henry on the floor of the print room, both watching Robert waltz out of the building, shoulders straight, head held high.

O O O

"Are you going to let him get away with it?" Patty asked after Jon had told her about the visit from his old nemesis, Robert Shepard.

"Wait, let me update you on the case against Chris Woods." Jon frowned, trying to find the right words. "Alec came by this afternoon after meeting with the DA. It looks like no one is particularly interested in prosecuting Woods. There's not much of a case there."

"That's okay," Patty said. "I don't care about any case against Chris Woods. I mean really, who's he? Nobody. I'd rather go after the guy behind it, Robert Shepard."

"No one at city hall wants to drag their police department through the muck." He silently shook his head, avoiding Patty's eyes. "More importantly, it looks like no one there really wants to pursue a case against their old friend, Robert Shepard, either."

"Their old friend and campaign donor, Robert Shepard. Isn't that what you really mean?" Patty asked, indignation bringing color to her cheeks and acid to her tone.

"Yeah," Jon answered. "I'm sure that's part of it. But look at it from their point of view. No real harm was done. Woods is gone, left town entirely. And Shepard knows we'll be on alert, watching for his next try."

"Next try!" Patty exploded. "First he tried to cheat you on supplies, then he tried to drive away all your ad revenue, and now he's tried to sabotage the big printing press. Why does he get another shot at you?"

"This is looking like a reality we might just have to accept. At least if I take him up on his offer to pay the deductible, I'm not out anything." Jon looked into his wife's dark eyes, the fireworks sparking within. "Come on Patty, be reasonable," he pleaded.

"Reasonable?" she repeated. "There's nothing reasonable about any of this."

TWENTY-FIVE

Monday afternoon, after all the customers had left the café, Patty emerged from the kitchen to find Care chatting with Doris, Wanda, and Barbara. When Trevor reported for work, passing through the café to clean up in the kitchen area, the ladies all fell silent, five pairs of eyes following him across the room, paying more attention to his phone than to them.

"Man, his mother was sure the topic of the day after church services yesterday," Barbara said, *sotto voce.*

Patty and Wanda exchanged a look, neither wanting to pursue this conversation. Doris examined her nails.

"What about her?" Care asked, leaning forward eagerly.

"Some old stuff," Barbara said, looking around the table for others to join in, tell the rest of the story. "It was all way before Trevor was born. Something about her boyfriend before Alec, something about the guy leaving town now. The town gossips seemed to make some connection to what happened years ago." She paused, searching the others' faces. "Without any background, it didn't make sense to me."

Doris cleared her throat, reluctant to be placed in a position to rehash any of this to newcomers. "It's all old news now. If Chris Woods hadn't left town so suddenly without any sort of explanation, tongues wouldn't be wagging again." She shot an angry glance at Wanda.

"She's a white girl, right?" Care asked, failing at a casual pretense. "Is that what's this is all about?"

"No." Wanda harrumphed. "It's more about how she herself left suddenly without a word to anyone, not even her own son, and without any explanation."

Doris put her hand on her friend's arm, looking toward the door to the kitchen, where that son had just begun his day's work, and spoke softly. "When she left, there were a lot of rumors flying around. I seem to remember it was Chris Woods who suggested she hadn't left at all, that Alec had done away with her."

"As if," Wanda huffed angrily.

"I know he's your friend," Doris said. "But those rumors got some traction at the time. Even my son thought they were worth reporting on at first."

"That's right," Patty said. "Robert still owned the paper then, didn't he?"

"Well," Barbara said. "What did happen? Why did she leave so mysteriously?"

"Who knows?" Wanda replied, with one quick shake of her head. "Whoever really knows what goes on in someone else's life, someone else's marriage?" She shrugged her shoulders, shifting her t-shirt which expressed her usual attitude, *Forget the dogs. Who let the idiots out?* "Alls I know is she was working out at the truck center next to the highway, met someone she liked better, and left."

"The truck center?" Barbara asked, frowning in confusion. She turned to Care. "Didn't you say you tracked your truck driving husband out here where he'd found a younger woman to take up with?"

In unison, Patty, Wanda, and Doris slowly swiveled to Care, their brains processing this new thought that had somehow escaped their attention.

"Care," Patty said to her employee and friend. "Is that right? Was it Alec's wife that took up with your husband?"

When Care didn't respond right away, Wanda pressed, "Was it your husband who left with Alec's wife?"

Care clamped her lips together, refusing to speak, but nodded.

"Why didn't you say anything before now?" Doris asked, reaching across the table to her friend. "Why didn't you tell us?"

"At first, I didn't know any of you," Care replied, looking around the table, meeting each of their eyes in turn. "I didn't know how you'd react. I saw Alec was friendly with all of you and I didn't want to insert my problems into that." She turned to Patty. "And then you hired Trevor. He's such a nice young man, I didn't want to be an unpleasant reminder of the loss of his mama. I couldn't bring myself to tell anyone." She shrugged her thin shoulders expressively. "I put it behind me."

"There is no 'behind me' in a small community like this," Doris said with a huff. "As all the gossip this weekend over Chris Woods reminds us, nothing in a small town is ever truly done and over with."

"Right," Wanda said with an emerging smile. "Anything you say or do will come back to bite you on your butt when you least want."

"Well, tell us now," Barbara asked. "Is Alec's wife still with your husband?"

"Ex, that's ex-husband, and yes, last I heard," Care replied. "As soon as I figured out I was better off without him, I stopped checking." She looked again toward the kitchen doorway and lowered her voice. "I'll tell you one thing though, I think I can explain how come she didn't take Trevor with her."

"Really? Why?" Patty asked, leaning into the conversation, anxious to hear this explanation.

"I'm sorry to say my husband has always been somewhat of a racist," Care said. "He never would have wanted anything to do with a child of mixed race. So maybe she did love her son, did want to take him with her."

"Not enough to choose him over a new guy," Wanda said, rolling her eyes.

"Racist, was he?" Patty asked, not unkindly.

"Yeah," Care said. "I never liked it but as long as he was gone so much of the time, it wasn't really much of an issue." She nodded. "Anyway, I can see him thinking he's rescuing this white girl from her mud-race husband."

"Like I said, you never really know what's going on in someone else's marriage," Wanda said, leaning back, crossing her arms over her ample bosom.

Patty packed up the day's leftovers for Doris to take to the food bank, closed up, and returned to the kitchen to start the prep work for tomorrow. As she worked with Trevor, who was learning sous chef responsibilities quickly, she strived to act normal. She was afraid her new knowledge about Trevor's mother would affect her relationship with him. And she didn't want that. Trevor'd already felt betrayed by the loss of his mother. She didn't want to make it worse.

When the prep work was as complete as it could be until tomorrow morning and Trevor had gone home, Patty headed upstairs. She followed her nose to the open door to the balcony off the living area where she found Jon grilling two thick steaks.

"Wow," she said. "What did I do to deserve this treatment? I may want to be able to repeat it every once in a while."

Jon came through the door, wiping his hands on his apron, and taking her in a warm embrace. He buried his nose in her hair, mumbling, "Mmm, you sure smell nice."

Patty pushed him away, just slightly, so she could look up into his eyes. "Okay, now I'm getting nervous, what's this all about?'

"Wait a minute," Jon said. "I need to check the potatoes and pull the salad out of the fridge."

Patty followed him into the kitchen where he used a hot pad to reach into the oven and pinch the potatoes, checking for doneness. Satisfied, he turned off the oven and opened the fridge where he grabbed the green salad, tossed and ready, along with some Stilton cheese to crumble into it, and added the dried cranberries and pumpkin seeds. He returned to the fridge for sour cream to put on the potatoes. "Would you rather set the table or finish up the salad and potatoes?" he asked.

"I'll set the table," Patty replied with a lilt in her voice. "I'm enjoying having someone else do the cooking for a change. I could learn to like this."

"Don't get too used to it," Jon said with a chuckle. "I've been so spoiled by your cooking over the years, this is about the extent of my repertoire."

"I'll take it. Gladly." Patty finished readying the table while Jon brought in the steaks, the salad, and the potatoes with all the fixings.

"Everything okay?" Jon asked once they were seated and served.

"Wonderful," Patty replied, gazing at the food and inhaling appreciatively. "Forgive me but I'm still just a little suspicious. What brought this on?"

"When I'm wooing a source for a story," Jon explained, "sometimes I have to take them out for drinks or dinner to get them to open up. It's a tried and true method. I thought it would work on you as well. And be much more enjoyable for me."

Patty chuckled. "Alright I'm sufficiently buttered up. Whatever story am I a source for?"

"When I walked through the café today after work, you girls were all talking about Alec, Darla and Trevor," Jon said, opening a bottle of wine and holding it forward so Patty could read the label.

"I didn't even see you pass through," Patty said, brow wrinkling.

"You were all pretty deep into the discussion," Jon said, passing the bottle to Patty.

"So I'm a source for decades old gossip? Why do you care about that?" Patty asked.

Jon put down his napkin and straightened. "I think I'm offended," he said. "Alec is my friend and I like Trevor, too, you know." His shoulders caved and he cast his gaze around the room. "Also, I think that old story may have something to do with the current mess, at least with Chris Woods, if not with Robert Shepard."

"Really? How so?" Patty asked.

"Alec came by again this afternoon to give me

an update on the status of the case. But he's really limited in what he can tell me, how much he can share." Jon paused. "I get that. I know how it works, the perp's right to confidentiality versus the public's right to know. And he told me their deal included a bilateral non-disclosure agreement. But I still don't think that's all there is to this. It felt like he was holding something back, something personal. I think maybe Chris Woods likes Alec about as much as Robert Shepard likes me."

"It looks like Chris Woods' leaving is somehow tied up with Alec's ex-wife. Maybe that explains it," Patty mused. "Okay, let's put together what Alec told you with what I heard this afternoon and see what we get. You first."

"That'll be quick, there's not a lot he could say you haven't already heard," Jon began.

"Just wait 'til my turn," Patty said. "I got at least one brand new juicy detail you haven't heard."

Jon narrowed his eyes, examining her smile.

"You first," Patty repeated, shaking her head teasingly and going to the freezer to retrieve some ice cream for dessert.

"Well, like I said," Jon said, as Patty passed him a bowl of hazelnut gelato with chocolate sauce. "Alec couldn't tell me much we didn't already know. Woods' agreement is a done deal and the DA says without proof of intent for Shepard, which we'll never get, the case drops from a felony to a misdemeanor."

"So?" Patty prompted.

"With a felony, the People, in the persons of the DA and the police, decide whether or not to press charges but with a misdemeanor, the victim has a say in the decision." Jon shrugged his shoulders and arched his left eyebrow. "So that's what Shepard's deductible offer is all about. But something about the way Alec was acting when he mentioned Woods' non-disclosure agreement made me think to look him up online."

"Oh, that's good," Patty said. "Why didn't we think of that?"

Jon pulled out his iPad and scrolled through his notes. "He grew up here, which is where I found a link to his older brother, Kurt Woods, so I switched over to his bio. Apparently the older brother was the captain of the football team, Homecoming King, and president of his senior class, a real Big Man On Campus type. After high school, he went to UC Berkeley but left there less than two years into it. He then joined the air force and soon after, died in a training accident. End of story."

"Oh, that's sad," Patty said.

"Yeah, so I switched back to Chris Woods. He was younger by eight years and his time in high school was nothing like older brother Kurt's."

"Well, yeah," Patty commiserated. "It must've been tough, following in his brother's big man on campus footsteps."

"Yeah," Jon said. "His big brother, the dead BMOC." Jon scrolled further through his notes. "Okay, let's see. It turns out his mother died less than a year after Kurt's accident. It didn't say whether she died by accident, disease, or suicide, just the date of her death."

"Oh that's worse," Patty said. "No mother, trying to live up to his big brother, his dead brother."

"Unlike Kurt, Chris Woods went to the local community college, for a two year criminology degree,"

Jon read. "And then, almost as soon as he finished there, his father died."

"If he had an undistinguished high school record he might have had difficulty getting into a four year program, certainly not Berkeley," Patty said, slipping the final bite of gelato into her mouth. "So is he the last of their whole family?"

"Yep," Jon said. "He gets hired on at the police department here by the previous chief, while Alec was still in the marines, and finally works his way up to detective. I found a lot of photos of that chief on the high school football team with Kurt. I can't prove it, but I wonder if he didn't hire Chris in the first place cause of his memories of the brother."

"Oh great," Patty said. "That can't be a happy situation. All alone, never living up to his big brother, a pity hire, not having much success anywhere."

"That's my update," Jon said. "What's your juicy detail?"

"Let me start at the beginning," Patty said, leading Jon over to the sitting area and settling into a comfortable seat. "We'll get to it."

Patty reminded him of how Chris Woods had spread the rumor that Alec had done away with Darla and how Robert Shepard had reported on that rumor until it was proven untrue. Finally, she told him how Darla had left with a man she'd met while working at the truck center near the highway. She leaned back, crossing her arms, watching Jon's face to see if he made the leap.

Jon's thick brows beetled. Married to Patty for a long time, he knew she was waiting for him to figure out something but he couldn't guess what it was.

"It turns out," Patty said, "wait for it, the man Darla left Alec for is none other than Care's ex."

Jon's jaw dropped, his eyes widened. "Wow. I did not see that coming," he said, unaccustomed to being caught so off guard. "How did we not put that together when she first told us about herself?"

"Well why would we?" Patty asked, smiling like a cat with a canary still struggling in its mouth.

"Small world," Jon said, still processing this new piece of information.

"What I don't get," Patty said. "Is why would the old news about Chris Woods and his big brother connect to Darla's leaving Alec?"

"Your guess is as good as mine," Jon said, rubbing his hands together. "Now that I know her name, maybe if I look her up I'll find a connection." Jon put his arm around his wife, nuzzling her hair again. "Good work, honey. You really brought home the goods."

"Enough of all this," Patty said. "I know I'll be glad to get back to everyone's fascination with crop circles," Patty said.

TWENTY-SIX

The next morning Jon came down to the café for breakfast, ordering only a blueberry scone and coffee. He just couldn't find his appetite, which was really unusual for him. He joined Nate at one of the round tables in the center of the bustling cafe, listening in on the discussion between Dr. Rasmussen, Eddie, and Spense. "No Kylie this morning?" he asked.

"She had some other mysterious lead to follow up this morning," Nate said. "She still doesn't share her leads with me. I don't get it. I'm not in the news biz anymore. It's not like I'm going to scoop her. So why's she so secretive?"

"Come on, man. You've been there," Jon said. "It's all part of the news competition. And you know she's ambitious." He tossed his chin toward the booth where Dr. Rasmussen, Eddie, and Spense had their heads together, discussing the crop circles. "What's new with them this morning?"

"It's above my head," Nate said, pulling out his notes. "Dr. R got some results back from that big lab in, let's see, uh here it is, in Michigan. It must be big 'cause that's all they've been able to talk about ever since."

Leaving the group of scientists, Spense joined Jon and Nate. "They're so caught up in the new lab reports, they may not even notice I'm gone," he said, with a merry twinkle in his blue eyes.

"So what is it that has them so excited?" Jon asked, interested in spite of himself. "Proof come in the crop circles are real?"

"Yeah, should we be on the lookout for ET?" Nate added, with his lopsided grin.

"Don't get them started," Spense said with a smirk. "No ET but it does look like the preliminary results from the BLT lab support the veracity of your circles." He took in a big breath and, looking over at Dr. Rasmussen, said, "You'll want to get the exact data from Dr. R, but in summary, the lab says the bends in the alfalfa could not be replicated so they think they're not human made."

"What does that mean?" Nate asked. "In terms a simple newsman can understand."

"The lab says there are genetic mutations within the cells of the alfalfa stems," Spense replied. "Then they went on to say the bit about the bends in the stems which could have only happened naturally in very young crops, early in spring when there's a lot of dew on the ground."

"Definitely not the case here," Jon said.

"No," Nate said, as he began furiously taking notes. "This kind of detail is just what I'll need for my book."

"Right," Jon said. "It gives it verisimilitude."

"Don't make fun," Nate said, elbowing him with a self-deprecatory chuckle.

"Anyway," Spense pushed on, ignoring their byplay. "Dr. R has the new lab results and Eddie has some follow up information about cell phone disruption in the area he's all excited about."

"What about you?" Nate asked, turning his focus

on Spense. "Anything new to report on cover-up efforts?"

Jon leaned back, settling into his seat and crossing his arms across his chest, to observe the conversation. He wanted to follow this, he needed it for next week's edition, but his eyes lost focus as his mind drifted.

Jon's attention returned at the commotion that accompanied Kylie's entrance. Nate got up to offer her his chair as he moved over one and Spense stood until she was settled.

She batted her camera ready made up eyes at Spense, "Oh my, such a gentleman! Aren't you just adorable?" she gushed at him.

Jon watched Nate's reaction to Kylie paying this much attention to Spense. Nate's eyes glowed with an almost paternal pride. But there was nothing paternal about the possessive way he put his hand on the back of her chair, marking her as his territory, reminding Spense what was what.

"What'd you get?" Nate asked her.

"Well I've already filed the story so I guess there's no harm in telling you now," Kylie replied. "I was doing my research, looking up old coverage on crop circles when I came upon a question posed by Carl Sagan in a 1995 Parade magazine article where he suggests that crop circles exist because they're a money maker."

"Money maker?" Spense asked. "Who? How?"

"Well now, isn't that what I've been doing all morning? Answering just those very questions?" Kylie responded, with southern accent to match Spense's.

Jon was surprised. Not at the turn of the story

but by Kylie's southern accent. He'd never heard it at all when she was on a broadcast but now it was strong, distractingly strong.

"So I, as they say, followed the money," she said, smiling at her own cleverness. Now she pulled out her iPad, scrolling through her notes. "There are some so-called researchers who deliberately keep people in the dark so they can keep producing merchandise." She looked up from her notes. "Not Dr. R or Eddie. They both work for universities and get paid either way."

"Surely there can't be much money in crop circle merchandise," Nate said.

"Right," Kylie said, nodding. "But apparently it's enough for some people. The real money goes to the hoaxers. They make money even on some circles it's been proven they couldn't possibly have made."

"Wait," Spense said, holding up a big square hand like a traffic cop. "Are you saying the hoaxers make money even when there's proof they couldn't be responsible? They claim to have hoaxed a circle, it's proven they couldn't have done it, at least not that particular one, and they still make money off it?"

"Exactly," Kylie said, nodding. "From speaking engagements, books, and merchandise."

"They can't be making much off books," Nate said. "There's not much money in books."

"I'm just telling you what I found," Kylie said, hands up in surrender.

"Maybe I need to consider changing the focus of my book," Nate said, blowing out his cheeks.

○ ○ ○

At 01:30 Patty snuck a peek into the dining area and, finding only two booths with diners still talking over their coffee and Doris and Wanda at their favorite booth by the door, decided she didn't need to start any more food for today. Instead, she packed up some leftovers for Doris to take to the food bank and headed in to join her friends.

Just as Patty entered the room, Doris got up and left without a glance, a word, or even a smile.

Watching the door close behind her friend as she reached the booth, Patty shook her head and said, "Well I know it wasn't something I said." But when Wanda didn't share her humor, Patty asked, "What's up with her?"

"She's upset about her miscreant son, Robert," Wanda said.

"What's up, what's new?" Patty asked, joining Wanda in the booth.

"She doesn't like what she's hearing about Robert's involvement in the mess at the paper."

"What!" Patty cried, then looking around, lowered her voice. "What has she heard? How could she hear anything? Only we and you guys at the police department know. We haven't said anything and I'm pretty sure you guys haven't. Right?"

Wanda snorted. "You know better. I'm pretty sure the leak comes from city hall, out of the DA's office."

"City hall?" Patty asked. "Who there would say anything?"

Wanda closed her eyes and shook her head sadly. "Are you kidding? They're politicians, flapping their gums is what they do."

"Yeah, I guess so," Patty agreed. "But why?"

"Good question," Wanda replied, narrowing her eyes. "I hadn't given it much thought. Politicians rarely do anything that isn't in their own interest. So let's find their interest."

"Money?" Patty asked. "Surely there isn't much money in city politics?"

"Right, the offices don't pay much," Wanda agreed. "But the influence that comes with election leads to power and money. People sucking up to the city council, for example, make campaign contributions or give their business to an elected official's business to influence his votes."

"Something to think about," Patty said, slowly nodding. "I never paid much attention to local politics. I never knew how all this works. But still, what's that got to do with the paper or Robert Shepard?"

"Humpf," Wanda said. "Our town's worst kept secret is that he's always wanted to run for city council. And now, with all this going on, coming out, there's not much chance of that happening for him."

"Wouldn't he've had a better chance of getting elected when he still controlled the local paper?" Patty asked.

"You'd think, huh?" Wanda said. "Too many people around here have always known what he's like so he never had a real chance. This is just the latest in a string of his dirty little tricks."

"I don't get it," Patty said, slumping back into her bench seat. "Doris is nothing like this. How did he turn out this way?"

"I don't know," Wanda said. "We weren't close

when he was growing up. By the time Doris and I became friendly, he was no longer living at home, no longer much in her daily life."

"He lives alone, right?" Patty asked. "Never married, no children?"

"Oh, he was married once," Wanda said. "For a very short time. She was someone he'd met in college and followed him here after his daddy's stroke. But she didn't take to the small town life and left him pretty quick."

"So really, his whole life fell apart then and he never got it back on track," Patty said.

"And he's been taking it out on everyone around him ever since, mostly his mama," Wanda said. "Cause she's the only one who's stood by him and is still around."

"I wonder if ...," Patty began.

Wanda put her hand over Patty's and shook her head. "She's his mama. She's going to go on standing up for him no matter what."

"That's too bad," Patty said. "I really like her. I don't want to lose her friendship over this."

"Give her some time," Wanda said. "After all, it's not like this is the first time she's had to back him up when he's done something indefensible."

"And I bet he doesn't even appreciate it," Patty said. "Doesn't even recognize her support."

"You got that right," Wanda said. "I think he sees it in her eyes and it shames him."

"And that's something he can't bear," Patty said.

○ ○ ○

The next day, the café was filled with hungry people discussing the crop circles, the county fair, the upcoming football season, and anything else on their minds. But one customer was missing, Doris.

It was a Wednesday so neither Care nor Jamala was scheduled to work, making the café seem even lonelier.

Customers kept Patty busy most of the day. She welcomed Trevor when he came to work midafternoon. They worked together, side by side, to get everything ready for the next day. Patty sighed. Their conversation seem stilted to her. *Please let this be just me being over sensitive,* she thought, worried about what the teen knew and understood about the talk around town involving his father, his mother, and some previous boyfriend.

At the end of the day, after Trevor had left, Patty collected the leftovers she'd packed up earlier to give to the food bank. She took them into the walk in fridge and placed them next to those from yesterday. Patty frowned at the two days' worth of leftovers sitting on the shelf. Her café had enjoyed such a good relationship with the food bank. She felt an involuntary shiver that had nothing to do with the temperature in the fridge.

TWENTY-SEVEN

Near close of business Thursday afternoon, Patty stuck her head into the dining area. Care was collecting payment from Dr. Rasmussen, Eddie, and Spense who were leaving the booth they'd made into their ad hoc local office. The only others remaining were Wanda and Barbara, sitting, chatting quietly. Patty watched Care saunter over to join them and then she did, too.

"What's up, boss?" Care asked, glancing up, readying herself to do her boss' bidding. "Everything pretty much taken care of?"

"Yeah, I guess so," Patty replied, frowning, looking around the empty dining room. "Did it seem quiet here today?"

"No, not really," Care said, taking out her order book. "I think we did about as much business today as ever on a Thursday."

"I guess by that measure, I probably made about as many meals as usual," Patty said, absently reaching for an errant lock of hair that was no longer there.

"The usual group from the yoga studio came in after class," Care said. "I always notice them 'cause they're all such good tippers."

"I think yoga is good for their temperament," Barbara offered. "It always works on mine. And I know you're not supposed to eat before class so they're

248

probably hungry afterwards." She turned to Patty and added, "That was really smart to put in a yoga studio right next to your café."

"All the usual suspects were in to discuss the latest developments on the crop circles," Wanda said. "I saw farmers and townies alike talking with our visiting scientists." She winked over a broad smile. "And not a few ladies talking to Spense for no other reason than just to be near him."

Care chuckled deep in her throat. "He pretty much always gets that reaction. I wonder if it has anything to do with why he's still single?"

"Interesting," Barbara mused. "I wonder how he stays grounded in the face of so much adoration."

Wanda shook her head. "There were some new folks in today, too."

"Yeah," Care said. "Two booths of couples, all dressed up nice, came in just past one o'clock. When they left, they headed into the dance studio."

"That's right," Patty said. "I remember Chris and Pat rented some extra time this week so they could practice for a big dance competition in San Diego this weekend." Patty frowned, her forehead creased, "I wonder if they're still there. I really wanted to sneak in to watch a little." She sighed. But she didn't get up.

Trevor opened the door, reporting for work. He held it open for a stranger, a young man dressed in a uniform matching the Fed Ex truck that had just pulled to a stop out front.

Trevor paused for a moment to ask Patty if there was anything special she wanted him to do this afternoon. "Nothing I can think of," she said listlessly.

As Trevor headed to the kitchen, the delivery

guy stepped up to take his place by the booth. "Which one of you ladies is Carole Gibbs?" he asked.

The ladies exchanged glances as Care held up her hand, "I am."

He passed her his electronic clipboard for her to sign.

"Wait, don't you want to know what it is first?" Wanda asked.

"Oh, I'm pretty sure I know what it is." Care answered, bitterness tinging her tone.

"Why is he bringing it here instead of to your home?" Barbara asked.

"If it's what I think it is," Care replied. "I didn't want him to use my home address." She returned the signed clipboard to the delivery guy who handed her a sealed cardboard envelope and thanked her before turning sharply and exiting.

Patty followed him to the door, closing and locking it behind him. She returned to the booth where Barbara and Wanda were staring at Care but not speaking.

"Everyone else may be too polite to ask," Wanda said. "But I'm not. What is it and why haven't you ripped it open yet?"

Care sighed, shoulders slumping. "It's from my attorney."

"Attorney?" Barbara asked.

"Yeah, attorney," Care turned to Patty. "A couple of months ago, shortly after I got settled here, I contacted a lawyer to initiate divorce proceedings. In all this time, I haven't heard a word from my ex asshole. I know my attorney followed up with him, I got the bills for his time to do it." She sighed, looking at the heavy cardboard envelope. "Now it looks like maybe he finally responded. I wonder if he signed the final papers."

"Girl, you are playing on my last nerve," Wanda said. She leaned forward to force eye contact with Care and smiled to soften the sting of her words. "Open it already. Let's see if he did."

Care grimaced as she ripped into the Fed Ex delivery envelope. She upended it and a thick, legal sized envelope slid out. She picked it up, put on her reading glasses, and examined the return address. "It's from my lawyer's office alright." She took in a deep breath. "Okay, let's see."

Care read through the long document as her friends waited. They watched a huge smile slowly stretch across her face.

"Well," Wanda said. "Looks like good news. Tell us already."

Care straightened, an invisible load lifted off her shoulders. "He signed it. I'm a free woman. For the first time in my adult life, I'm free." She gazed around the group of friends, shrugging her incomprehension. "I don't remember why I married him in the first place. I was eighteen, it was a small town in the south in the late 60's. It seemed like it was time for me to get married, all my friends were doing it. And he was the only one asking."

Patty patted her hand in a there, there gesture.

Care looked at her with gratitude. "After that, with him gone so much of the time, it just seemed easier to stay married to him. You know, the path of least resistance." Her posture straightened again as she cast a fond smile around the booth. "But I'm free of him now, no looking back."

"That's good," Patty said, Barbara and Wanda murmuring their congratulations as well.

"But wait, there's more," Care teased. "Just like in those old late night info-mercials. My lawyer did good for me. It says here I'm entitled to half of the proceeds from the sale of our old property in Georgia." She waved a check in the air. "This just might be enough for a down payment on a condo or townhouse around here."

"That's wonderful," Barbara said.

"Terrific!" Wanda yelled.

"Are you thinking about settling here, then?" Patty asked, hope lifting her voice. Until that very moment, Patty hadn't realized how much she wanted Care to be a permanent part of her community.

"Yeah, I guess I am," Care replied, surprise coloring her tone and a smile rejuvenating her face. "I'm ready for a fresh start. New home, new friends, no more secrets, no more baggage from my ex." She stood up and danced, practically floating. Finishing one last turn with a flourish, she said, "I gotta get out of here. I need to get my hands on some real estate flyers."

Barbara and Wanda chuckled to see her so happy, getting up to leave as well. Patty heaved herself up to go into the kitchen to work with Trevor on preparations for tomorrow's menu.

While Patty worked on chopping, mixing, and kneading, her mind returned to Care's exuberance at the idea of starting a new life here. She remembered feeling just like that less than a year ago. It hadn't always been easy but it was what she'd wanted to do.

She and Jon had left their old lives behind on

purpose. They'd wanted to move toward a better life for both of them.

"You don't need me here, do you?" Patty asked Trevor.

"Naw, Boss, I got this," he replied, folding the fennel seeds and fresh rosemary into the pizza dough.

Patty tossed him the spare set of keys. "Lock up when you leave. Okay?" Then disappeared through the doorway without waiting for an answer.

○ ○ ○

Patty pushed open the door into Jon's office and rushed in. She knew Thursday afternoons were the busiest time for him, putting the paper to bed for the next day's edition, but she went in anyway.

Jon looked up from his computer, raising one hand and saying, "Not right now. I gotta get this in to put this week's edition to bed."

"No," Patty said. "I have to say this now before I change my mind."

Jon turned to her in surprise. In twenty-five years of marriage, he'd seldom heard that tone in his wife's voice. He hit the 'save' button and turned to study Patty, as she paced around his office. "Okay, honey. You got my full attention." Jon said, head swiveling to follow her. "What is it?"

Wringing her hands, Patty turned to him. "Just sign the agreement, accept the deal. Do whatever you have to do to put an end to this."

"This?" Jon asked.

"This limbo," Patty said, pausing her pacing mid-stride to face Jon, her eyes imploring. "I can't take it. I just want it over."

Jon got up and walked Patty over to the little couch in the corner of his office. "I don't understand. Just a couple of days ago you were dead set against letting him get away with it. Why the change?"

"It's too much," Patty said, her words in a rush. "Remember? You asked me to be reasonable. I'm ready to see reason where there is none. I just want it to end, the sooner the better."

Jon leaned away, considering her. "Doris still not coming to the café? I know you miss her but it's only been a couple of days. Why the sudden change of heart?"

Patty slumped, hanging her head and slowly shaking it side to side. "Yes, it's Doris. But it's more."

"Okay," Jon said, putting his arm around her, pulling her into his chest. "What else is there that has you so upset?"

"This is not us, not who we are," Patty said. "This is not why we moved here."

"Explain," Jon said.

Patty blew out a big breath. "When we left LA, left our previous lives, this is what we were trying to leave behind."

"I'm going to need more," Jon said. "I'm not seeing it yet."

"Don't you remember?" Patty asked. "You were fed up with the situation at the paper, always feeling disposable, wondering who'd be the next to go?"

One side of Jon's mouth quirked up. "I recognize that part alright."

"And I was tired of navigating all the red tape just so I could teach my students." Patty looked up into

Jon's eyes. "We moved here to get away from all that."

"Yeah, that's right," Jon said, smiling into her eyes. "Living in the big city, we'd become isolated."

"And we wanted to live a small community lifestyle, all interconnected," Patty said.

"Right," Jon said, his shoulders slumping, his tone regret tinged. "But for me and the paper at least, this is the price of living a small community life."

"I don't get that," Patty said. "What'd you mean?"

"Any of those local stories, the one about the change to the trash collection system or the scandal in the city manager's office. I could've covered those stories in LA without a second thought." Jon blew a breath through his nose, looking around his little office. "But here, any of that is too close."

"I get it," Patty said slowly. "Here, you could literally run into those people in the public restroom at the city park."

"Or sitting in your café."

"Oh," Patty said.

"Yes, oh," Jon repeated.

"This mess has us pitted against the rest of the community." Patty counted out on her fingers. "Your friend Alec knows stuff he can't tell us because it's an active case. Wanda's not coming to the café as often and when she does she's uncharacteristically quiet which makes me think she knows more than she's telling. We can't mention any of it to anyone. And now Doris has cut us off altogether. This whole thing affects both of our businesses, our friendships, and our lives. Everything."

"And it's news I can't even report," Jon said. "I don't know that ever happened while I was just a reporter." He paused to run his big hands through his thick wavy hair. "But then how would I know if the publisher was quashing some story?"

"I know," Patty said. "And the café is no longer what I wanted it to be, a place for people to sit around, lingering over their food, chatting. A real social center. At least not for me."

"Yeah, even I've been avoiding it," Jon said. "It's no fun when everybody's talking but nobody's talking about what's on my mind."

Patty burrowed more deeply into the soft, leather sofa back. "It feels like some sort of an emotional amputation, cut off from others like this."

Jon sighed loudly. "And Doris is the phantom limb you're missing?"

"Yeah, I guess," Patty said softly. "But it's really all of it, the whole atmosphere of the café, the ease, the comfort level." She shook her head. "I'm ready to let the Shepard situation go so we can get our lives back." Patty looked around, her mood as dark as Jon's windowless office. "I'm past ready."

"I thought it made sense," Jon said. "To pursue it, to not to let him get away with anything."

"And what for?" Patty asked. "In spite of their intentions, they didn't do any actual harm."

"Chris Woods is gone and Robert's political aspirations have been effectively ended," Jon added.

"The sooner we put an end to this," Patty said. "The sooner we can begin healing." She smiled, beginning to see a light at the end of this long dark tunnel.

"It would be good to get back to normal, or as normal as our life ever was," Jon said, smiling.

TWENTY-EIGHT

Patty was surprised to see Jamala standing by the kitchen door, waiting to talk with her. She wasn't scheduled to work on Wednesdays and, between her classes and Max's care, she didn't usually come in on her days off. She stood very still, her eyes cast down, no expression leaking from her face.

Patty smiled at her, waving her arm to coax her further into the kitchen. "Come in," she said. "It's an unexpected pleasure to see you this morning."

Jamala came in and sat but still didn't speak, so Patty continued. "Is there something you need to discuss with me?"

"Yes, please Miss Patty," Jamala said quietly. "Please excuse me for imposing. I know that you are very busy."

Patty brushed her hands off on her apron and came over to sit, giving Jamala her full attention. "Don't apologize. If you have something important enough to come in on your day off, I can make time for you. What is it?"

"I went in this morning to speak with the people from the literacy services program at the library as you suggested," Jamala said, folding her hands on her lap. "I came to tell you what they said."

"That's wonderful," Patty said. "I do hope they can help you with the citizenship test, the application process, the whole thing."

"No Miss Patty, they said I do not qualify for their program," Jamala said, her shoulders slumping as she released a soft sigh.

"What!" Patty cried. "That's ridiculous. You're in the country legally, you qualify for college. The English is excellent. What do they mean you don't qualify?"

"Exactly, Miss Patty," Jamala said, raising her right hand and shaking her head slowly. "My English skills are exactly why they say that I do not qualify. They said my English is too good, I do not need the training in reading, writing, speaking, and listening they provide."

"Oh," Patty said, settling back into her seat, frowning. "I didn't think about that. Your English is probably better than some of their tutors. Okay." she nodded. "That may make sense but I'd still like to see you get some help with the whole citizenship thing. Did they offer any ideas?"

"They suggested I apply at the International Rescue Committee in San Diego," Jamala said, her dark eyes clouding over.

Patty stretched a hand across the counter to pat Jamala's arm, consoling her. "Surely we can find you some help without your having to drive all the way there to get it." *Or risk running into your ex or any of his friends.* "Do you know if assistance is available through your college?"

"No madam, I do not. I wanted first to tell you about the meeting at the library."

"Alright then," Patty said, standing up. "That's our next step. You check with the college and see what, if anything, they offer. You have classes today, you'll be on campus this afternoon, right?"

"Yes, Miss Patty," Jamala said, standing up as well and turning toward the doorway. "That is where I am headed now."

"Good," Patty said. "You go talk to them and I'll see if I can come up with any other ideas." Patty watched Jamala cross the dining room to the front door, a slim straight figure, appearing taller in her determination.

o o o

Friday afternoon, Patty struggled up the stairs, laden with leftovers for their dinner. The café had been busy today and she was tired. In general, business had been good and the mood was upbeat. But Doris had yet to return.

No sooner did she hit the top step than her phone began to ring. She glanced over toward Jon, lounging in the sitting area, his feet up, playing a video game but he made no move to help her. "Don't worry, I'll get it," she muttered. Dumping the leftovers on the counter, Patty answered the phone without checking the caller ID.

"Patty, is that you?" the caller asked.

Patty's free hand flew to her throat as she collapsed onto one of the bar stools at the counter. "Yes," she said. "Doris, it's good to hear from you."

Patty heard a brief silence on the other end of the phone. Finally, Doris continued, "Yes, uh well, our food bank is really running low. I-I wonder if the café has anything you'd like to contribute?"

So we're just not going to discuss any rift. Is that

how you want to play it? "I sure do," Patty said. "I have several days' worth. I finally had to throw out some of the first days' bags. They were too far over the hill."

Patty's shoulders relaxed in relief at hearing her old friend's familiar warm chuckle. They talked for a little while until Doris said, "Well, if I'm going to come over to pick everything up, I'd better get my other chores done and out of the way. I'll let you go now and see you in a couple of hours."

Hanging up, Patty glanced at the disheveled pile of leftovers on the counter before abandoning them in favor of joining Jon on the sofa. "Well, that was certainly a surprise," she said.

"What?" Jon asked without looking away from his video game.

"That call," Patty replied. Frowning at Jon's lack of interest, she continued, "I just got a call from a party of aliens. They're all tired out from creating crop circles and want to make dinner reservations."

"Hmm," Jon said. "Wait. Dinner reservations? The café doesn't do dinner. Don't they know that?"

"Well Jon, since they're aliens from a distant galaxy there're probably lots of things about our planet they don't know."

Responding to her tone, Jon put the game away. "I was losing anyway, probably going to die in the next round." He tried his most winsome smile out on her, to little effect. "Alright, you have my undivided attention. What was the call really about?"

"It was Doris," Patty said, opening her eyes wide, signaling the significance.

"Okay, now you really have my full attention," Jon said, turning toward her. "Is this the first time you've heard from her since she walked out?"

"Yes," Patty said, closing her eyes to check her mental calendar. "It's been about that long."

"Well, don't keep me in suspense," Jon coaxed. "What'd she want? Did she apologize, explain?"

"None of the above," Patty replied. "She just asked for leftovers for the food bank. Didn't mention a thing about her absence, not a word about why I have so many leftovers taking up space in my walk-in fridge."

Patty watched Jon's face closely. She could almost see his agile mind processing the call, trying to figure out the meaning behind Doris' reluctance to bring up the rift. "So," she said. "What do you think?"

"I'm not sure," Jon said slowly, clearly still analyzing. "How'd you end it? Are you taking stuff over to her?"

"No, she's coming here," Patty said, glancing at her watch, "in a couple of hours."

"That's good," Jon said, nodding. "It'll get her back in the door."

"Good, good," Patty said. "I can invite her up here, offer her some of her favorite tea and some of the leftover lemon cookies I brought up for us. See if I can get her to go there, talk about it."

"Why?" Jon asked.

"Why?" Patty asked, shaking her head, sitting up straight and turning to look Jon in the eye. "Why? Why not? I thought that was the idea, to get her to talk about it."

"Okay," Jon said. "But why? What purpose will that serve?"

"Oh," Patty said, closing her eyes and running her fingers through her short, brush cut hair as she sank back into the soft, comfy pillows. Finally, she took in a deep breath and slowly opened her eyes. "Yeah, okay I see that. Bringing it up, forcing the issue, is not going to change anything, not going to do anything to strengthen the friendship." She blinked rapidly a couple of times. "But won't leaving it there, unresolved, won't it just fester and grow? How will I ever be able to trust that something like this won't happen again?"

"I don't know," Jon admitted. "Why don't you take it one step at a time?"

"I can do that." Patty nodded. "I can just be her friend and let her know, not say anything, let her know just by being there, that I'm available if she wants to discuss anything. It's going to be hard, not telling how she hurt my feelings, not sure I can trust the friendship."

"She's been Robert's mother for more than sixty years," Jon said. "Think about it, isolating herself every time she has to back him up must be harder on her than on anyone else. This is probably not the first time backing him has meant crossing someone off her friend list."

"Well it's not going to go that way this time," Patty said with a curt nod. She looked at her husband, lounging in his sports shorts and rumpled t-shirt boasting, *Grammar Police - to serve and protect the English language.* "Are you going to be here? Hanging around?"

Jon snorted a laugh. "No, I won't be here to embarrass you or cramp your style." He glanced at his watch. "Alec's coming by in a little while for our evening run, bringing Trevor."

"Really?" Patty asked. "You're starting that up again? That's great. Why don't you invite them to stay for dinner?"

"Thanks, *Mom*," Jon said with an indulgent chuckle. "You sound like a mother proud of her child for making a new friend."

Patty joined him, laughing. It felt good to be here together laughing at themselves. "Yeah well, laugh if you want to, but I have corn chowder and Stroganoff stuffed potatoes, if anyone's interested." She pulled herself up from the sofa and went to the kitchen where she began sorting the leftovers, some for the fridge, some for the microwave.

○ ○ ○

Patty and Doris were emerging from the café kitchen with bags and boxes of leftovers as Jon, Alec, and Trevor returned from their evening run. "Here," Trevor said. "Let me help you get those to your car." Patty and Trevor walked Doris out while Jon and Alec headed upstairs to freshen up.

"You know," Alec said to Jon. "I almost can't believe the changes I see in my son since he began working here."

"He's a good kid," Jon said.

"Don't get me wrong," Alec said quickly. "He was always basically a good kid. But next April will be his eighteenth birthday. That's the same age I was when I joined the marines with no idea what I was going to do with my life. Since working here, Trevor not only knows what he wants to do, he's halfway to a plan to get there."

Joining them upstairs, Trevor helped set the table and pour drinks while Patty heated the soup and the stuffed potatoes for their dinner.

"Doris didn't want to stay for dinner?" Jon asked, his tone trying for casual but his tightly focused eyes signaled his interest. "Everything okay?"

"Yes *Mom*," Patty replied. "It was a good talk. I told her what the literacy people had told Jamala and she said she'd contact Jamala to offer private tutoring. Otherwise, nothing of any real substance but really comfortable. I'm giving it time."

"Private tutoring," Jon said. "That's good, good for Jamala, good of Doris."

"Jamala's going to get private tutoring?" Trevor asked. "In what? She's a great student."

"Just for the citizenship application process," Patty said. "To smooth the way for her."

Alec shot Jon a meaningful look over Trevor's head. "Doris is a good person. Always has been."

TWENTY-NINE

Patty brought a Devil's Food cake out to the dessert display stand, the third one that morning. She leaned back to admire it and then turned to survey the crowd in her café. Cranberry/orange scones and bacon/brie frittata wedges had been disappearing quickly all morning so she was surprised to find the atmosphere subdued.

"What's that scowl about?" Care asked her.

"I know it's been a pretty busy morning but something feels off," Patty said. "What is it?"

"You're missing Dr. R and Eddie," Care replied. "New crop circles were reported in southern England and they left town last night. Spense says they got all the samples they need from here anyway and they can continue the investigation, even from off site."

"England?" Patty said. "But that's so far." Patty's hazel eyes did a quick search of the café, landing on Jon, sitting at a center table with Spense and Nate. "Gone?" Patty whispered. "How can they leave? We still don't have an answer about the crop circles."

"Sugah," Care drawled, gently cupping Patty's shoulder. "All around the world, questions about crop circles go unanswered. Welcome to reality."

"Well, I don't like it," Patty said, her jaw set. "What's going to happen to my business with them all gone?" Patty's instant fear and anguish produced audible stress in her voice. "Oh well, I see at least Spense and Nate are still here."

Care looked at Spense and smiled warmly. "Yeah, Spense is still around, still drawing in female customers."

Patty gazed around the café again. "Are we low on anything or can I take a short break with Jon?"

"Sure Sugah," Care said. "Your Devil's Food cake is very popular. It was the only thing we're about out of."

Patty sauntered over to Jon's table and put her hand on the fourth chair. "Mind if I join you?"

Jon looked up and nodded a welcome but it was Spense who jumped up to pull the chair out, holding it until Patty was settled.

"Go on," Jon said to Nate. "I want to hear the rest of that."

Nate turned to Patty. "I was just telling the fellas that Kylie left town before dawn this morning. She has interviews scheduled this morning in San Francisco and then later in Seattle."

"Network?" Jon asked.

Nate chewed at his lip. "No, I'm afraid not. Still local. But at least they're both in larger markets." He paused to thank Care for the refill and take a cautious sip of his hot coffee. "I'm pulling for San Francisco. My home base is there and it would be really convenient for me. But we were up late last night figuring out ways to keep our thing, whatever it may turn out to be, going wherever she lands."

"Well, that's new," Patty said, liking Nate a little more to see him care. "Good for you."

"Yeah," Nate's face lit up in a smile. "I think she's

worth it. Our backgrounds mesh and we're no longer in competition for stories." He sighed and his smile turned wistful.

Spense gave Nate's shoulder a fist bump and Jon nodded to him. Patty waited but neither man offered any words of encouragement. *Men!* she thought, *and two of these guys are in the word business!*

Patty looked up as Barbara came to stand by their table. Spense jumped up to pull a spare chair from a nearby table for her. "About ready?" he asked.

"Almost," Barbara said, her eyes roaming the cafe's customers. "I have a couple more people I want to touch base with before I leave."

"Leave?" Patty asked, straightening. "Not you, too. I don't understand how everyone is leaving and we still don't know anything for sure about the circles."

"Sorry pretty lady, that's just the way it goes," Spense said, eyes a-twinkle. "And about Barbara leaving, I'm afraid that's my fault. My Air Force contact finally came through with an interview at Area 51." He puffed up with pride and female heads turned at every table in the café.

"He's very excited," Barbara said, an indulgent smile lighting her usually muddy green eyes. "But first, we're going to fly a detour."

Spense grew even more animated, waving his hands and all but levitating in his seat. "Barbara said she'd fly me over the Blythe Intaglios as we head east to Nevada."

"Blythe Intagly whats?" Nate asked. "Never heard of 'em."

Barbara chuckled. "Few people have and I don't

know why. They're spectacular."

"They're geoglyphs, gigantic figure drawings, in the Colorado Desert near Blythe," Spense explained. "They've been dated to sometime between 900 BCE and 1200 CE but nobody much knew about them until air travel."

Patty's face asked her question for her, so Spense continued his explanation. "They're so big, you can't tell what they are from ground level. You have to get a bird's eye view to recognize them."

"There are three human figures, two four legged animals, and a spiral," Barbara said. "I first saw them when I was in pilot training and I've been fascinated ever since."

"There are so many fantastic things on the planet, unexplained things," Nate said. "I have a feeling I have the material for several more books."

"Here come Wanda and Doris," Barbara said, "I couldn't leave without saying good-bye to you and Care and the two of them. I've never known a community as welcoming as you have been." She and Patty went together to join Wanda and Doris, immediately followed by Care.

"Good to see you," Care said to Doris. "I've missed hearing your commentary on all the town's goings on."

Doris sent a smile toward Patty. "It's good to be back. I've missed all of you, too."

The five ladies settled in, talking over the mugs of hot coffee and thick slices of cake Care had brought them. Patty watched their faces, ignoring the chatter for a moment. This is the community of friends I've craved, she thought. *So sad that I'm appreciating it only now,*

now when people are leaving.

She noticed how well Doris' shirt, - *Good girls with bad habits make the best friends* - in fancy script over a crowded circle of cartoon women holding full wineglasses, reflected her personality. She let her gaze drift to Wanda whose shirt today pictured a big red and white circus tent with a troupe of monkeys running wild all over the words, *Not my Circus. Not my monkeys.* in bold red print. Patty smiled to herself. Wanda might pretend to be uninvolved but she always ended up right in the midst of whatever was brewing.

Her attention turned next to the newest member of their circle, Barbara. Today, her shirt read simply *AV8R* in bold white letters on a cloud filled sky blue background. Just like her, Patty thought, bold, direct, and high in the clouds. Finally, she turned to Care who wore the perfect shirt to capture her essence, *I used to be a people person, but people ruined that for me.* In spite of everything Care said, she was the ultimate people person, proving it every interaction.

This is my tribe, Patty thought, happiness flowing through her. *We belong to each other as surely as to any blood relatives.*

After what seemed like an incredibly short period of time, Spense appeared at their table. "Jon left for the paper and Nate went to finish packing," he said. "Isn't it time we got going, too?"

Everyone, all the ladies, got up together, exchanging hugs and promises to keep in touch. "Promise me you'll come back for a visit real soon," Doris pleaded.

"Yes, soon," Patty echoed.

"I will, I know I will," Barbara said. "I miss you

girls already and I haven't even left yet."

Patty hadn't noticed how close to 2:00 it'd gotten. She gazed around the almost empty dining room. Care had been quietly excusing herself to refill coffee and collect payments while Patty had been too absorbed in the conversation to notice. She took a big breath and gave a one shoulder shrug. Business was pretty much over for the day, no need for her to return to the kitchen until Trevor showed up to begin prep work for tomorrow. She collapsed back down onto the booth bench with Wanda and Doris. Care soon rejoined them.

"You've been awfully quiet," Care said to Wanda. "What's up? Something wrong?"

"Wrong?" Wanda said, swallowing a big lump. She wet her lips and pressed them together. She shook her head and tried again. "Yeah, I got a call from my brothers last night."

Doris immediately reached across the table to pat her friend's arm. "Your mom?" she asked.

"Yeah, she's getting worse and my brothers are pretty much worthless taking care of her." Wanda's chin dropped to her chest. "No, that's not fair. They've taken care of her just fine up 'til now."

"Pardon me for asking, but what's wrong with her?" Care asked.

"Well she's almost ninety," Wanda said. "And pretty much what you'd expect to be wrong with any ninety year old black woman. High blood pressure, diabetes, and memory problems. Plus, she doesn't want to need help and she's really stubborn."

"That apple didn't fall very far from the tree," Doris teased.

In spite of herself, Wanda smiled. "Just picture the two of us under one roof, trying to make it work."

Already reeling from the loss of Dr. Rasmussen, Eddie, Kylie, Nate, Spense, and Barbara, Patty's hand flew to her throat. "Will you go there, to Chicago is it, or will she come here?"

"I don't know yet," Wanda said, squirming in her seat. "I know it would be easier for her if I moved there, but ..." Wanda shook her head slowly. "It gets really cold in Chicago. In the summer. Never mind the winters. And I know in theory, my brothers would be closer to help out when needed, but that's in theory. Who knows how it would work out for real."

"Just let us know how we can help," Care offered. "I've been collecting a stack of real estate ads if you need 'em."

"Thanks," Wanda said. "If we end up here, I may need to look for a bigger place. We'll see."

Oh please stay here, Patty thought. *I'm not ready to lose anyone else right now.*

By the time Trevor arrived for his afternoon shift, a much subdued group of ladies were ready to go their separate ways. Beyond the effect on her business, Patty worried about her tribe. Suddenly aware that all relationships are very fragile.

o o o

Upstairs that evening after dinner, over coffee and dessert, Patty brought up the subject she'd avoided while they ate. "Now that all the people studying the crop circles have left town, do you think my café will still have enough customers to stay in

271

business?"

Jon sputtered into his coffee. "I didn't realize you were worried about that," he said. "Surely you have enough repeat customers that you don't need to worry."

"I'm not so sure," Patty said, sinking deeper into the sofa cushions, gazing out at the fading sunset. "A lot of those people came in almost daily to hear the news, what was going on with the circles. What if they stop coming in? What happens when all the ladies find out Spense is no longer there every day?"

"You're right," Jon said. "Cafés all around the country go out of business every day for lack of Spenser Elliott." He smiled at Patty then turned serious. "A lot of customers did come in at first because our visiting specialists hung out there. But now that they've tasted your food and enjoyed the cafe's casual atmosphere, they keep coming back. I think you'll be okay. Besides there'll always be new things to be discussed."

"The rental income from the dance and yoga contracts covers the payments for the remodeling loan," Patty said, not yet ready to be mollified. "As long as I don't lose those, all I have to worry about is groceries. And payroll. I'd hate to have to lay off any of my employees. They're part of what makes the café what it is." She blew out a puff of air. "Enough about my problems. What's new at the paper?"

Jon sat up and turned to Patty, talking with his hands as he gave her the first clues to the new story he was pursuing. "The city council wants to make a change to the election process. They want to change it so they would be elected by district instead of representing the city in general," he told her.

"Wait a minute," Patty said. "Isn't this going to be another point of local controversy? Do we want to put ourselves right back in the middle? Didn't we just barely escape that?"

Jon rubbed the back of his neck as his gaze bounced around the room, window to window. "You know that's the nature of running a paper. Everything is, by definition, controversial. There's going to be someone to disagree no matter what stories the paper covers. Should I stop covering anything that matters?"

Patty saw the anguish in his eyes. "It doesn't matter if we want to stop. You couldn't do it anyway. I'm just asking, do we want to be in the middle of that again, so soon?"

"Now I understand why so many small local papers turn into little more than forums for ads with a little high school sports thrown in, leaving the real news to the big guys," Jon said. His smile wavered. He pressed his lips together in a tight grimace.

"That's not you," Patty said, lightly stroking his hand. "I couldn't ask you to give up what you love just so we can be a little more comfortable." A long time history teacher, Patty's mind flew to a favorite quote from Benjamin Franklin. "Those who would give up Essential Liberty to purchase a little Temporary Safety, deserve neither Liberty or Safety," she said, repeating the quote to Jon.

"I was going to tell you later, but I guess now's as good a time as any." Jon faced Patty squarely. "I've gotten an offer to buy the paper from one of those big conglomerates. I didn't take it because I believe that business taking over papers is what has destroyed journalism." He shook his head. "Maybe I need to rethink that?"

"What would you do?" Patty asked. "If you sold the paper, what would you do?"

Jon arched his left eyebrow. "The offer would include me and Henry staying on to run the day to day operation."

"Great," Patty said, with a quick dismissive snort. "All the responsibility without any of the authority." She took in Jon's hangdog expression. "You could leave the paper business altogether and come work in the café."

Jon flinched, physically recoiling from the very suggestion.

"So that's not going to happen," Patty said, love and humor coloring her tone. "I think you're just going to have to make case by case decisions about what stories your paper carries."

"Maybe I can re-look at the op-ed page," Jon offered, standing up and shrugging his left shoulder. "I'll think about that tomorrow. Tomorrow's another day," Jon said in his pathetic imitation of Scarlett O'Hara.

As they headed toward their bedroom for an early night, Patty said, "Oh I almost forgot to tell you I do have some good news. Trevor wants to go to the CIA, instead of college."

Jon stopped in his tracks. "The CIA? Straight outta high school? Don't you have to be recruited for that, political science majors out of college, or specialists out of the military?"

When Jon stopped suddenly, Patty ran into him, noticing how well his evening runs with Alec had toned his previously softening middle. It reminded her of how much her own middle was spreading because of all the time she spent in the kitchen, tasting and testing. She smacked his shoulder lightly. "Not that CIA, silly. The Culinary Institute of America. There's a branch in San Francisco, and even if he doesn't get accepted there, there are other good cooking schools he could attend."

Jon's tensed body relaxed. "Great. I want to ask him to take charge on Friday so we can celebrate our anniversary with a late morning in bed. You haven't had a day off since you opened the café."

"That does sound nice. I'll ask him."

THIRTY

Patty awoke to bright sunshine in her eyes. After a moment of panic, she realized she hadn't overslept, she wasn't late to get breakfast out to the café customers. She was taking a well-deserved day off. She got herself up to go to the bathroom. Upon returning she found Jon standing in the middle of the room with a breakfast-in-bed tray.

"Get back in bed," he said, smiling broadly, his dark brown eyes twinkling. "How can I serve you breakfast in bed if you're up wandering around?"

"This is a special treat," Patty said, tucking her feet under the covers and fluffing her pillows into position so she could sit up. "But at some point, I'm going to need to go check in on Trevor, see if he needs any help."

"I just came up from there," Jon reported as he brought the tray over. "With Care's help, he has it all under control." He took off his shoes and settled himself in next to Patty. "Relax, right now he's still hovering between sheer terror and thrill of a lifetime." Once he'd settled himself, Jon explained, "I'm a little later with this than I'd planned. I had to stop off to feed our squirrel family."

"Oh, I'm sorry I missed that on my one day sleeping in," Patty said. "It's usually still dark when I head downstairs, so you get all the fun with them and I miss out. All I get is early morning birdsongs and that's not every day." When they'd put up the bird feeder on their little balcony, the birds had come but the neighborhood squirrels soon followed. So Jon had gotten a supply of nuts to feed them separately. Their balcony was really small, only room for Jon's grill and a couple of chairs, but it was just right for them, the birds and squirrels.

Patty's eyes roamed over the array of foods on her tray. "Judging from these, Trevor's doing fine. It looks like you brought up one of everything on the Friday morning menu."

"Yeah, I'm hoping to eat whatever you don't want." Jon rearranged his pillows until he could settle in with a deep sigh and reached for the second cup of coffee on the tray. "What a difference a year makes, huh?"

"A year?"

"Don't you remember?" Jon asked. "It was our anniversary weekend last year when we planned the trip up here 'just to look'?"

Patty put her fork down and passed the wedge of spinach and feta quiche to Jon. "You don't mind? I'm feeling like the roast veggie frittata today."

"Not at all," Jon said. "It's one of my favorites."

Foodstuffs distributed, Patty took Jon's hand. "I had forgotten. Not our anniversary. Don't worry big guy, I've already gotten your present." Patty's eyes involuntarily shot to the top drawer of her dresser. "But I had forgotten we made our first trip here for our anniversary last year."

"Like I said, what a difference?" Jon repeated.

277

"Who could've imagined then how our lives would change?" Patty asked, thinking about all the changes in her life – her home, her career, even her relationship with Jon, and everything else that came from taking charge of her own life.

"I know. Neither of us did," Jon teased, taking a sip of his coffee. "I seem to remember quite a bit of second thoughts and not a little bit of outright panic."

Patty gazed around their bright, sunny master bedroom, comparing it to the darkness that had surrounded them in the unfamiliar hotel room as they struggled with the decision to move here and start over. "From dark to sunny," she said, the smile clear in her voice. "From the unfamiliar to the home we've made our own."

"It hasn't all been sunny," Jon said.

"A lot of it hasn't been easy," Patty said. "But right now, it sure seems to have been worth it."

"On the whole, I gotta say we've had more ups than downs," Jon said. "Don't you think?"

"Yes, of course," Patty quickly reassured him. "Although, I think I'm more than a little worried that the café will fall out of favor without the crop circle visitors as an attraction. I know I'm still stuck on that but what happens if business drops off dramatically?"

"What happens if the paper folds because I'm not covering local news? We'll face those bridges if they come," Jon said. "Money problems should be the least of our worries."

"I know, but I worry when things are doing well, waiting for the other shoe to drop."

Jon leaned over to plant a gentle kiss on the top of her head, smiling at the tickle of her brush cut hair.

"You've got the rental income to cover the loan payments. We'll manage if things get a little rocky. So far, so good."

Patty's shoulders relaxed incrementally. "And you can revisit editorial decisions as you go. I know you're right, you gotta cover that stuff. It still makes me nervous, but I trust you. So far so good."

"Besides, if this morning is any sort of gauge, business at the café isn't going to drop off." Jon shook his head emphatically. "When I went down to get our breakfast it was busy as ever." He stopped to chuckle. "One customer asked where you were."

Patty's head jerked around, fork frozen on its path to her mouth.

Jon quickly patted her arm. "Not to worry. Care handled him. She pouted at him and asked him if her company wasn't good enough," Jon said, mimicking Care's familiar tone. "The man just about collapsed under her stare, stuttering that he was just asking."

Patty smiled. "That Care, she sure turned out to be a treasure."

"All the staff are," Jon said. "Trevor's learning to prepare your recipes almost as well as you. Care handles all customers in her own style and Jamala is a pleasant respite from Care's spicy tongue."

Patty nodded. "They're golden. I struck gold when I stumbled onto each one of them. Like you did when you inherited Henry."

"Oh yeah," Jon replied immediately. "I don't think I could get the paper out without him. He's the best part of the deal with Robert Shepard. He had no idea of Henry's value."

"Yes, Henry is good," Patty said. "But he's

B K Robinson

blossomed under your respect for him, growing into the responsibility. And don't forget, you were the one who thought to consult with the computer science folks at VCC. Those changes you made really made a difference."

Jon took a big breath and swallowed hard. "I had no idea how steep the learning curve would be," he said. "Going from writer to publisher. Whew, what a year."

"But you did it," Patty said, nodding. "You're a marvel."

"Me?" Jon asked. "You've gone from no idea what you wanted to do with yourself to a successful restauranteur. Do you know how amazing that is?"

"Yes, it has been an amazing year," Patty said. "Even if Chris Woods and Robert Shepard won't face jail time.

"Even if we never find any definitive answers about the crop circles," Jon added.

"We have a new home we love," Patty said, stretching and sinking into their soft, warm bed.

"We each have careers we enjoy," Jon added, taking her hand and snuggling in deeper next to her.

"And new friends," Patty added, through her satisfied smile. "We've found some really great friends, people who make our lives worthwhile." She frowned. "I hope we'll see Barbara again. And Nate. And Spense. I really liked each of them."

"They're good people," Jon said. "We met them and others mostly 'cause your café is exactly what you wanted, a place for people to gather." Jon held Patty's hand to his chest and heaved a great sigh. "Pretty good year, if you ask me."

"Pretty good life," Patty echoed. "All the better because we created it for ourselves. We risked it all and made it happen."

"Uh-hmmm," Jon murmured.

Patty heard the drowsiness in his voice. "Wait, before you fall asleep, what are the plans for the day?"

"I knew we couldn't afford the time or the money for a return to the French countryside," Jon said, stifling a yawn. "But I did what I could to recreate it for you. I researched the best French restaurants in San Diego and made our dinner reservations at Pamplemousse near Del Mar."

Patty perked up, her eyes growing big and round. "I've heard of that place and I've been wanting to go there." She hugged Jon awkwardly around the breakfast tray. "That's so perfect! Want to split this sticky bun so I can get rid of the tray."

"No thanks," Jon said giving in to a yawn. "I ate a whole one while I was downstairs waiting for Care to put this tray together."

"Okay, all mine," Patty said.

"Oh wait," Jon said, turning back to Patty for a moment. "I almost forgot. JJ called. He's planning to come here for Thanksgiving."

Patty's smile lit up her face. "Wonderful ... Wait, there's nothing wrong is there?"

"Stop being such a mother," Jon teased. "His second year teaching fifth grade is still good, in spite of the school's high risk neighborhood. He said he got something special for us for an anniversary present but he wants to wait to deliver it in person. Is that okay?"

"Of course," Patty said, a mother's loving smile warming her voice. "I'll call him to confirm and see if I can pry some clues out of him. I can't wait to show him my café, to introduce him to everyone. I just wish Barbara and Nate and Spense were still around. Oh well, I can at least take him out to see what's left of the circles."

Jon didn't answer and soon Patty heard his soft snores. "It looks like both of us are pretty tired out from this last year."

Patty let her eyes close as a kaleidoscope of memories drifted past her mind's eye, starting with their first visit to 'Aunt Maude's old place' and proceeding through many of the highlights of the past year. She shook her head, comparing that pathetic continental breakfast from their first visit to what her café served.

She remembered the remodel of their living quarters upstairs which led to memories of the remodel of the café space. The pie contest, the flight over the crop circles, meeting Jamala on campus after a ceramics class, Care hiring herself, Trevor's first attempts at following her recipes, and many, many conversations with friends in her café. Her cruise down memory lane ended on the vision of sitting and chatting with Doris, Wanda, Barbara, and Care just yesterday.

Being Patty, the happy memories filled the biggest part of her thoughts, allowing only a few moments for any bad ones. She gave very little time to thoughts of Chris Woods, Robert Shepard, or Doris' brief absence.

Patty sighed deeply in satisfaction, at last succumbing to the rhythm of Jon's snores. "What a year," she whispered, snuggling in, spooning Jon. "I can't wait to see what comes next."

CAFÉ Du JOUR MENU/PLACEMAT

	Breakfast Bread	Frittata	Quiche	Soup	Stuffed Potato	Pizza	Sweet
M	apple walnut muffins	Cajun (crab/shrimp/cayenne)	sausage/roasted red peppers	creamy butternut squash	beer/cheddar chowder	veggie	date nut cookies
T	blueberry scones	Denver or western	Cajun (crab/shrimp/cayenne)	wild mushroom medley	Reuben	shrimp and banana pepper	angel food cake
W	lemon poppy muffins	spinach mushroom	bacon/broccoli	baked potato	mushroom and onions	pepperoni/sausage	Dutch apple pie
TH	cranberry orange scones	bacon/brie	caramelized onion	broccoli	sour cream and chives	BBQ chicken	devils food cake
F	pecan sticky buns	roast veggie	spinach/feta	corn chowder	stroganoff	3 cheese/rst red peppers, olives	lemon cookies
SA	carrot raisin muffins	sun dried tomato/herb	ham/asparagus	chili	BBQ chicken	meatball mushroom	seasonal fruit pie
SU	cinnamon rolls	sausage/cream cheese	Lorraine	beer/cheddar chowder	chili and cheese	everything	red velvet cake

B K Robinson

If you, like Patty, can't wait to find out what comes next, turn the page to read an excerpt from the next book in the Café Du Jour series, due out in 2018.

B K Robinson

One

Patty Townsend's hazel eyes circled the prep area of her cafe's kitchen as she worked. Something felt off about this very familiar space. The light streaming through the west window was lower than usual. She was used to seeing it in the morning or early afternoon. Her café was only open for breakfast and lunch, from 07:00 to 02:00. Every day, before opening and after closing, she and Trevor Harrison worked here preparing for each day's menu.

This afternoon was the exception. They were serving a special menu for a private event. The menu was different but the warm yeasty aroma leaking out of the oven as the bread baked was certainly familiar. The intense, intoxicating cocoa fragrance wafting off the chocolate butter cream frosting she was spreading, was new. The event had been booked by Henry Walker, Patty's husband's primary employee. He was Jon's employee but this dinner was the direct result of something Patty had done.

Two years earlier, their son Jon, Jr or JJ, had given both Patty and Jon gift certificates for 23 and me, the DNA ancestry testing service, for an anniversary present. JJ had wanted to know more about his own history which meant learning more about his parents' origins. Jon was easy. His parents had been part of JJ's world right up until their early deaths by a drunk driver. But Patty had been adopted. Although her adoptive parents had been loving people who had given her a wonderful life, JJ wanted to know about her biological heritage for his own reasons.

What Patty had learned through that process had inspired Henry, also adopted, to pursue his own ancestry test. What he'd discovered had connected him to a brother and two sisters he never knew he had, and all of their extended families. They'd been in touch by phone, email and text message but now they were all coming to get together in person and Henry had arranged this dinner for their first meet and greet. From what Henry had told her, theirs was quite a story. Patty was more than a little curious to meet them herself.

A ringing phone interrupted Patty's musings and Trevor's chatter. Patty looked to Trevor who patted his pocket. No it wasn't his cell phone. It rang again. Patty turned to the land line on the wall next to the door.

"The land line?" she asked. "Who would call on the land line?" She pulled out her own cell phone to confirm she hadn't missed any calls as she stretched across the counter work surface to snag the land line.

"Café Du Jour," she answered, unconsciously straightening her posture, running her fingers through her thick brunette hair, as though the caller might see and judge her. "How may I help you?"

"Is this Patty Townsend?" the middle aged female voice asked before being interrupted by a smoker's cough.

"Yes," Patty replied, her voice short, impatience creasing her brow. *Someone else trying to sell me something I don't want or need. I swear I put this number on the 'Do Not Call' list. Lotta good that did.*

"This is Elsa Blaisdell from the Valley Center Fire and Rescue Services Department," Ms. Blaisdell continued.

Oh goody, Patty thought, *not even a sales call. It's a donation request.* "I'm sorry, Ms . . ." Patty began.

"Is Jon Townsend your husband?" the caller asked, speaking over Patty. "Are you the next of kin for Jon Townsend?"

"Jon? Next? W-what is this about?" Patty asked. At forty-nine years old, Patty was still barely two inches above five feet tall and her weight had ballooned to 125. She leaned heavily against the counter.

"You are his emergency contact?" Ms. Blaisdell reiterated.

"Y-yes, yes," Patty said. "What's happened? Is Jon okay?"

Trevor dropped the vegetables he'd been washing into the sink and came to Patty's side, his hand supporting her back.

"Chief Rodriquez himself asked me to call to let you know Mr. Townsend has been transported to emergency services at Valley Center Hospital," she said. "You can call there to check on his status."

"The emergency room?" Patty asked, voice breaking. "What happened?"

"I don't have that information, ma'am," the caller replied. "I can't tell you any more than that. Please contact the staff at the hospital. Have a nice day."

"Nice day!" Patty exclaimed, returning the handset to the base unit.

Trevor pulled over a chair for her to collapse onto but before he could ask any questions, his own phone began to ring. Seeing Jamala Dirie in the caller

ID, he quickly answered. "Where are you," he asked, his voice rising. "Are you at work at the hospital?"

"Yes, Trevor. I am," Jamala said, her lyrical voice soft, calm. "Are you with Patty? Is she at the café?"

"Yes," he answered.

"Jon is being treated at the emergency room." Jamala said. "She should come here."

"Treated? For what?" Trevor asked. "Never mind, no time for questions. I'll bring her. See you in a minute."

"Come on, Patty," he said, gently pulling his boss, and substitute mother, to her feet. "I'm going to take you to the hospital."

"Hospital?" Patty said, looking up into Trevor's face. At twenty years old, Trevor's 5'11" frame was now lean and angular but his face still had a softer roundness surrounding the deep dimples in his liquid caramel skin.

"Hospital, yes," he said. "That was Jamala. She's with Jon at the hospital. Let's get you there, too."

"Right," Patty said, standing up tall and shaking herself out of her frozen state. She glanced at her watch and surveyed the half done prep work, quickly returning to her usual take charge persona. Reaching under the counter, she pulled out her purse and patted her pockets until she found her keys. "I'll get myself to the hospital. It's not far. You finish up here." She looked around once more, nodding and ignoring Trevor's protests. "I promised Henry a nice dinner for his family and I will not let him down."

Minutes later, a blaring horn startled Patty. She'd been driving more or less on auto pilot and had shot right through a red light, barely avoiding hitting some cross traffic. "Get it together, girl," she commanded herself. "Jon needs you. This is no time to fall apart."

She executed a right turn, entering the hospital parking lot and left her car in the first open space she found. She didn't remember getting into her car or driving here but now that she was here, she had to take the next step. "You can fall apart later," she promised herself. "There'll be time for that later."

She recognized the words "Emergency Services Entrance" in huge red letters over the doorway, ambulances blocking the lanes. She wasn't sure if it was alright for her to enter through that doorway, but in mission mode, Patty marched in anyway.

She approached the young woman manning the desk and summoned the unfamiliar words, "My name is Patricia Townsend. I'm looking for my husband, Jon Townsend." The woman held up one finger, asking Patty to wait a moment while she concentrated on the caller on her headset. How the woman could hear anything over the PA announcements and constant chatter around her, Patty couldn't begin to imagine.

Before she got a response, Fire Chief Benny Rodriguez's handsome head poked out of the nearby curtains. Patty rushed toward him. He held her away from the enclosed treatment bay but she could see past his shoulder.

Patty didn't recognize Jon at first. Recognize him? She didn't see him when she first looked into the bay. The space was filled with blinking lights, beeping machines and by several people dressed in scrubs busy over an elderly man in the hospital bed in the middle of the semi-organized chaos. *That's Jon?* No color infusing the gray pallor of his skin against the stark white of the sheets, no tone to his slack muscles, no twinkle in his half lidded eyes, no familiar smile quirking his lips, no movement. *That can't be my Jon. He's barely fifty years old.* Patty's eyes closed against the glare of the bright white space, the harsh lights shining off the hard surfaces. She fell back against Benny.

A middle aged man in blue scrubs looked up at the commotion. "She can't be here while we're working on him. Get her out of here."

"My fault," Benny said, turning Patty away and ushering her toward the waiting room, to a chair off by itself. "Wait here. I'll let you know when we know more."

Patty sat staring straight ahead, her eyes unblinking, images from her twenty eight year marriage to Jon cascading through her mind. She tried creating a quiet place within her mind, undisturbed by the swirl of commotion around her. It wasn't working. She felt cold, stiff, out of place, and badly frightened.

That's how Jamala found her a few minutes later. "I called JJ," Jamala said softly, as she gracefully lowered her slight, twenty-two year old self into the next chair and took Patty's hand. "I left a voicemail and an text message for him."

Patty glanced at her watch. *How could so little time have passed?* "He's probably still in class or maybe on his way home," she said, none of her usual energy in her voice.

"Here comes the doctor," Jamala said, standing. "He is one of the best here. Jon is in good hands."

Patty rose to stand, feeling the blood drain from

her head to her feet, facing the same man who'd ordered her away from Jon's treatment bay.

The short, balding man came to a stop before her, still wiping his spotlessly clean hands on a towel. Barely glancing at Jamala, he focused on Patty. "You're next of kin for Jon Townsend?"

Patty nodded, but couldn't form any words. Her eyes searched his watery blue eyes for some clue of what he was about to tell her. Without his mask and disposable paper head cover, she could see he wasn't as old as she'd thought. The permanent lines of stress around his eyes had made him seem older than his years.

"He's stable for now," he said. "It's his good fortune his incident occurred right across the street from the fire station where the emergency services unit is housed. They were able to get to him really quickly and I believe he was only without oxygen for a little over one minute."

"W-without oxygen?" Patty whispered. "Does that mean he was dead?"

The doctor's eyes shot around the waiting room. "Right. He suffered a SCA, a sudden cardiac arrest, with syncope, loss of consciousness. The EMTs, emergency medical technicians, revived him using a defibrillator. Once they had him stabilized enough for transport, they brought him here." He paused, taking in a breath. "We lost him briefly again but we were able to bring him back without having to open up his chest." He continued speaking, offering more details.

Patty saw his mouth moving, knew she needed to listen to what he was saying but all she heard was white noise, the blood pulsing through her brain, past her ear drums.

"See, Miss Patty," Jamala said, her voice silky smooth, soothing. "I told you he is one of the best doctors here. Mister Jon will be fine."

The doctor glared at her, taking in her nurses' aid uniform, her dark skin, her stilted speech. To Patty he said, "He's stable. It's too soon to say he's out of the woods. We want to move him upstairs and keep a close watch on him for at least the next twenty-four hours." To Jamala he said, "You should know better than to make promises, young lady. I don't recognize you, are you assigned to emergency services?"

"No, sir."

"Then get back to where you belong before I report you."

"I'm off duty, sir."

Patty held on tight to Jamala's hand. "She's here as a friend." She turned to Jamala. "But he's right, dear. If you're off duty, you should get out of here. Trevor needs your help tonight since I can't be there. Please, go now."

"Are you sure that is where you want me tonight? At the café, not here with you?"

"Yes, I'll be alright. You go help Trevor, for Henry." She turned back to the doctor. "When will you know more?"

"Probably not before morning," he replied.

"Can I go sit with him?" Patty asked.

"He's being moved to a bed in the Cardiac Intensive Care unit," he said. He cocked his head toward the PA system, alerting to hearing his name. "I have to go now," he said. "The nurses will notify you when you can go up."

Jamala gone, the doctor gone, not yet time to go to Jon, Patty stood still in the middle of the waiting room, people and activity surrounding her, for a moment. The wide automatic doors opened, shifting the air pressure and catching her attention. She turned toward the doors where she saw a tall backlit figure searching the room briefly before heading straight for her. Tall, dark, and handsome, quiet but strong, Alec Harrison, the chief of police, Trevor's father, and Jon's best friend, came to Patty and folded her into his arms.

Patty allowed herself to cry, helplessly, freely.

B K Robinson

ACKNOWLEDGMENTS

I am immensely grateful to my husband for his support throughout the writing process. He insists he has liked each of my books, even the first one.

Once again, I'm thankful for the encouragement and suggestions from my writers' group - Barbara Eknoian, Nancy Mary, Mushroom Montoya, Carol Anne Perini, and John L Stacy.

New for this book, I am truly grateful to Michelle. You've been enjoying the benefit of what I think of as the Michelle effect throughout this story. Her support, constructive criticism, and positive editing suggestions improved this book by orders of magnitude.

I will never tire of hearing from readers who love Tuffy and all his squirrel friends, who continue to send me pictures and stories. I love them all and each of you.

Not surprisingly, the appreciation for the Three Sisters is more nuanced, more serious, and more deeply felt.

I thank you all for taking these journeys with me.

B K Robinson

E. Elizabeth Watson is a writer and mother. She earned her Bachelor's Degree from the University of Texas at Austin in anthropology and her Master's Degree from Newcastle University, United Kingdom in archaeology. The history, folklore and architecture of England and Scotland inspired the *Prince of Lions* series. For more information on new releases, giveaways, and appearances, or to sign up for her newsletter, visit her website at:

www.eelizabethwatson.com

For those interested in further learning about crop circles, I recommend:

Crop Circles: Quest for Truth (© 2002) - a documentary film by Academy Award nominated documentary film maker William Gazecki

Crop Circles, Exploring the Designs & Mysteries by Werner Anderhub and Hans Peter Roth, published by Lark Books, a Division of Sterling Publishing Co. (© 2002)

Alien Art, Extraterrestrial Expressions on Earth by Sarah Moran, published by CLB International, an imprint of Quadrillion Publishing Ltd. (© 1998)

There are many resources available **online**. I suggest you start with cropcircleresearch.com where you will find biographies of leading crop circle researchers and can follow the branching links to the topics of most interest for you. Or, you may simply enter Crop Circles into your search engine and go wherever that leads you.

Searching for a crop circle design to use in *Café Du Jour*, I selected the Cissbury Rings, found in England in 1995. You should able to see them for yourself by entering that name, location, and year into your search engine. Do you see a cone or a funnel?

www.ingramcontent.com/pod-product-compliance
Lightning Source LLC
Chambersburg PA
CBHW021213250626
47155CB00008B/2790